A Test of
Faith

A Test of Faith

MAXINE BILLINGS

BET Publications, LLC
http://www.bet.com

NEW SPIRIT BOOKS are published by

BET Publications, LLC
c/o BET BOOKS
One BET Plaza
1900 W Place NE
Washington, DC 20018-1211

All Kensington Titles, Imprints, and Distributed Lines are available at special quantity discounts for bulk purchases for sales promotions, premiums, fund-raising, and educational or institutional use. Special book excerpts or customized printings can also be created to fit specific needs. For details, write or phone the office of the Kensington special sales manager: Kensington Publishing Corp., 850 Third Avenue, New York, NY 10022, attn: Special Sales Department, Phone: 1-800-221-2647.

ISBN: 1-58314-466-8

First Printing: April 2005
10 9 8 7 6 5 4 3 2 1

Printed in the United States of America

This book is dedicated to my sister Charlotte,
her husband Charles, and their children Joshua, Jay, and Devaree.
It is also dedicated to all the other people throughout the world
who have ever lost a loved one in death.

ACKNOWLEDGMENTS

My heavenly Father Jehovah: thank you for the gifts of life and writing and all the many other wonderful blessings you bestow upon me and my family every day.

My family, especially my husband Tony and our children Tasha and Stefan: thank you for your ongoing love, support, patience, and encouragement.

Special thanks to my sister Lisa Nelson: thank you for the help you gave me in setting up my computer. I couldn't have done it without you.

Other individuals who have helped me in different ways: Jacquelin Thomas (cousin and author), JoAnn Turner (friend), Deidre Knight and Pamela Harty (agents), Glenda Howard (editor) and the entire BET staff, Janice Sims (author), Wayne Jordan (*Romance In Color*), Sue Waldeck (*Road to Romance*), Shunda Leigh (*Booking Matters Magazine*), Lisa Zachery, (Papered Wonders, Inc.), Yolanda Parks (Barnes and Noble) and staff, Rodney Shumake (former editor of *Times–Georgian* newspaper), Georgia Department of Juvenile Justice staff, and Suzanne Watson (Villa Rica, Georgia Public Library). Thank you for the generosity you have extended in helping me to get as far as I have.

Reviewers, readers, and book clubs: thank you for your encouraging reviews and letters. I would also like to offer a special thank-you to those of you who attended my Sign and Dine last year, which was my first book signing event.

As always, this list could go on and on because I have so many people in my life who have shown me that I have their support. However, it's not possible to mention every name. Please know that although you don't see your name here, the memory of your love and support is imbedded in my mind and heart. I wouldn't be where I am without you.

SOMEONE WHO CARES

When you feel lost and alone,
When you feel all hope is gone,
There is someone who cares for you,
Someone who is a friend forever true.

Someone who'll share a kind word or two,
Someone you can count on to be there for you,
Through the good and the bad, the sun and the rain,
To share your smiles of joy and hurt when you feel pain.

Though they can never know exactly how you feel,
Remember there is one who can your sorrow heal,
He's our Father, our Creator, who knows us inside out,
So remember that He cares for you beyond the shadow of a doubt.

Maxine Billings

Chapter 1

The October weather was sunny and pleasantly cool, as rustic colors of autumn waltzed throughout the countryside. Rays of sunshine that streamed through the trees, bouncing off the front entrance of the Hamilton home, seemed to cry out to all who passed by. It was a beautiful time of year. A day to be relished—by other people—but not by the family and friends of Clayton David Hamilton.

Lizzie Hamilton's face exhibited grief and anxiety as she joined the other relatives in the family room. She had not felt her sixty-seven years until recently. A few days ago, she was so full of vigor. Now she felt as though her life was leaving her in slow, agonizing breaths. The pain of losing a child in death was more intense than she had ever imagined. As she entered the room, all eyes turned to her.

Her eldest son, Devin, was the first to speak. "How is she, Mama?"

Lizzie sat down beside Devin. "Not good," she stated, shaking her head slowly. "She's just sitting there, staring out the window. Anna and Leah are in there now trying to talk to her."

Lizzie's husband, Edward, spoke without turning his head from where he stood next to the huge bay window. "She'll be fine. It's going to take some time." Then he added, "For all of us."

Everyone sadly nodded in agreement.

In the master bedroom, Andrea Hamilton sat on a blue and white plaid armchair and rested her feet on the matching ottoman, as she stared despondently out the window. Her mother, Anna Washington, and her twin sister, Leah, both sat on chairs on either side of her and tried to console her.

It was obvious to everyone that Andrea and Leah were identical twins, each possessing caramel-colored skin. Nevertheless, their tastes in styles of clothing and hair were somewhat different. Andrea wore her shoulder-length hair layered in soft curls, while Leah preferred a shorter, curlier style.

Anna held her daughter's hand as she spoke. "Andrea, honey, I know you're hurting. We all are. Everyone loved Clay very much."

Before Anna could speak further, Andrea respectfully reminded her mother, "I know, Mama, but he was my husband. We were married for ten years, and all I feel now is a big hole in my heart."

Leah attempted to offer her own words of encouragement. "Mama and Daddy will be here another week, and you have three more weeks before you have to return to work. Go back with them to Brooklyn like they suggested. Kayla's teacher will work with you as far as her schoolwork goes. You can get her assignments, and she can do them while you're gone."

Leah looked at her twin, hoping she had made some headway. Andrea would listen to her. After all, they had always had a close bond. Nothing would break it—not even this.

Andrea slowly shook her head. "I don't want to go to New York. I want to be at home."

Leah protested, "But you love New York. You said you and Clay and Kayla had a good time when you went last year."

Andrea quickly prompted, "That was different. We were a family then. We were together. Everything has changed." More tears spilled down her cheeks.

Leah was not going to give up. "Andrea . . ."

Leah had come into the world fifteen minutes before Andrea. The thirty-five-year-old twins had very distinct personalities. Andrea was considered the mighty one who could handle any situation. Leah was domineering and possessed very strong powers of persuasion. Nevertheless, Anna felt now was not the appropriate time for Leah to try to master them over her sister. Anna looked at Leah and gave a slight shake of her head.

Outside, Andrea's five-year-old daughter, Kayla, sat on the swing of the huge front porch of their traditional Georgia home. Kayla's maternal grandfather, William Washington, eyed his granddaughter reverently as the two swung back and forth.

Little Kayla looked up at her grandfather with the biggest, prettiest brown eyes he had ever seen, even more spectacular than her mother's. "Paw Paw, I'm gonna fix you and Mee Maw and Poppy and Nanna breakfast in the morning."

William smiled. "You are? What are you gonna fix?"

Kayla returned her grandfather's smile, revealing the spaces where two of her top teeth were missing. "Oh, scrambled eggs, bacon, grits, biscuits." She threw up her tiny hands, shrugged her shoulders, and added, "Whatever you want."

William chuckled as he leaned down and kissed the top of Kayla's head. "You're too good to me. I don't know what I'd do without you. I love you."

"I love you, too, Paw Paw." Kayla moved closer to her grandfather and buried her face in his side.

"You okay, sweetie?"

The little girl's voice was muffled, but William could make out her words. "I miss my daddy."

William pulled her closer. "I know you do, baby. You know, your daddy loved you very much. I want you to promise me that when you get sad from missing him, you'll think about the time when you'll get to see him again, when God brings him back to life. Think about how happy he'll be to see you. How he'll hold you in his arms and hug you and kiss you and make you laugh. Do you think you can do that?"

Kayla looked up at her grandfather. "I can, Paw Paw."

"That's my girl."

William continued swinging back and forth. This sure was a beautiful place Andrea and Clayton had here. He still remembered when they had found the land out in the country. Andrea was so excited that she had brought him and Anna to see it when they were visiting once. Even though there was nothing but trees on it at the time, Andrea pointed out where the house and each room would be.

As he looked around, William admired the purple, white, and yellow pansies in the flower beds scattered throughout the front yard that his daughter, son-in-law, and granddaughter had planted only a week ago. He remembered how delighted Kayla had sounded when she had told him about the flowers during their telephone conversation. Clayton had been a family man. He believed in spending time with his family. Even if they hadn't had this house on such beautiful property, Andrea still would have been happy. As long as she was with Clayton, she would have been happy living in a one-room shack.

A few minutes later, William heard Kayla's soft snoring. He ceased swinging and painstakingly pulled himself up off the wooden swing. Gently lifting her into his arms, he carried her inside.

As soon as Leah saw them, she made her way toward them. She placed her hand gently on Kayla's small back and took a peek at her face. "Did she fall asleep on you, Daddy?"

"Yeah, she did. She's tired," her father answered.

Leah started to remove the sleeping child from her father's arms. "Let me have her, Daddy. I'll put pajamas on her and get her into bed."

"Okay. Here you go," William responded as he released Kayla into the arms of her aunt.

William joined Leah's fiancé, Devin, and Edward in the family room. Devin and Clayton had only been a little over two years apart in age. Devin was forty-one, and Clayton had been thirty-eight when his life was tragically taken from him.

William took a seat on an orange floral chair, sat back, and propped one leg on top of the other. "How's Andrea?"

The two men on the sofa looked more like brothers instead of father and son. They were both bald with toffee-colored skin and neatly trimmed moustaches. Edward, on the other hand, also wore a goatee. He had obviously taken very good care of himself, for he did not look his sixty-nine years. He was two years older than William.

Devin spoke as he shook his head. "Not good."

Edward agreed. "She's really taking it hard, but that's to be expected." He paused, then continued. "I know what she's feeling is normal, considering she just lost her husband. Clay was my son, and it's killing me that he's gone. You know, a parent never expects to outlive his children, and believe me, if I could give my life to get his back, I'd do it in a heartbeat."

Devin patted his father's knee. "We know you would, Pop. I feel the same way. It's not fair. I'm so angry. Why do people insist on drinking and driving? That one irresponsible act has changed our lives forever. You know, he was gonna be my best man." As soon as the words were out of his mouth, Devin jumped up and stormed over to the window with his back to William and Edward.

The two men started to get up at the same time, but William sat back down to let father and son console each other.

Edward stood beside his son and put his arm around Devin's shoulders. "I know Clay was going to be your best man."

Devin didn't take his eyes from the window. Tears streamed down his face as his mind gravitated without effort to the day that he and Leah had given their family the news of their engagement. His baby brother had nearly picked him up off the floor in a big bear hug. The couple had immediately requested that Clayton be the best man; Andrea, the matron of honor; and Kayla, the flower girl. In talking to Leah the day before, Leah had somberly informed Devin that since Andrea was now an unmarried woman, her title had been changed to maid of honor. He still couldn't comprehend some of the terminology associated with weddings; therefore, it made no difference to him what Andrea was called, as long as she could still have a part in their nuptials. "How can Leah and I get married without him? It won't be the same."

"You're right," his father said. "It won't be the same, because he won't be there—but, son, don't you think Clay would want you to be happy?"

"I know he would, but it's so hard to let go."

"I know, but we've got to for now."

When Leah entered the room and saw the two men, she quickly approached them. She placed her hand lightly on Devin's back. "Baby, are you okay?" When she saw his tear-soaked face, she gently pulled him into her arms. As they held each other, Edward rejoined William.

Leah gently rubbed the back of Devin's head as more tears soaked his face. She spoke consolingly. "It's gonna be all right. It's okay. Let it out."

As Leah comforted her husband-to-be, Edward and William removed handkerchiefs from their pants pockets and wiped the tears from their own eyes.

The next morning, the enticing aroma of breakfast filled the air of the Hamilton home. As William turned the corner into the kitchen, he spotted Anna and little Kayla busy cooking. He attempted to spy on them without their knowledge. His wife was still beautiful, even at sixty-four. Their girls favored her. Kayla, with flour all over her face, sat on a stool at the counter and assisted her grandmother in cutting biscuits into medium-sized circles.

Kayla looked up and caught her grandfather spying on them.

"Paw Paw!" she exclaimed. "I told you I was gonna make you breakfast."

William laughed as he entered the kitchen and kissed Anna's cheek. "Good morning, my sweet."

"Good morning," Anna cheerfully replied. "How did you sleep?"

"Pretty good. How about you?"

"All right."

"Paw Paw, you forgot about me," Kayla complained. "Where's my good morning kiss?"

"How could I forget you?" William joked as he strolled over to his granddaughter. "I'm coming. You know I move slow for my age." He put his slippered feet together and slowly shuffled them over the red, brick-patterned, ceramic tile floor.

Kayla giggled. "Oh, Paw Paw, you're so silly."

When William finally reached Kayla, he plopped a big kiss on her floured cheek. "Why aren't you in school today?" he asked.

Kayla held her head back as she laughed again. "Paw Paw, it's Saturday. I don't go to school on Saturday."

William stood up straight, folded his arms, and asked in a playfully stern voice, "Well, why not? I remember one time when your Mama was little she had to go to school on Saturday."

Kayla could not stop giggling. "That was in the olden days."

"The olden days," William repeated. "I beg your pardon. And just what do you know about the olden days? You're only four years old."

"Paw Paw," Kayla laughed. "I'm not four. I'm five." She held up five floured fingers.

"Five!" William exclaimed. "Oh, you're just a baby."

"I'm not a baby. I'm a big girl. Tell him, Mee Maw. I'm a big girl."

"You certainly are," Anna proudly replied. "Babies can't cook like this."

They were all laughing when Andrea staggered in. She held on to the counter as she leaned over.

7

Anna and William immediately ran to their daughter. "Honey, what's wrong?" Anna inquired. They helped her to a chair at the kitchen table.

Andrea sprawled her fingers over her forehead and eyes. "I feel weak and nauseated."

Kayla attempted to get down from the stool. William saw her and moved quickly to assist her. She ran to her mother's side. "Mommy, are you okay?"

"Have you been throwing up?" William asked.

"Yes. I think it's a stomach virus or something. I feel awful."

Anna started to lift her daughter by her arm from the chair. "Come on. I'm taking you to the doctor."

It was obvious that Andrea was feeling poorly, for she did not argue with her mother about getting medical attention, but only stated, "My doctor's office doesn't open on Saturday. We'll have to go to the emergency room."

"All right. Do you need me to help you get dressed?"

"No, I can do it. Daddy," Andrea called out over her shoulder. "Will you keep an eye on Kayla?"

"Sure, baby. You know I will."

After Anna helped Andrea to her bedroom, she returned to the kitchen where William and Kayla had just finished putting the biscuits in the oven.

"Honey," Anna said to her husband, "please keep an eye on those. Don't let them burn. I wanted to have everything done when Edward and Lizzie got up, but . . ."

William wouldn't let his wife finish. "Don't worry about a thing. Kay and I will finish." He looked at Kayla and smiled. "Won't we, Kay?"

Kayla replied, "You can count on us, Mee Maw. We won't let you down."

Anna leaned down, put her hands on Kayla's little cheeks, and kissed the tip of her nose. "I know you won't. Take care of Paw Paw and keep him out of trouble. Okay?"

Kayla replied in a serious tone, "I'll try, but I warn you, it won't be easy. You know how he can be sometimes."

Anna and William let out snickers. Anna kissed her husband quickly and went to check on Andrea. As she went in search of her daughter, her mind promptly averted from her two tricksters in the kitchen. She was extremely concerned about her daughter's health and well-being. They had just buried her husband the day before and now this. What was next?

Chapter 2

At the hospital, Andrea had not wanted her mother to accompany her to the examination room. The waiting area was extremely crowded. Anna thought that everyone who lived in the small, but developing, Georgia town of Villa Rica must have been at the hospital.

Anna attempted to look at a magazine. She wasn't remembering anything she read, so she tried to watch a news show on the television. She couldn't keep her mind focused on that either, so she prayed silently. She was engrossed in her thoughts when she saw a nurse rushing toward her.

The nurse approached Anna. "Are you Andrea Hamilton's mother?"

Anna stood up. "Yes, I am. Is she all right?"

"She'll be fine. We just need your assistance. Please follow me," the nurse kindly but firmly ordered.

Anna obeyed but wanted to know what all the fuss was about. "Are you sure she's okay? What's the matter?"

"Ma'am, please just follow me," the nurse repeated.

Anna wanted some answers at that moment. *Why do these hospital people always do this? They get you all in an uproar and then won't tell you anything.*

They finally reached Andrea's examination room. What Anna saw tore at her very core. There in the bed lay Andrea in a fetal position crying and trembling frantically. The attending physician was leaning down beside her, attempting to console her with words of reassurance.

As Anna started to rush over to her daughter, she almost sent the nurse who had accompanied her tumbling to the floor. Not pausing to beg the woman's pardon, she pressed on. "Andrea? Honey, what's wrong?"

Andrea didn't answer. All she could do was tremble and moan in grief.

Anna looked at the doctor. "What's wrong with her? Is she that sick? Did you give her some awful news about her condition?"

The doctor attempted to explain. "I'm Dr. Hicks. Your daughter is four weeks pregnant. When I told her, she got extremely upset."

Anna couldn't believe her ears. She felt the urge to join Andrea and scream at the top of her own lungs.

Anna turned her attention back to her daughter and managed to grab hold of Andrea's hands. "Andrea, listen to me, honey. Everything will be okay. I know this is a shock to you. It is to me, too, but you'll get through this. We're all going to get through this together."

Andrea looked at her mother and managed to speak through all the pain and tears, shaking her head. "I can't, Mama. I can't do it without Clay. How can I? I need him. I want him here with me."

"Yes, you can do it, and you won't be alone, because you have your family. Think about it. Kayla, your father and me, Edward and Lizzie, Leah and Devin. We'll always be here for you." Anna gently took Andrea by one arm. "Come on. Let me help you up."

Much to Anna's surprise, Andrea allowed her to aid her in getting out of the bed. Anna informed the doctor that they had buried

Andrea's husband the day before. Dr. Hicks advised them that they should call Andrea's gynecologist the first thing Monday morning and make an appointment. Then, before giving them Andrea's release instructions, he gave them some information on counseling groups for help in dealing with the loss of a loved one.

On the ride home, Andrea simply stared out the window. Everyone they passed along the way appeared so happy. She didn't know happiness anymore. Her world had been shattered into a million pieces, and she didn't know how or if she could ever put it back together.

"Mama, why is this happening to me?"

Anna was shocked. She had never heard words such as those come from her daughter's mouth, but then again, Andrea had never experienced anything as traumatic as what she was going through now. They had a strong religious background and knew from their study of the Bible that time and chance happened to all people, God's servants included. Was now the time to remind her grieving daughter of Ecclesiastes 9:11? She was about to, when Andrea spoke again.

"Clay was a good man, Mama. The best. He never hurt anybody. We had been trying for months to have another baby. We didn't say anything because we didn't want to get everybody's hopes up. I had forgotten my period hadn't come this month. My cycles are sporadic sometimes. We've had false alarms before, so I just didn't think anything of it. Why did it have to happen now after he's gone? He wanted a son so badly. That was all he talked about." Andrea's lips began to quiver.

Anna had tears pouring down her face and could hardly see through them to drive. She managed to grab some napkins from the console. She gave some to Andrea and wiped her own face with one.

Anna attempted to comfort her daughter. "Baby, I know it's hard, and I hate to see you hurting like this. It won't be easy, but you don't have to go it alone. God will help you through, and so will your family. You're strong, Andrea. You always have been. You know that."

Anna stole a quick glance at Andrea but received no response. She continued, "Now our family has an emergency situation. We've got to pray for endurance, because that's the only way we're going to make it through this. We all have to be strong for each other, and you've got to be strong for your babies."

"I know, Mama, but I don't know if I can. I want to."

Anna looked at her daughter again. "Well, that's a start. You want to. And if you want to, you can do it."

Inside the house, everyone rushed to Andrea, each taking a turn at embracing her. They went into the family room and sat down.

Leah and Devin held hands as Leah spoke. "When we found out you went to the emergency room, I called the hospital, but they said you'd already gone, so we rushed over here. Are you okay? What's wrong?"

Little Kayla wanted to know, too. "Yeah, Mommy, what did the doctor say?"

Andrea looked at her mother. Anna stared back at her. Neither said anything.

Lizzie mistook their looks to indicate something terrible. She immediately put her hand to her chest and gasped, "Oh, my Lord. What is it?"

Andrea sighed. She thought she might as well let it out here and now with everybody present, including Kayla, who was five going on thirty. She spoke in a delicate tone. "We're having a baby."

"Really, Mommy?" Kayla was excited. "A real live baby?"

Andrea nodded her head. "Yes, sweetie, a real live baby."

Once again, everyone took turns hugging Andrea.

"A baby," Lizzie whispered against her daughter-in-law's cheek. "That's wonderful."

"Mommy," Kayla said, "I'm gonna be a big sister." She pointed to herself.

Andrea smiled. "Yes, you are. And you're going to be a wonderful big sister."

The room was filled with laughter and chatter about the news of the baby. Andrea could feel the love in the air, and she knew she was truly blessed to be surrounded by such a loving family. However, despite the happiness everyone else was feeling, the hole in her heart felt like it was getting bigger and bigger. Could she make it through this?

Later that afternoon, Andrea laid her head against her father's shoulder as they sat on the porch swing.

William patted his daughter's arm. "You're going to be all right."

"I don't know, Daddy. How am I going to raise two children on my own? I'm scared."

"I know you are, but you won't have to do it alone. You know that. Your family will help."

That wasn't what she meant, and Andrea knew her father was aware of that. Everybody kept telling her she wasn't alone. What she needed was her husband.

Andrea said, "I've never hurt like I'm hurting now. I just want it to end."

"And it will," William reassured her. "But it'll take time. Right now, you probably feel that there is no way you can ever be happy again, but you will. God will help you through."

Andrea sighed. "I know He'll help me, Daddy. And I know I have the hope of seeing Clay again, but right now, the Resurrection seems so far off to me."

"That's because we don't know the exact day or hour. So, no, it won't happen soon enough for you. But it'll happen when God says it's time."

Andrea thought for a moment. She knew what the scriptures said regarding the Resurrection. She had heard them all her life. In fact, she had quoted verses such as John 5:28-29 many times, especially when offering comfort and words of hope to other bereaved families. Now it was her turn to receive some solace. She never understood until now why some grieving people, although they had faith, felt as though that faith could not sustain them. The pain of losing a loved one in death was more horrible than she ever imagined.

Andrea's mother interrupted her thoughts. "Andrea, do you want to eat your lunch out here on the porch or inside?"

Andrea did not want to escape from the comfort of her father's arms. She raised her head just enough to respond to her mother's inquiry. "I'm not hungry, Mama."

Anna opened the glass storm door wider and stepped out. A cool breeze swept across her face. She stood beside her husband and daughter as she wiped her hands on a yellow and white towel. She looked down at Andrea. Her voice was firm, yet loving. "Andrea, you need to eat. Remember you're not just eating for yourself now. It's important that you eat. You've got to keep up *your* strength, too."

Andrea didn't dare look at her mother. "I know. I'm just not hungry."

Anna knew her daughter was in a lot of pain, but she would not give in to her this time. "Andrea, we've still got some leftovers from yesterday, and I fixed a few of your favorites. Come on. You and your father can sit over here at this table you've got fixed up so pretty." Anna motioned behind her at the round table covered in a green-and-white-checkered gingham tablecloth with matching wicker chairs. "I can bring the food, and we can eat out here. It'll be nice."

William nudged his daughter. "Come on. Your mother's right. You need to eat, and it'll be nice."

"Okay," Andrea murmured.

"You two go on over there and have a seat," Anna ordered. "I'll be back in a jiffy."

Anna dashed back into the house. When she came back with a

basket of sliced, hot, buttered French bread and a dish of baked macaroni and cheese, she found William and Andrea at the table. She placed the food next to the flower centerpiece. "I have a couple more things to get. I'll be right back."

William started to rise. "I'll help you."

"Sit back down," Anna tactfully ordered. "I've got it." She burst back through the front door.

Andrea looked at her father. "You better mind her," she joked. "I've already got her all riled up. You don't want her on you, too, do you?"

William teased his daughter as he leaned toward her and whispered. "You better hush before she hears you, or she'll be on both of us. You know, I think she can take us on, too."

Andrea let out a snicker, even though her inclination was totally against it. Her father could make her laugh no matter what the situation. They were still at it when Anna returned with a pitcher of sweet iced tea and a platter of fried chicken. She plopped them down onto the table.

"What are you two giggling at?" Anna inquired. She reached into her apron pocket and pulled out silverware and paper napkins. "Never mind. I'm just glad to see you smiling, Andrea." She waved her hand in a playfully dismissing manner at William. "As for your father, he's always joking. He's a regular comedian."

William just smiled. He knew his wife loved his sense of humor. It helped keep their marriage from being stale and boring.

As Anna sat down, Andrea took on a serious demeanor. She grabbed both her parents' hands. "Mama. Daddy. I don't know what I'd do without you. I love you both so much." Then she leaned over and kissed each one on the cheek.

Anna squeezed Andrea's hand and smiled. "We love you, too. You stay strong. Things'll get better." She glanced at her husband. "Won't they, William?"

William agreed. "Yes, they will." To Andrea, he said, "You'll see," and gave her a wink.

"Okay," Anna said. "Let's let your father say the blessing so you can get some food in your stomach before you pass out on us."

Still clutching each other's hands, they bowed their heads as William offered a prayer of thanksgiving.

Chapter 3

Kayla glanced up with big, brown eyes at her mother as Andrea walked into the child's room. The little girl sat on a petite footstool as her grandmother tied a pink satin ribbon on a bit of loosely curled hair on top of her head. The rest flowed in soft curls below her shoulders.

"Look at Mommy's baby. You look so pretty," Andrea bragged. She took a seat on one of the matching white, twin-size canopy beds, both of which were decorated in a floral, watercolor pattern.

Aware that her mother, still bedecked in her big, fluffy, white, terry cloth robe, wasn't dressed in her Sunday best, Kayla inquired, "Mommy, you're not going to church with us?"

"No, sweetie. Mommy's not going today."

"Are you sick?" Andrea's inquisitive little one wanted to know.

Andrea looked at her mother who met her gaze. Anna didn't say a word as she pulled her fingers loosely through Kayla's curls.

"No, honey, I'm not sick. I just don't feel good."

Anna patted Kayla's arms. "Okay, pumpkin, you're all done and ready to go. Your Mommy's right. You do look pretty. Now give me some sugar."

Kayla giggled, jumped up off the stool, and kissed her grandmother's cheek. "Thank you, Mee Maw." As she caught a glimpse of her reflection in a white, oval-shaped mirror, she gently patted the sides of her hair and said, "Mommy, see how Mee Maw fixes my hair? She makes me look like a big girl, not a baby."

Andrea let out a tiny snicker. "I beg your pardon. What do you mean?"

"You know, Mommy. You twist it like this." Kayla put her tiny hands above her head and attempted to imitate the way her mother usually styled her hair.

Andrea and Anna both let out chuckles. Andrea playfully swatted Kayla's bottom against the satin, white dress sprinkled with tiny pink rose petals. "You just won't do."

Kayla laughed. Looking at her grandmother's pink sweatshirt and pants, she exclaimed, "Mee Maw, I know you're not wearing that, are you?"

Anna smiled. "I'm going to stay here with your Mommy today since she's not feeling good. Is that okay with you?"

"Yes," Kayla agreed, "as long as you'll be looking after Mommy."

A few minutes later, William, Edward, Lizzie, and Kayla left for Sunday morning service.

Later that evening, everyone sat around the rectangle-shaped dining room table, which was covered in a soft lilac, damask tablecloth, and held hands with heads bowed.

William's voice filled the quiescent space. "Father, we thank you for allowing us to wake up to another day of life and for the opportunity to serve you yet another day. We're appreciative for the food that we are about to partake for the nourishment of our physical bodies. Please help us to remember that just as we need physical food, we also need spiritual food to feed our hearts and minds.

"This is a sad time for us all. We've lost a dear loved one. Please sustain us by means of your promise of a resurrection, our family, and our spiritual brotherhood. We love you so much, Father. We love your Son, Jesus, and appreciate the sacrifice that you both made for all mankind. So help us please to remain strong, and keep our complete trust in you. When we fall short of your righteous requirements, we beg for your forgiveness and ask that you help us to extend the same to others. It's in Jesus' dear name we pray. Amen."

"Amen," everyone concurred.

When William saw the tears streaming down Andrea's face, he squeezed her hand. "Thank you, Daddy," she whispered.

Gently tightening his grasp, he nodded his head before releasing her hand. Andrea swiped her napkin from the table and quickly wiped her face as everyone passed around the platters of food.

"Kayla, you looked beautiful today in your pretty little dress and hair in curls," Devin bragged. "You looked like a little princess."

Kayla placed her corn on the cob on her plate and licked her fingers. "Thank you, Uncle Devin. See? I told you, Mommy. Mee Maw knows how to do my hair good. You do it good, too, but Mee Maw's a professor."

Everyone started laughing. "Honey, I think you mean *professional*," Andrea politely corrected her little one.

Kayla looked at her mother and held her hands open in front of her in a questioning gesture. "That's what I said."

Leah chuckled. "No, sweetie, but you were close."

Kayla shrugged her shoulders and grabbed her corn again. "Oh, well." Her two missing front teeth did not hinder her from taking another huge bite of the crunchy vegetable.

She had everyone at the table laughing. She was oblivious to it, though, and kept right on eating.

As everyone else talked, Andrea stole glances at her daughter, thinking of how much she was like Clayton. Clayton had a wonderful sense of humor, like his father, and had kept Andrea and Kayla laughing all the time. It was a trait that had been passed on from father and son to Kayla. Everything Kayla did and said seemed to remind Andrea of Clayton. Was that going to be good or bad? Every time she thought about the good times they had, it made her miss him that much more.

Andrea was still lost in her thoughts when Leah put her hand on her arm and shook it slightly. "Andrea, did you hear what I said?"

Andrea stared at her sister. "What? What did you say?"

"I was just saying how everyone at church was asking about you today. The brothers and sisters are all very concerned about you. They want you to know that."

"I know. I appreciate it. I miss them. I hope to see them soon."

"They want to come by to visit. They said they'd call first."

"That's fine," Andrea sighed. "I don't feel much like being social right now."

Leah patted her sister's hand. "I know."

After dinner, Edward and Lizzie gathered up their belongings for their trip back home to Birmingham. Andrea retreated to the bedroom, where she was spending the majority of her time lately. She sat in her chair, her mind racing.

She was so glad that both her and Clayton's parents had been able to stay with her and Kayla during this difficult time. When she and Clayton had selected the design for the house, they had both agreed they needed a one-story, four-bedroom home. Whenever their parents came to visit, they wanted them to have their own rooms. They didn't want steps for their parents to have to climb as they got older.

Andrea would surely miss Edward and Lizzie when they left. She couldn't have asked for better in-laws than them. She had always heard nightmare in-law stories from her friends and coworkers, but her relationship with hers was not like that. She needed to have a few more minutes alone with them before they left. She eased up out of her chair and went down the hall to their room. The door was open, but she tapped lightly before she entered.

Lizzie turned around and smiled when she saw Andrea. "Hey. Come on in." She held out her arms, and the two women embraced. Then Andrea and Edward hugged. All three stood in a tiny circle holding hands.

Andrea's heart wept at the thought of their leaving. "I'm gonna miss you two," she confessed. "You know that, don't you?"

Lizzie concurred, "We're gonna miss you, too."

"We wish you and Kayla would come to visit soon," William said. He motioned with a nod of his head at Andrea's stomach. "Maybe before this little one gets here. If you don't want to drive with just the two of you, we'll come pick you up and bring you back home when you're ready."

"Yeah, that's a good idea," Lizzie agreed. "Come here." She broke their circle and pulled Andrea and Edward toward the bed to sit down, with herself in the middle.

Lizzie swept Andrea's hair behind her right ear. "Andrea, you know we love you. You're the daughter we never had. When you and Clay chose each other, you picked the best. I know you need some time to yourself. You deserve that, but you also need your family, your friends, and your church. Don't isolate yourself too much. Sometimes when we're going through personal suffering, we tend to go into seclusion. I know things are hard for you right now. You want to be alone sometimes. You've got a lot on your mind. Am I right?"

Andrea nodded in agreement. "Yes, you're right. Sometimes I'm so afraid of being alone, and other times, all I want is to be by myself. I don't feel like being around people the way I used to, because deep down inside I'm not happy anymore, and I can't laugh the way I once could. Is that how the two of you feel?"

Edward and Lizzie nodded. The three talked a few more minutes. Then Devin assisted his father in carrying the luggage to the car, while everybody else followed them outside. Good-byes were said quickly so that Andrea and Kayla could have more time to say theirs. Tears streamed slowly down Andrea's face as she hugged her in-laws one more time. "I'm gonna miss you," she repeated.

Lizzie gently touched Andrea's cheek. "We'll miss you, too."

Then she grabbed Andrea's hands and added, "You take care of yourself and Kayla." She placed her hand on Andrea's stomach. "And this little one."

As Kayla swung her hand back and forth in Edward's, she looked up at her grandmother and assured her, "We'll be okay, Nanna. Don't worry. Paw Paw told me when I get sad to think about when I can see Daddy again."

Edward agreed. "Paw Paw's right. You pray and ask God to help you do that, and He will, you know."

Kayla smiled.

Edward reached down, picked Kayla up, and squeezed her tightly as he hugged her. "I love you, Pooh Bear."

"I love you, too, Poppy Bear." Kayla wrapped her tiny arms around her grandfather's neck and squeezed him with all her might.

After Edward and Lizzie were in the car, Andrea and Kayla stood beside the vehicle on the driver's side, with Edward at the wheel. Andrea reminded them, "Don't forget to call and let us know you made it home okay." Ever since Clayton's accident, she was even more apprehensive.

"We'll call," Lizzie promised.

As they pulled out of the driveway, they all waved good-bye until the car was out of sight.

Andrea and Kayla walked back toward the house. Leah and Devin stood beside Devin's burgundy Maxima and held hands. Mother and daughter stopped in front of the couple.

Andrea moaned, "Don't tell me you're leaving, too."

"Yeah," Leah answered. "We've got to go. I'll call you tomorrow. Maybe while Mama and Daddy are here, we can go to lunch one day."

"Okay."

The two sisters hugged. "I love you, girl," Leah said.

Andrea replied, "I love you, too."

Leah leaned down so that she was eye level with Kayla. "You be good. Okay, June Bug?"

Kayla grinned. She loved it when her family called her by the nicknames her father had given her. "I will."

Leah and Kayla hugged. "I love you, Aunt Leah."

"I love you, too, sweetie."

Andrea looked at her brother-in-law. "Devin, thanks so much for all your help." As the two hugged, she reminded him, "You're a terrific brother-in-law. I love you."

"You're welcome. I love you, too."

"I love you, too, Uncle Devin," Kayla assured her uncle.

Devin smiled and picked up his niece. "I know you do, little lady, and I love you."

Anna and William stood on the porch, smiling at all the *I love you's* being exchanged. It was obvious that there was a lot of love in this family. They hoped that, along with their faith, it would help sustain them.

As Leah and Devin drove away, Kayla ran to join her grandparents on the porch. Andrea walked slowly toward the house. *Thank God my parents are still here.* They were leaving the following weekend, though. What would she and Kayla do when they had to come home every day to an empty house with no expectations of seeing their loved one? It would never be the same.

Chapter 4

Anna pulled away from Kayla's school and went through the old part of town on Highway 78. As she drove, her mind wandered back to the conversation she'd just had with her granddaughter. Kayla was a bright child. Her parents had taught her well, but she was so innocent and had a lot of honest, warmhearted questions. *They'll get through this,* she thought. *God will see them through.*

Anna reached the strip on Highway 61, where stores and buildings now stood in place of the trees of long ago. Villa Rica, Georgia, known as the City of Gold, looked so different. She was amazed at how much the small township had grown since she and William had lived here. She had been born and raised in this little city and had lived here all her life until she and William had moved to Brooklyn a few years ago.

Never in a million years would she have believed that she would leave the comforts of her hometown and move to the hustle and bustle of a big city. If her older sister, Doreen, hadn't been sick and too stubborn to move in with them at the time, they never would have left. Anna hadn't been too thrilled about relocating at first, but William had convinced her that it was the right thing to do. After all, Doreen was her sister and the only close family she had.

However, they loved New York so much that, even after Doreen's death, they had decided to stay.

Anna observed the city with admiration. There had been no fast-food restaurants, hotels, or large discount stores when they had lived here. Now there was a Super Wal-Mart, fast-food restaurants, and convenience stores everywhere, and the area was still growing. She shouldn't have been surprised, though. After all, the town sat right off Interstate 20 which made all the expansion accessible to everyone, including travelers.

Everything was changing. Andrea and Kayla were practically going to have to start their lives all over again. It would be an adjustment, but Anna had confidence that God would help them through it. She headed toward Carrollton to the Goodwill store, which was only about twenty minutes away.

Anna arrived at the store before it opened. She waited in the car, passing the time away thinking about her family and praying. Finally, she was able to leave the items of clothing that had belonged to Clayton and head back to Andrea's. She got back to the house about fifteen minutes before ten and found William in the family room reading the newspaper. She kissed his cheek and sat down beside him. "Where's Andrea?"

William refolded the paper and placed it on the coffee table. "She went back to bed. She's not feeling good."

Anna sat back against the chair and took her husband's hand. "We have to get her out of this house. She's gonna go stir crazy if she stays cooped up in here."

"She told me this morning that she and Kayla may be moving."

Anna was surprised at first, but then realized she'd probably feel the same way. "Where to?"

"She didn't say. I don't think she knows what she wants to do at this point. I didn't tell her, but personally, I think it's too soon for her to be making major decisions such as that. She said she'll think about it and talk to Kayla."

Anna slowly nodded her head.

William saw that his wife's face was overshadowed with more anxiety. "What is it?"

"Kayla," Anna sighed heavily. "She doesn't understand why God let her Daddy die. We talked yesterday about Job and why God allowed him to suffer. I reminded her of the Resurrection hope. I suppose she and Andrea are getting pretty tired of everybody doing that, because it's not making their pain go away."

William agreed, "Yeah, I guess so. How was Kayla after you talked to her?"

"Well, she seemed fine, but you know how it is. One minute, they're okay, it seems. The next minute, who knows?" Anna laid her head on her husband's shoulder. "William, what are we going to do? Maybe we should move back here so we'll be closer and can offer to help more, especially since she's talking about moving. This is going to be harder than I thought."

William put his arm around Anna. "Maybe you're right. Perhaps we should move back. She's really going to need some help when the baby gets here. I think we should give it prayerful consideration when we get home."

"Okay," Anna said as she stood. "I'm gonna go check on her."

Andrea was sitting on the side of the bed.

"Hey, honey. I thought you were asleep."

"Hey, Mama. I was. I just woke up."

"How are you?"

"Okay."

Anna sat on the bed beside Andrea and looked intently into her face. "Did you call the doctor?"

"Yes. I have an appointment this Friday at ten-thirty."

"Good. I'll drive you. Listen. Why don't you, me, and your father go somewhere—riding, shopping, to the mall, or something? You need to get out."

"I really don't feel like going anywhere."

"Come on. You said you wanted some mums for the porch. Let's go to Douglasville to Lowe's or Home Depot and get some. It'll help keep your mind occupied. We can stop and eat lunch. You know I'm not taking no for an answer."

Andrea looked at her mother. "You're very persistent, aren't you? I have to take a shower," she said, standing.

"Okay. While you're doing that I'll put your things in these drawers."

"That's fine." Andrea went into the bathroom.

While Anna put some of Andrea's clothes where Clayton's once were, she thought about the possibility that she and William would be moving back to Georgia. They loved New York, but family was more important, and right now, theirs needed them. She would go to the ends of the earth for her family. It would be nice to be closer to them. Maybe she and William could find a small, two-bedroom apartment or house, so when Kayla and the baby spent the night, there would be enough room for them. *This'll be good. It'll work out. Everything will work out just fine.*

"Mama!" Andrea called out as she leaned down to pick up a pot of golden orange mums. "Do you like these?"

Anna walked down the Home Depot aisle toward Andrea and William. "Yes, they're beautiful. You like them?"

"Yes." Andrea pointed. "These yellow ones are pretty, too. I think I'll get some of these as well."

"Oh, yes," Anna concurred.

They filled the shopping cart with eight plants—four orange chrysanthemums and four yellow ones. William got another cart and put in eight flowerpots.

They decided to eat lunch at Souper Salad. About halfway through their meal, Anna noticed that Andrea had become extremely quiet. Something seemed to have captured her attention. At a nearby table, a man, woman, and little girl were about to sit down. The child looked to be about three or four. The woman was pregnant.

Andrea appeared forlorn. She hadn't realized she was in a daze until she felt her mother's hand on hers. "Andrea."

She looked at her mother, but said not a word.

"Honey, are you all right?" Anna already knew the answer, but didn't know what else to say.

"I'm fine," Andrea lied.

Her parents attempted to engage her in conversation, but she simply picked at her food and remained quiet during the remainder of the meal.

On the way home, Andrea was silent as she sat in the front with her head against the headrest and her eyes closed as her mother drove. When they reached the house, she quickly exited the vehicle and ran inside.

Once outside the car, William and Anna looked at each other, anxiety apparent on their faces. William stated tenderly, "Go check on her. I'll get the flowers."

Anna took off quickly after her bereaved daughter. She tapped lightly on the closed door of Andrea's room. She just barely heard a stifled, "Yes?"

"Andrea." Anna leaned against the door. "It's Mama. Can I come in?"

"Not right now," Andrea sniffed.

"Honey, I just want to make sure you're okay," her mother reassured her.

"I'll be fine. I just need some time alone."

Anna didn't like what she was hearing, and she was equally unhappy that Andrea was shutting her out. However, she knew she had to respect her daughter's wish, so she simply stated, "Okay," and reluctantly walked away.

Andrea lay on her side on the bed facing the wall in a fetal position as tears streamed down her face. She had seemed fine until she saw the family in the restaurant. Was this how she was going to react every time she was in public and witnessed a husband and wife together with their children? In her heart, she knew that seeing families together would only serve that much more as a reminder of how lonely she was without Clayton.

Oh, God, I thought I could do this, but now I don't know if I can. Please help me.

Her tears became as rushing waters until, finally, she cried herself to sleep.

Chapter 5

The next few days were difficult for Andrea. She was thankful for her parents' love and support. Having them around made her feel a little better, but they couldn't stay forever. As a matter of fact, it was Friday, and they were leaving the next day. What would she do then? *Go on living,* a tiny voice inside Andrea's head reminded her, as she and her mother sat in the waiting area of Dr. Gina Murphy's office.

She flipped through the pages of a parenting magazine, but Andrea's thoughts were elsewhere. All around her, she took in the sights of happy men and women together, anticipating the births of their children. Her mind wandered back to six years ago when she and Clayton had sat together, in this very room, bubbling over with excitement about the little bundle of joy that would soon be theirs. Now here she sat, years later, pregnant and alone, except for her mother. She realized she was indeed blessed to have such a loving and supportive family, but what she wanted and needed was her husband.

Andrea felt her mother's hand on her arm. "Andrea, they're calling your name."

She had been so consumed in her contemplations that Andrea

had not even heard her name called. She placed the magazine on the table beside her, got up, and walked toward the nurse who was waiting for her.

While Anna waited, she tried not to think about her and William's departure the next morning. Andrea was so melancholy. She hated to leave her in this state.

Anna breathed a heavy sigh. *Oh, God, sometimes I don't know what to do or say. Do I say too much? Not enough? When she was young, I could do or say something to make whatever she was going through all better. But not this time. I feel so helpless.*

Thirty minutes later, Andrea was ready to go. The hair salon Leah worked at was in Carrollton, and Andrea and her mother had plans to meet Leah for lunch at twelve at Valentino's. As the two women walked to the car, Anna pulled out her cell phone and called Leah to let her know that she and Andrea would be on time.

At Valentino's, Andrea, Leah, and Anna went through the pizza and salad buffet line. When they returned to their table, they held hands as Anna offered the blessing for their meal.

After they whispered "Amen," Leah gleefully blurted out, "So what did the doctor say?"

Andrea answered, "My due date is June twenty-fifth."

"Oh, that's great." Leah smiled. "That's six months before the wedding." She squirmed in her seat and rubbed her hands together. "This is wonderful."

Anna looked at Leah and smiled. "That's the same thing I was thinking."

"What else did the doctor say?" Leah went on. "Is everything okay?"

Andrea had just taken a sip of tea. She allowed the cool, sweet liquid to slide down her throat before answering. "Everything's fine. Considering I had a normal, healthy pregnancy and delivery with Kayla, everything should be okay."

Leah was concerned. She touched her sister's hand. "You're going through a lot right now, and I'm worried about you."

"I'll be fine," Andrea assured Leah. She hoped she had convinced her sister better than she had herself. "Dr. Murphy wants me to take childbirth classes. I told her I don't see the need for that. After all, it's not like I haven't had a baby before."

"Honey," Anna chimed in, "that was five years ago. I'm sure there's a lot of up-to-date information that will be beneficial for you. You're under a lot of stress. When you get ready to deliver this baby, you'll need to know how to relax and be comfortable during the labor and delivery. I think it's a good idea."

Andrea put her fork down on her plate. "When I was pregnant with Kayla, Clay and I went to every class. I think he was more excited that I was. This time, I don't have him. I'm alone," she stressed.

As soon as the words were out of Andrea's mouth, an intense feeling of guilt washed over Anna. She had not been thinking. The way Andrea had been reacting lately around other couples, Anna should have known that attending childbirth classes would be the last thing she wanted to do.

Leah interrupted her mother's thoughts, reminding her sister, "You're not alone. I wish you'd stop saying that you are. I know it won't be the same as having Clay, but *I'll* be your partner."

At Leah's words, Andrea almost choked on a bit of salad she had just placed in her mouth. She covered her mouth with her napkin as she coughed uncontrollably.

Anna and Leah gently patted Andrea's back. "Are you all right?" they asked in unison.

Andrea nodded her head and reassured them, "I'm fine."

"What happened?" Leah asked. "Did your food go down the wrong way?"

"No, I'm okay," Andrea said, placing her napkin on the table. "It's just that when you said you'd be my partner, it caught me by surprise."

Leah looked at her sister, a serious expression covering her face. "Why are you surprised? I'll do it."

Andrea and her mother glanced at each other. Anna knew why Andrea had reacted as she had and was bewildered that Leah seemed to have no clue. Everyone who knew Leah was aware of what a weak reaction she had to medical issues.

Andrea didn't want to hurt her sister's feelings, but she shook her head. "That's okay."

"Well, why not?" Leah ceased eating and glared at her sister.

Neither Andrea nor Anna spoke.

Then it dawned on Leah. "Oh, I get it. You don't trust me. I'm hurt." Then she grabbed a clean plate from their table, got up, and walked away mumbling, "Pass out once and nobody thinks you can do anything."

When Leah returned, Andrea was smiling. "I'm sorry. I didn't mean to hurt your feelings. It's just that you get weak at the knees from something as minor as a paper cut." She covered her mouth with her hand as she let out a snicker.

Leah faked a frown. "Very funny," she said, as she stabbed her fork into her salad and crammed a portion into her mouth.

Andrea couldn't stop laughing. "I'm sorry." She looked at Anna. "Mama, can you see Leah in the delivery room with me about to give birth? I can picture the hospital staff now when they see her turn green and pass out."

When Leah and Anna saw how hard Andrea was laughing, they joined in. It was the first good laugh Andrea had had in almost two weeks.

Andrea dabbed at the corners of her eyes with her napkin. "I'm sorry, Leah. I didn't mean to make fun of you."

"I'm serious," Leah said. "I really do want to do it. I know my resumé for handling emergency situations doesn't look good, but I'm willing to try. Give me a chance. The first time I pass out, you can fire me."

Andrea asked, "Are you sure about this? I don't know."

"Yes, I'm sure. Trust me."

Andrea thought for a moment. "I trust you. Okay."

Leah's face lit up like the sun.

Anna smiled. She felt confident that Leah would do her best to live up to the commitment she'd just made to her sister. However, she'd give anything to see the expression on Leah's face during the childbirth film. Leah had no idea what she had just gotten herself into, but why tell her now and ruin the excitement?

Andrea was gloomy on the ride from the airport. She was in an obscure world of her own as Kayla chatted away from the backseat. Seated behind the steering wheel, Leah exchanged a few words every now and then whenever Kayla would let her get a word in edgewise. By now, Anna and William were on the plane headed home.

Andrea missed them already. What would she do now that they were gone? She wished she was a little girl again, safe and secure in the comfort of her parents' arms. Their good-byes at the airport had been tearful indeed.

Kayla's little voice brought Andrea out of her reverie. "Mommy, did you hear me?"

Andrea turned slightly to look at Kayla. "What is it, sweetie?"

"Can I spend the night with Aunt Leah tonight?"

"No, not tonight."

"I'm hungry." Kayla fidgeted in the backseat. "Can we stop at Mickey D's?"

"You'll have to ask Aunt Leah. She's driving, and it's her car," Andrea reminded her daughter.

Kayla poked her head forward in an attempt to see her aunt. "Aunt Leah, may we go to Mickey D's? Please?"

Leah turned quickly to look at Kayla and smiled. "Of course. When you ask like that, how can I resist?"

"Thank you, Aunt Leah. I love you."

"I love you, too," Leah concurred.

"I love you, too, Mommy."

"I love you, too, sweetie."

After lunch at McDonald's, they stopped by the grocery store. Then Leah took Andrea and Kayla home.

While Kayla played in her room, Leah helped Andrea put away the groceries.

Leah asked, "Why don't you and Kayla come home with me? Stay for a week or two."

Andrea shook her head. "No, I want to be in my own house. It'll be hard at first, but we have to get used to it."

"Well, I'll stay with you for a couple of weeks."

"That's sweet, but you've got your own life. Don't worry about us. We'll be okay."

"But," Leah protested, "I want to. I don't mind."

"I know you don't, but I do. I know you're trying to help, and I appreciate it. I really do, but we'll be all right. Stop worrying."

Leah felt tempted to pressure her sister, but she simply stated, "Okay. Whatever you say."

Leah spent the remainder of the day with Andrea and Kayla. Anna called to let them know that she and William had made it home safely. Later, Leah prepared a quick supper. By seven o'clock, she reluctantly prepared for her departure. Kayla gave her a hug and kiss good-bye.

When Andrea walked her to the door, Leah demanded, "You call me if you need anything. I mean it."

"Yes, ma'am." Andrea hugged her sister. Then she was gone.

Andrea and Kayla were exhausted. After Kayla had her bath and said her prayers, Andrea read to her from her Bible storybook. Kayla was soon fast asleep.

The house was quiet. Andrea felt strange. The loneliness she felt was a painful reminder that Clayton wouldn't be walking back through the doors they had built together. She felt a huge lump in her throat as she fought back the tears.

Without even realizing what she was doing, Andrea began walking through each and every room of the house. When she stopped, she was standing in the midst of the master bedroom.

I can't do this. I can't stay in this house. It's so full of memories. Memories of Clayton. Things will never be the same.

Andrea managed to shut the door before she crumpled to the floor in a heap and burst into tears. She crawled over to the bed, reached up, and grabbed a pillow. Pulling it off the bed, she buried her face in it to keep her wails contained inside the bedroom walls, so as not to awaken and frighten her daughter. As she sobbed uncontrollably, the painful sounds she heard coming from within her frightened her. She could not remember ever crying like this. Her heart was throbbing; it felt as though her life was being drained from her body. She lay there paralyzed in agony and wept for several minutes.

Finally, Andrea was able to pull herself up. She went into the bathroom and grabbed some tissues to wipe her face, then chose to take a hot bubble bath. After her bath, she put on her silk, lavender pajamas and decided that spiritual healing was what she needed.

She went into the family room, grabbed her Bible off the table, and stretched out on the sofa. She knew how the scripture read, but could not recall exactly where it was. She turned to the dictionary-concordance in the back of the Bible and turned to the *r*'s. She started at the top of the page and slid her index finger down slowly until she found the word *resurrection*. Upon seeing the scripture she was searching for, she opened her Bible to John 11:25 and read in an undertone.

Jesus said unto her, I am the resurrection and the life: he that believeth in me, though he were dead, yet shall he live.

Comforting words. Oh, how she needed them. Andrea closed her eyes for a moment to reflect. The shrill ring of the telephone broke her concentration. She quickly answered it. It was Leah. Andrea tried again to reassure her sister that she was fine. They talked for a few minutes before ending the call. When Andrea went to bed, sleep didn't come, but the tears did.

Chapter 6

Andrea's full attention was focused on the words of Minister Alexander Knight as he spoke from the church's podium, gesturing with his hands every now and then as he spoke the word of God. Alexander and his wife, Ellen, were cherished friends of Andrea and Clayton. In their late fifties, they had no children, but plenty of spiritual ones. The two couples had spent a tremendous amount of time together. Being part of a racially mixed assemblage, it hadn't mattered to them that the Knights were white and the Hamiltons were black. They loved each other as though they were family.

Kayla sat quietly beside her mother, her own personal copy of the Bible open in her tiny lap. A strange feeling had come over Andrea as soon as she and Kayla had walked through the church's doors. This was the first time Andrea had stepped foot inside the building since Clayton's funeral here over a week ago. Everyone had immediately run to her and Kayla with hugs, kisses, and kind words of sympathy and encouragement.

Alexander was speaking on the subject of "Finding Happiness in a Troubled World." He asked the audience to open their Bibles to 1 Corinthians 10:13. As Andrea flipped through the scriptures, she glanced now and then to see if Kayla needed assistance in locating the text—but even though she was only five, Kayla was highly adept at locating the books of the Bible.

Alexander began reading. Andrea followed along, each word making an impression in her mind.

There hath no temptation taken you but such as is common to man: but God is faithful, who will not suffer you to be tempted above that ye are able; but will with the temptation also make a way to escape, that ye may be able to bear it.

All her life Andrea had heard the scripture, especially from the older generation. Her mother had made reference to it just recently, the day in the car on the way home from the emergency room. *God does not put any more on us than we can bear.* Andrea had always believed it—until now. Her heart grew heavy with anxiety as the tears began to well up in her eyes. She didn't want them to come—not here in front of everyone. She didn't want to be the grieving widow. She struggled to conceal her emotions, but wasn't successful.

Andrea bounded up from her seat, turned up the aisle, and walked as fast as she could without running. She wanted no one's attention focused on her at the moment. She promptly dashed into the restroom. It was empty. *Thank goodness.* She sat down on the gold-trimmed bench and let the tears flow.

Before she knew it, she was joined by two women. One of them, an older woman, grabbed a couple of tissues from the tissue box on the counter and offered them to Andrea. The other one, about Andrea's age, placed her hand on Andrea's back and gently patted it. "It's gonna be okay, Sister Andrea," she spoke consolingly. "God will help you through your pain."

"That's right," the older lady added. "And you have your family and all of us, your spiritual family. We're here to help and encourage you. Go ahead and cry. Let it out."

Andrea sniffed as she wiped her face and blew her nose with the tissues. "It's just so hard," she confided. "I don't know if I'm gonna make it. I just want to curl up somewhere and die. When we read that scripture, all I could think about is how not having Clayton is more than I can bear. I used to believe in that verse, but not anymore. I've never hurt so much."

The older sister spoke again. "You take it to God, honey. He knows your pain, and He'll hear your prayers. He'll give you comfort. We all love you, Andrea. You know we'll do whatever we can to help."

Andrea knew her church family would be there for her. Their congregation was one filled with love. Her crying subsided, and she wiped her face again as she stood up. "Thank you." She hugged the two women. "It means a lot to me that you care so much. I know everyone loves me. I love you all, too." Andrea smoothed down her dress with her hands and dropped the wet tissues into the wastebasket. "I'm okay now. I'm going back to my seat."

Just then, another woman popped her head in the door. It was Ellen Knight. "Andrea, are you okay?"

Andrea attempted to smile. "Yes, Ellen. I'm fine. I was just going back to my seat."

Ellen placed her hand on Andrea's shoulder, asking consolingly, "Are you sure?"

"Yes," Andrea answered.

When Andrea returned to her seat, there was Leah sitting in Andrea's spot beside Kayla. She was thankful that her sister had sat with her little one. Leah looked at Andrea as she vacated the seat.

Andrea smiled, whispered, "Thank you," and sat down.

"You're welcome," Leah murmured back and returned to her seat across the aisle.

Andrea was able to sit through the remainder of the service without incident. However, she really did not feel much like socializing afterward, so she grabbed Kayla's hand and immediately started for the door. She had almost made it, when she felt someone's hand on her shoulder.

She stopped and turned around to see a tall, thin, slightly bald man. It was Alexander. "Andrea, it's so good to see you." He hugged Andrea.

Andrea smiled. "Hello, Alex. It's good to be here."

The man leaned down and took Kayla's tiny hand in his large one. "It's good to see you, too, Kayla. How are you today?"

Kayla smiled. "I'm fine."

Alexander returned the child's smile. "Well, that's just wonderful. Are you helping your Mommy out at home?"

Kayla smiled even harder. She liked it when the older ones talked to her on their level. She thought she was just as grown as them. "Yes," she answered.

"Well, that's good. You keep up the good work."

"I will," Kayla promised.

Alexander turned his attention back to Andrea. "Is it okay if Ellen calls you tonight to see what the congregation needs to help you out with at home?"

"Sure. That'll be fine. Thanks so much."

"You're welcome."

Andrea said a hasty good-bye, grabbed Kayla's hand, and bolted for the exit again. She knew they were loved, and it wasn't that she didn't appreciate everyone's concern. She just wasn't ready to be surrounded by too many more people. This time she made it to the parking lot and had her hand on the car door handle before she felt someone beside her. She jumped. It was Leah.

"Hey," Leah said. "Whatcha doing this afternoon?"

Andrea opened the door and pressed a button to unlock the other doors so Kayla could climb in. "Kayla and I were just gonna hang around the house."

"Come to my house," Leah prodded, "and have dinner with me and Devin."

"Not today. Maybe another time." Andrea just wanted to be at home with Kayla.

"Come on. I made your favorite. Pork roast, sweet potatoes,

turnip greens, and cornbread. And for dessert, Kayla's favorite, strawberry shortcake. Please?"

Andrea hated it when her sister begged. She always gave in to her when she did.

"All right, but let us go home and change first. I want to get comfortable."

"Okay."

After Andrea had driven away, Leah stood a few minutes staring after her. She was worried about her sister. She had never seen Andrea lose it like she had today. She realized it was normal behavior, considering she'd just lost her husband, but it was hard seeing her sister like this.

"I'm fine," Andrea's voice sang out as she placed her glass of water on the table between her and Leah. They had just finished eating dinner, and the two sisters sat on Leah's front porch watching Devin play kick ball with Kayla and Kayla's friend, LeaAnn, who lived in Leah's neighborhood.

Leah had not been aware that her stares had been observed by her sister, and she pretended to be clueless as to what Andrea was referring to. "What?"

"Don't play dumb. You know what I'm talking about. You've been staring at me all afternoon. You did it during dinner, and you were doing it just now. I'm fine," Andrea reiterated.

"Sorry. I didn't know I was that obvious," Leah finally confessed. "After what happened during service this morning, I'm just worried about you."

"I'm fine. I'm just having . . ."

"Look at me, Mommy!" Kayla called out as she kicked the ball Devin had rolled her way.

"Wow!" Andrea yelled. "Good kick, honey." Andrea clapped. "Way to go!" She turned her attention back to her sister. "I'm just having a tough time right now."

"What are you going to do for the next two weeks while you're off work?" Leah was concerned. She didn't want her sister moping around the house. That would depress her even more.

"I don't know," Andrea admitted. "I'm just thankful that I work for one of the best doctors in town. One who's patient and understanding when it comes to other people's feelings."

Andrea had worked for Glenn Taylor for fifteen years. She loved her job as a dental hygienist. As a matter of fact, that was how she and Clayton had met. He had come in one day to get his teeth cleaned. The strange thing was she did not even like him at first. He had kept commenting about how pretty her teeth were. She thought he was just running a line by her like most men did, but she soon found out that he was a true gentleman at heart. He possessed all the qualities she longed for in a husband. It was not long thereafter that they had both fallen head over heels in love with each other.

Andrea didn't realize it showed on her face that she had left planet Earth and gone into her own little world, until she heard Leah ask, "What is it?"

Andrea answered sadly, "I was just thinking about the first time Clay and I met in Glenn's office. We were both young. I was twenty. He was twenty-three. I didn't like him at first. I thought he was arrogant."

Leah's mouth fell open. "No. . . ." She was shocked. She didn't remember this story. "Sweet Clay. Why in the world did you think that about him?"

Andrea smiled. "It was his attitude. I was young and inexperienced in the field. He wasn't rude. He just kept making little comments about how young I looked. Telling me how pretty my teeth were. I kidded him after we were married that he was trying to flirt. He just laughed and told me I fell in love with his teeth before I fell in love with him."

Leah smiled. "That's so sweet. I hope Devin and I are as happy in our marriage as you and Clay were."

"You will be. And just wait 'til you have kids." Andrea looked at the threesome playing on the lawn. "Look at him. I believe he's having more fun than Kayla and LeaAnn."

"He's good with kids. And people, in general. I think he'll make a wonderful father if and when that time comes. You know me and pain," Leah reminded her sibling. "It's gonna be hard enough seeing you go through it."

"Children are gifts from God," Andrea declared, "and when you see that new life come into the world, it's just an awesome feeling. You're not getting cold feet on me, are you?"

"Oh no. I know you think I'm gonna chicken out, but I'm not. I'm here for you."

"I know you are." Andrea knew all too well her sister's tolerance for pain and blood. She'd seen her get weak at the knees on many occasions. She and Leah always had the other's back, and deep down inside, Andrea had no reason to believe that this time would be any different.

Chapter 7

Monday morning, Andrea arose at six o'clock and fixed breakfast for Kayla. She wasn't hungry herself, but her mother's previous advice regarding her own strength and the health of the baby continued to echo in her ears, so she finished off the scraps of toast and bacon and the spoonful of grits Kayla left on her plate.

Andrea took Kayla to day care and hurried back home. When Ellen had called the night before to see how the congregation could assist, Alexander had also inquired as to whether or not she felt up to him and Ellen visiting her this morning. Andrea appreciated their companionship and the brotherly love that existed among them. They had really been there for her during this dark moment in her life. They weren't due to arrive until eleven o'clock. She still had three and a half hours in which to occupy herself.

There was no cleaning or laundry to be done, as her mother had done all that before her departure the previous week. Andrea still had one more week left before she planned to return to work. What was she going to do with all the time? She was thinking that perhaps she should return to work next week instead. She was not used to having so much free time on her hands.

She decided to go for a walk in the neighborhood. When she returned home, much to her surprise, Andrea felt energized. She took a bubble bath and dressed in a pair of baggy jeans and a T-shirt and pulled her hair up in a claw clip. She still had a couple of hours before the Knights' arrival so she baked some homemade chocolate chip cookies. They were still warm when Alexander and Ellen arrived promptly at eleven. After they had been seated in the family room, Andrea excused herself briefly and came back with a tray of cookies and cups of steaming hot coffee.

Andrea set the tray on the coffee table and invited her guests to help themselves. Before digging in, Alexander said a brief prayer, thanking God for another day of life, for the food that Andrea had so graciously prepared, and for her inviting them to her home to share some more encouragement with her.

Fifty-nine and fifty-seven respectively, Alexander and his wife looked as though they were made for each other. Andrea loved the way the flecks of silver in Ellen's hair glistened like shiny, new silver dollars.

Alexander looked over at Andrea where she sat across from him and his wife. His concern was evident on his face. "Andrea, our hearts go out to you and Kayla. Not just ours, but the entire congregation. We miss Clay, too. He was our brother in Christ and a very dear friend. But we realize it's a deeper loss for you and Kayla. So tell us, how are you feeling?"

This was just like Alexander. Always worrying about others. Forever having a listening ear. He and Ellen had been among the first to run to her side when they'd heard about the accident. Andrea felt she could talk to them about anything, because they never judged people. They lovingly shared scriptural encouragement from God's Word.

Once Andrea opened her mouth to speak, all of her feelings gushed out like water through a broken dam. "I still feel numb. Like it's not really happening. Every morning when I wake up, I think I'll find Clay lying beside me. Everyone keeps telling me if I just stay strong, I can see him again in the Resurrection, and I know that's true. The thing is, each day that I have to live without him makes the Resurrection seem that much farther away."

Andrea could see that she really had her friends' attention, and that pleased her because she desperately needed to share her feelings with someone other than her own family members. Her family was ready for her to get over her loss. They didn't like seeing her hurt. She knew how much it pained them seeing her in such intense agony, but she couldn't make it any less or make it go away for them. They had to understand that.

Andrea continued, "I found out the day after the funeral that I'm pregnant."

At the news of her pregnancy, the Knights' faces showed a combination of happiness and sadness, for they knew how much Clayton had wanted another child. However, they didn't say anything. They let Andrea finish speaking.

Andrea went on. "The baby's due in June." A lone tear fell down her cheek. "I want this baby so much, but I'm scared. Scared of having to raise him alone. Of course, my family keeps reminding me that I won't have to do it by myself." As the tears came, Andrea wiped them away with the palms of her hands. "And I know they'll be there for me just like they always have been, but it won't be the same. I just feel so lost. . . . I don't know what to do." More tears fell.

Ellen grabbed a handful of tissues from the Kleenex box on the table, took them to Andrea, and sat down beside her.

Alexander leaned forward with his fingertips together and looked tenderly at Andrea. "Please be assured, Andrea, that what you're feeling is normal. And although you're looking forward to the Resurrection, you still need to mourn Clay's loss. Don't try to hide your grief. If you feel you need to let it out, then do so. Remember the faithful men of old like Job and David. They didn't bottle up their feelings.

"Even Jesus wept bitterly upon hearing of the death of his friend Lazarus, and Jesus was a perfect man. But he still had feelings, and he felt pain just like we do. So if he expressed grief and sadness, how much more so we as imperfect humans must and will express it."

Andrea thought about what Alexander had just said. He was right. Sometimes she felt so guilty for grieving the way she did. In the back of her mind, she felt she was displaying a lack of faith in God and His promises.

"How long will I feel this way?" Andrea asked. "Kayla keeps telling me, 'Mommy, we have to be strong.'" As she repeated the words of her precious little one, more pain became evident as she cried harder. "I'm trying, but it's just so hard."

Alexander looked at his wife. Ellen was a wealth of encouragement in situations such as this.

Ellen took Andrea's hand and spoke consolingly. "It may last longer than you think, but you have to be patient with yourself. Just remember you'll have good days and bad days. One minute, you may be feeling up. The next minute, something may trigger memories of Clayton, and your feelings may shift. But Andrea, one of the best ways to handle it is through prayer. Psalms 55:22 tells us to cast our burdens on the Lord and He'll sustain us. And when you cast something, you throw it. You throw it with force."

Ellen gestured with her free hand as if she were throwing an object with great strength. "God will give you the strength you need to go on, but you have to let Him. Throw all your burdens on Him."

Andrea knew from other personal experiences that Ellen was right. Yet, she still needed to hear it. "You're both right. I know everything you just said is true."

"Yes," Alexander said. "It's true because it's not coming from us, but from God's Word, the Bible, and we know God can't lie."

Before the Knights departed, Alexander gave Andrea a brochure titled *When Someone You Loves Dies*. Then they prayed together. Alexander and Ellen reassured Andrea of their love for her and Kayla before they left.

After the Knights had gone, Andrea went to the privacy of her bedroom, knelt beside her bed, and poured out her heart to God.

"I have good days and bad days. Just taking one day at a time," Andrea spoke into the telephone, as she filled Glenn Taylor in on her condition.

"Well, that's all you can do—take one day at a time. We miss you. All your patients are asking about you. They miss you, too. You're the best hygienist I have. The office doesn't seem the same without you. Everybody misses your laughter—the way you keep us in stitches."

"I miss you all, too. I'm glad you called, Glenn. As a matter of fact, I was thinking of calling you. You know, I have one more week left before I'm scheduled to come back to work. I'm about to go crazy. I know this is short notice, but do you mind if I come back to work on Monday?"

"I don't mind, but that's four days away. Are you sure you're ready?" Glenn didn't want Andrea to push herself too hard.

Andrea stared across the room out the window into a world that no longer offered her any happiness. She conceded, "To tell you the truth, I'm not sure about anything anymore. All I know is, if I don't get back to my normal routine, I'm gonna go crazy."

Glenn sympathized with his friend. "You know if you want to come back sooner, all you have to do is ask. You've already done that, so I'll let Marcie know to start scheduling some appointments for you. Do you want to just try half days for a couple of weeks?"

Andrea thought about her present state of affairs. She had to tell Glenn. He had been so good to her. She had to let him know that eight months from now she would need more time off. Glenn was a family man himself. She knew it wouldn't be a problem. She just felt obligated to tell him now.

"No," Andrea answered. "Just put me back on the schedule full time. I have something else to tell you. I'm pregnant."

Glenn was shocked. He didn't know how to respond. "What? Are you serious?"

"Yes, it's true. I found out the day after the funeral. My due date is June twenty-fifth. I plan to work up until the baby is born, just like I did with Kayla."

After hearing this latest news, Glenn was somewhat surprised that Andrea was holding up as well as she was. His heart went out to her. She was a spiritual person. He knew her faith was strong, as she had shared it on many occasions, not only with him but the entire office staff. Everyone liked her. She just grew on everybody she came in contact with.

Glenn acknowledged, "I know how much you and Clay wanted another child. So how do you feel about it now? I imagine at this point it must be extremely difficult for you."

"It is," Andrea admitted. "It's bittersweet."

The two talked for a few more minutes. Andrea was thankful that she worked for such a sympathetic, understanding person.

Chapter 8

The sound of Christmas music and bells jingling could be heard throughout the entire mall. Andrea and Ellen sat in the food court eating their Chinese food.

"So how are you doing?" Ellen asked.

Andrea had just placed a forkful of noodles in her mouth. She chewed, swallowed, and breathed a heavy sigh. "I'm just trying to get on with my life, and it's taking some time."

Ellen looked sympathetically at her friend and touched her hand. "I know. Just remember, you have to be patient with yourself. You're still adjusting to the change in your life. Things'll get better. It's a slow process, but it'll happen. So how's work?"

"Fine. Glenn is such a good person to work for. I think I've finally gotten back into the swing of things. I really missed my patients while I was away, especially the children. You know how funny kids can be. They always make me laugh."

Ellen smiled. "That's nice. Speaking of children, how's Kayla?"

At the thought of her little one, Andrea smiled. "She's fine. She's spending the day with Leah and Devin. You know, she keeps me on my toes. If it wasn't for her, I think I would have given up already.

Children are so resilient. Something can hurt them—almost tear them apart—yet they bounce back so quickly. I wish I could be like that."

Ellen knew exactly what Andrea was saying, for her own life had been shattered many years ago when she had lost her first husband and two young children in an automobile accident. It was a painful experience she had put behind her and rarely ever discussed with anyone who didn't already know.

For a fleeting moment she considered sharing that part of herself with her spiritual sister and friend. Instead Ellen expressed sympathetically, "You spent a lot of years with Clay, just the two of you, before Kayla came along. Therefore, it's going to take you a little bit longer to get over your pain. The more time you spend with people, the more it hurts when they're no longer around. So stop being so hard on yourself. Relief will come."

Andrea was quiet as she finished off the remainder of her chicken and noodles.

Ellen tried to think of something to cheer up her friend. "Hey, I saw a cosmetics booth downstairs where they're giving free makeovers. Let's go get our faces done."

Andrea squinched up her nose and shook her head as they put their trash in the trash can. "No, I don't want to."

Ellen grabbed Andrea's hand and started pulling her toward the escalator. "Come on. It'll be fun."

They were already going down the escalator, so Andrea couldn't get away. By the time they made their exit, Ellen had Andrea laughing as they made their way to the booth.

The first thing Devin noticed about his beautiful fiancée when he opened the door to his apartment was that her arms were flooded with various sorts of catalogs and magazines, in addition to the video she'd rented from Blockbuster for them to watch. They usually went out on Saturday night. However, he wasn't in the mood to venture anyplace this evening. The pizza he had ordered would be delivered shortly.

As he quickly pecked Leah's right cheek, Devin obligingly relieved her of some of the items. "Hey. Whatcha got here?"

After gratefully expressing a quick thank-you, Leah followed Devin into his small bachelor apartment where she dropped her goodies onto the coffee table with the others he had placed there and joined him on the living room sofa. "Just . . . some magazines," she panted as she attempted to catch her breath after climbing the twelve flights of steps to his apartment. "I wanna show you something." Grabbing one of the catalogs from the coffee table, she flipped it open to a page marked with a yellow Post-it note and pointed to a bridal gown. Eyeing Devin, she grinned proudly as she awaited his glowing approval. "Do you like it?"

All Devin could observe at the moment was the four-digit number gazing back at him: *$1,500*. "Yeah . . . it's . . . pretty."

Devin's response disgruntled Leah. He didn't sound the least bit impressed. This was a gorgeous gown. Sighing, she slumped over slightly as her hands hastily left the pages of the catalog, only to come back down just as quickly. Staring at him, she queried, "Is that all you have to say? I think it's gorgeous. Don't you like it?"

Devin responded, "I like it. I said it's pretty."

Not taking her eyes off her fiancé, Leah heaved her back against the sofa. "You don't sound very convincing. What's wrong?"

Devin turned slightly and looked into Leah's warm brown eyes. Anxiety laced his voice. "Leah, we said we wouldn't go overboard with this wedding." He glanced down at the book, still open in her lap. "This dress costs fifteen hundred dollars. Can't you find something cheaper?"

Leah folded her arms. "I like this one. Devin, this is my wedding. I want it to be nice. I've been dreaming about this day practically all my life. When you see me coming down that aisle, I want to be the most beautiful bride you ever saw."

The last thing Devin wanted was them arguing over what dress she would wear to their wedding. He took the book, placed it back on the coffee table, and took Leah's hands in his. "Listen," he said, "I know this'll be a special day for you—for me, too. It's not just *your* wedding. It's *our* wedding," he kindly reminded her. "You can wear a burlap sack if you want to. You'll still look beautiful to me."

Leah laughed, "Yeah, right. I can see me coming down the aisle in a burlap sack. You'll be destroying everything in your path trying to get as far away from me as possible. You'll be the black tornado."

Devin smiled gently.

Leah went on. "Baby, I love this dress. If I get it, I'll keep down the costs on everything else. Deal?"

It was obvious to Devin that Leah adored the gown. He wanted their wedding to be special. He wanted her to be happy. "Okay. Just don't forget our agreement." Turning his thoughts to his sister-in-law, he inquired, "How does Andrea seem to you?"

"Okay, I guess. Sometimes it's hard to tell. I don't know what to say to her. I'm afraid I may say the wrong thing, and then she'll bite my head off."

"Well, she's going through a lot," Devin reminded his fiancée.

"I know," Leah agreed. "And that's the time when people change on us, and anything can happen. I just try to be real careful about what I say to her."

Devin didn't say anything as he sat back and relaxed against the plush brown leather sofa.

Leah turned to observe the handsome face of her fiancé, her eyes brimming with unquestionable concern. "Are you okay?"

Devin stared straight ahead. "Yeah, I'm fine. I've just got a lot on my mind."

Leah was keenly interested in what her future husband was thinking. "Tell me."

"Kayla asked me today if I miss her Daddy. The truth is," Devin confided, "I think about him every day. I think about when we were kids and how he used to get on my nerves, and then one day it seemed like we became best friends. And we stayed that way until the day he died. I'm so angry. I want the person who took his life to

55

suffer like we are. It's scary. I've never felt this way about anyone. I don't like it. I don't want to go around having these kinds of feelings. I pray every day and ask God to help me get rid of them, but it's so hard."

Leah's heart went out to Devin. "Baby, you just have to keep asking God to help you. He knows what you're going through. He'll give you the strength to do what you have to do."

Devin reached over and took hold of Leah's hand, pulling it to his lips and brushing it with a delicate kiss. "Yeah, you're right." When there was a knock at the door, he rose as he gently released her hand. "Pizza's here."

After paying for the pizza and tipping the driver, Devin grabbed some paper towels from the kitchen while Leah popped the DVD into the machine. They enjoyed the movie and their savory Italian dish. Two hours later when the video ended, Leah prepared for her departure.

Devin offered, "Let me drive you home. I'll pick you up in the morning for church."

"No," Leah said, gathering up her assortment of catalogs. "I'll be fine. You get some rest. I'll see you at church."

As they walked to the door, Devin teased, "You need a wheelbarrow for your books. I'll help you take them to your car." He reached out to retrieve some of the catalogs.

Leah politely declined his assistance. "I got 'em. Thanks though."

"You sure?"

"Yeah."

"Okay. I'll see you tomorrow. Call me when you get home."

Leah smiled. "I will."

They quickly kissed good night, and then she was gone. Leah thought about Devin all the way to her house. When he had talked about Clayton earlier tonight, her heart had melted for him like a chunk of ice on a sizzling hot summer day. She telephoned to assure him that she'd arrived home safely. Before she went to bed, she prayed and asked God to heal his broken heart as well as her sister's.

Chapter 9

With love and support from their family, friends, and church members, Andrea and Kayla had managed to make it through the Christmas holiday and into the new year. January was usually when the South received its harsh snowstorms.

Andrea had just completed her last cleaning for the day and was preparing to leave the office, when the recently turned fifty-year-old Dr. Glenn Taylor stuck his head in the door.

"Hey," Glenn said. "You know, the weatherman's been talking all day long about us getting three inches of snow by tomorrow morning."

Andrea turned to face her friend and employer. She frowned. "Do you really think we'll get that much?"

"I don't know. They say it's gonna come in late tonight, and the ground'll be covered by morning. Anyway," Glenn continued, "if it's as bad as they say, don't try to come in tomorrow. We'll close the office. Usually, patients don't try to come in anyway for appointments when there's a lot of snow, but just to be on the safe side, I had Marcie call all our appointments for tomorrow and inform them."

Andrea grabbed her coat and gloves. She wished it wouldn't snow. She, Clayton, and Kayla always played in the snow. She wouldn't mind if she never saw another snowflake for the rest of her life. "Okay, Glenn."

As she prepared to leave, Glenn asked, "So how are you? You holding up okay?" He was deeply concerned.

Andrea pulled her black leather insulated gloves over her hands. "I'm trying. Like we said, it's one day at a time. Being back at work is helping. If I don't keep my mind busy, I'll go crazy. Thanks for asking."

Glenn patted Andrea's back. "Good. Well, drive carefully on your way home. Hopefully, we'll be able to reopen the office on Friday. I'll call you. See ya."

Andrea smiled. "Okay. You be careful, too. Bye."

When she got in her car, Andrea considered stopping by the grocery store to pick up a few items. Then she recalled how crowded the stores would be with everyone trying to stock up on food and other essentials in case they got snowed in. She smiled to herself. That was one thing about the South. Just mention the words *snow* or *ice*, and people went crazy. She promptly concluded that a trip to the store was unnecessary. She and Kayla would make do with what they already had.

Andrea stopped by the day care center, picked up Kayla, and headed for home. Kayla was all excited about the weatherman's forecast for snow.

She chatted away. "Mommy, did you know it's gonna snow tonight? That means no school tomorrow. And you won't have to go to work, and we can build a snowman. We can lie in the snow and make snow angels. I can't wait, Mommy. Can you?"

Andrea did not share her daughter's enthusiasm regarding the latest forecast. However, she refused to burst Kayla's bubble, so she smiled and said, "No, I can't wait either."

After supper, the two nestled up together on the sofa in front of the roaring fire they had built together. Andrea decided to take the moment to discuss with Kayla the possibility of their moving.

"Sweetie," Andrea began, "I've been thinking about something, and I want to get your feelings on it. I've been thinking about selling the house and finding someplace else for you and me and the baby to live. How do you feel about that?"

Kayla turned purposely and stared up into her mother's face. "I don't wanna move. I love this house. I've lived here my whole life. Why do you wanna move, Mommy? Is it because you still miss Daddy and you're sad?"

Andrea was somewhat apprehensive about sharing her fears with her young daughter. She did not wish to pass on her own anxieties to Kayla. She was a well-adjusted little girl, and Andrea wanted her to remain that way. Nevertheless, she had to be up-front and honest with her.

"Well, honey, I do still miss Daddy, and I'm still sad, too. You and Daddy and I have a lot of happy memories here. Sometimes it's a little too painful for me when I think of them."

Kayla said matter-of-factly, "But, Mommy, even if we move, the memories will still be in your head. You can't make them go away. Our memories are good ones. Daddy said that's what memories are for—to be cherished."

Andrea could not help but smile. Once again, her daughter had taken a mountain and made a molehill of it. "Yeah, Daddy did say that, didn't he? He was right. What if we stay a while longer and see how things work out?"

"That sounds like a good idea, Mommy."

Just then, Kayla felt Andrea's stomach move. Her eyes grew huge as saucers. "Mommy, was that the baby?"

Andrea smiled. She was four months into her pregnancy. This baby was a lively one. "Yes, that's your little brother or sister."

Kayla felt Andrea's stomach move again and started giggling. "Did I used to move like that when I was in your stomach?"

Andrea rubbed her daughter's head. "Yes, all the time. You never stayed still. I'd be trying to sleep at night and you'd just be kicking away. It felt like you were dribbling a basketball inside my stomach."

Andrea and Kayla were all over the sofa laughing and giggling.

Andrea thought, *Life is worth living. Clay will live on in our children. Every time I look at them, I'll see a part of him, a part that will live forever in my heart.*

The next morning, the ground was covered with snow. It seemed the weatherman's prediction had been accurate. Kayla was so excited she could hardly sit through breakfast.

"Mommy, when do we get to go outside?" she asked as she hastily shoved a spoonful of grits in her mouth.

"Slow down, Kayla," her mother warned. "Don't eat so fast. We'll go out a little later. Not right now. First, we have chores to do inside. You've got to make your bed and straighten your room."

"Okay, Mommy." Kayla would do whatever it took to be able to go outside and play in the snow. She'd clean the entire house if that was what was required.

After breakfast, the two busily set about their chores. Andrea had never seen a child work so hard. *Maybe it needed to snow every day,* she thought. Then she thought again. *Nah.*

Outside, there were kids everywhere—on sleds, building snowmen, and just running around in the snow. Andrea and Kayla put the finishing touches on their snowman. Andrea placed an old navy blue Atlanta Braves baseball cap of Clayton's on its head, and Kayla wrapped a red-and-black-checkered scarf around its neck. Next, they lay down in the snow and made snow angels. Andrea dashed into the house, grabbed the camera off the kitchen counter, and came back outside flashing pictures. These would go well in the scrapbook she and Kayla were making.

Later, the two came inside, changed into some dry clothes, and warmed their feet in front of the fireplace. When the telephone rang, Andrea was too tired to get up, so Kayla answered it.

"Mee Maw!" Kayla yelled into the telephone. "We got snow just like in New York," she stated excitedly. She was shaking her head up and down. "Yes. A whole bunch. Me and Mommy built a snowman and made snow angels."

After Kayla talked to both her grandparents, she handed the telephone to her mother.

"Hey, Mama," Andrea said into the phone. "We're fine. Well, I guess you heard on the news about our snow. Yeah, she's really excited. She's been up since five o'clock. If she'd had to go to school, I would've had to drag her out of bed."

Andrea listened as her mother spoke. Then she asked, "How do y'all deal with all the snow up there? If we just get a few flakes here, everything shuts down."

Andrea and her mother talked for a few more minutes. Then she talked to her father. A few minutes later, Leah called.

Andrea and Kayla made cheesy beef enchiladas for supper, with a salad on the side. After dinner, Andrea listened to the evening news. The weatherman predicted that temperatures would drop overnight, thereby causing an accumulation of icy patches on the roads. Area schools would be closed again tomorrow.

Glenn called a few minutes later and informed Andrea that the office would be open for business the next day. She would not get to spend another day with Kayla. Fortunately, Leah did not have to go into the salon, so Andrea would drop Kayla off at her house in lieu of day care. To Kayla, spending the day with her Aunt Leah almost made up for not having the time with her mother.

Later, after Kayla had taken her bath, said her prayers, and been tucked into bed, Andrea grabbed Kayla's Bible storybook from her bookshelf and climbed underneath the warm covers with her daughter to read.

Kayla was knocked out before Andrea could finish the last sentence. She placed the book on the nightstand and carefully brushed some stray strands of hair behind her daughter's ear. She leaned down and kissed Kayla's warm cheek.

Andrea had no desire to leave just yet. She surveyed the solemn look on her little one's face. So innocent. So at peace. So lovable. This little girl lying here made life worth living. How could someone so tiny have such a huge impact on another person? *She's a gift from God*, a wee voice echoed inside Andrea's head. *You need her as much as she needs you. You complete each other.*

Andrea smiled as she snuggled up beside her baby. Before long, she, too, was lost in a deep slumber.

The next morning when Andrea went to wake Kayla, Kayla felt extremely warm. Andrea rushed to the bathroom and came back with the ear thermometer. The child's temperature was 101.6. She would have to take Kayla to see her pediatrician. She prayed the office would be open today. If it wasn't, she'd take her to the emergency room.

Andrea gave Kayla some children's liquid Tylenol. Then she called Leah, informed her of Kayla's condition, and advised that she would not be bringing Kayla by, as she had to take her to the doctor.

Leah instructed Andrea to bring Kayla to her house anyway. Andrea could go to work, and Leah would get her to the doctor or the emergency room and take care of her. Andrea thanked her and said a quick prayer, thanking God for her sister.

All the while Andrea was helping Kayla get ready, she was mentally scolding herself for permitting her daughter to go outside in all the snow the day before. She should have known better. She decided she had used extremely poor judgement.

Leah was successful at obtaining an early morning appointment for Kayla. When they finally saw the doctor, his diagnosis was strep throat.

As the two sat in the waiting area of the pharmacy awaiting the antibiotic the doctor had prescribed, Kayla leaned her head against Leah's arm as she slept. It was quite evident the poor child was ill, as she was usually energetic and talkative.

After the prescription had been filled, they went back to Leah's house. Leah warmed up some soup while Kayla lay on a blanket on the floor watching a children's video.

Leah joined her little patient on the floor. Kayla sat up and frowned when she saw the soup. "No pizza?" she asked.

Leah shook her head. "No pizza. Remember, the doctor said you need some warm liquids for your throat."

Kayla looked innocently at her aunt. "Pizza's warm if you heat it up."

Leah drew in her mouth and shook her head once more. Even sick, Kayla was trying to be sly. "Sorry. Not a liquid."

"Oh," was all Kayla could say in response.

As difficult as Leah had anticipated it would be, she managed to get most of the soup down Kayla before she dozed off again.

Kayla had gotten two snow days from school. By Saturday, nearly all of the snow and ice had melted and everything was pretty much back to normal. Andrea hated for her baby to be sick. She would rather be ill herself. She wished Kayla was up and wearing her out instead of lying around sick.

Andrea did some chores while Kayla napped. As she sat on the side of the tub cleaning it, she felt the baby stir inside her stomach. She stopped what she was doing, placed her hand on her belly, and began to talk to the baby.

"It's okay, little one. You're in a nice, warm, safe place. Kayla and I can't wait to see you."

Andrea felt the baby move again at the sound of her voice. A wide grin unfolded itself across her face.

"You're really a kicker, aren't you? Are you gonna be a football player? Huh?"

As Andrea sat there, she contemplated the future of her children. Even though their father was gone, she felt confident they could still grow up to be healthy, happy individuals. She prayed they would.

Chapter 10

Spring was just around the corner with trees and flowers awakening from a long winter's nap, painting the earth in an array of vivid colors. Andrea was almost in her sixth month of pregnancy. On Monday, she and Leah would start attending childbirth classes.

Leah wanted to do some shopping for the baby. Personally, Andrea thought it was too soon to be buying things. Dr. Murphy kept assuring her that she and the baby were progressing well. Still, Andrea was somewhat anxious. Since Clayton's death, she always expected something bad to happen. Leah was so excited, though, that Andrea gave in to her. They were going to Babies-R-Us, but first, Andrea was just dying for a taste of something sweet at the mall.

The two sisters had just purchased their cinnamon buns and turned to walk away, when Andrea felt a sharp jolt in her stomach. She'd never felt the baby kick this hard.

She flinched—not from pain, but exhilaration. "Ooh," Andrea let out.

Leah stopped beside her. "What's wrong?"

Andrea smiled from ear to ear. "Nothing. The baby just gave me a hard kick."

Leah was scared. "Did it hurt? Are you okay?"

"No, it didn't hurt," Andrea assured her sister. "I'm fine."

They sat down on a nearby bench. Remembering that her sister had not yet felt the baby move, Andrea took Leah's hand and placed it on her protruding midsection. She was bigger with this baby than she had been with Kayla at this stage. "Do you feel it?" she asked her sister.

Leah shook her head. "No, I don't feel anything."

"Well, don't move your hand," Andrea ordered. "You'll probably feel it in a minute."

Leah complied. They sat quietly for a few seconds. Then out of the blue, Leah yelled, "I feel it!" She was so excited, she was jumping up and down, announcing to everybody who walked by, "I felt the baby move! I really felt it! I can't believe it!"

Passersby simply gazed at Leah and smiled. Andrea attempted to calm her down and tugged on her arm to make her sit.

"Okay, Leah. That's nice. Now the whole mall knows you felt the baby move," Andrea joked, "and probably the whole county."

Leah burst out laughing. "I can't help it. I'm so excited. Do it again," she demanded.

Andrea laughed as she threw back her head. "Well, I can't make it happen on demand. Leah, you're so silly."

The two sisters ate the remainder of their pastries while they laughed and talked. Andrea hadn't felt this happy in a while. It felt so good to really laugh again.

As Leah spoke excitedly to the florist about the huge assortment of flowers she wanted at the wedding and the reception, Devin began to feel the throbbing sensation of an oncoming headache. Smiling wryly, he looked at the florist and requested, "Can you please excuse us for a minute?"

The lady smiled. "Certainly. Just let me know when you're

done." She walked away. She had been able to ascertain while Leah was talking that Devin was experiencing some anxiety. She'd seen it many times—the conservative husband-to-be and the spontaneous wife-to-be—the woman caught up in the revelry of *her* perfect day, as the man sat by with a troubled expression on his face because of all the expenses involved in fulfilling his love's wishes.

A look of confusion washed over Leah's face. "What's wrong?"

Devin was quick to remind his fiancée, "Leah, we had a deal. If you got the dress, we'd cut back on the other expenses. We don't need all these flowers you're asking for."

Leah quickly protested, "Devin, we need flowers for the wedding *and* the reception."

"Not all these. You're gonna have so many flowers, there won't be room for anyone to sit. There'll be more flowers than people."

Leah didn't appreciate her fiancé's dry sense of humor. Nevertheless, she replied, "You're right. We had a deal. I'm sorry, but I've always wanted to have lots of flowers at my wedding and reception. I don't care about the cost."

Devin quickly interjected, "Yeah, it's quite obvious that cost isn't one of your concerns."

Leah attempted to lower her voice, although sounding a bit irritated. "Well, Devin, it's not like we can't afford it. We both have jobs that pay good money. If we can't enjoy it and spend some on our wedding, what's the point?"

Devin was eagerly contemplating their future lives together. Once he and Leah were married, he didn't mind moving from his apartment to her home as they had agreed, but perhaps they would later decide that they wanted or needed to make a transformation. "Just because we have the money to spend, it doesn't mean we have to go crazy. We may have children one day. We might want to sell your house and build one together."

When Leah opened her eyes wide, they looked like two huge

headlights on a car traveling down a country road on a dark and dreary night. "I'm not selling my house."

"I said we *might* want to sell it. I didn't say we would. That's not the point. We have to consider our future. Just because we have money today doesn't mean we'll have it tomorrow. I don't wanna spend a bunch of money on this wedding. We agreed we wouldn't. As far as I'm concerned, we can forget the whole wedding scenario, go to the courthouse, and find a judge to marry us."

Leah couldn't believe what Devin had just uttered. If his sell-her-house notion didn't take the cake, his idea of a courthouse marriage sure did. "What? Are you serious? I'm not getting married at any courthouse. I want a wedding. Devin, after you and I are married, I don't ever plan on getting married again. I love you. I want our wedding to be special."

Devin thought about reminding her of the numerous people who had made the same statement about their wedding, but had gotten carried away with the expenses, only to find themselves divorced a few short years later; however, he didn't think it was a wise assertion to make at the time. He loved Leah with all his heart. Like her, he wanted this to be his one and only marriage. "Our wedding will be special because *we'll* be there—you and I. Our family will be there, but even if it's just you and me there, I don't care. And it makes no difference to me if we have flowers or anything else, as long as we have each other."

Leah knew that Devin had meant every word of what he'd just shared from his heart. However, her desire for a fairy-tale wedding still lingered in her heart. "I appreciate how you feel, but can't you please try to understand my feelings, too?"

Devin looked at his wife-to-be, as all the love he felt for her made his heart swell with fullness. Without giving an answer, he rose and walked over to the florist.

When he and the woman returned to their seats, Devin said, "We'll take the flowers."

Leah's smile was so wide that it could have stretched from there to China. Entwining her arm in his, she whispered, "Thank you."

Devin was thrilled that once again he had made Leah happy. He prayed that he could survive the next eight months of planning the wedding.

As Andrea and Leah walked up the sidewalk leading to the hospital, a cool evening spring breeze swept across their faces. A light mist of rain had just begun to descend. Once inside, they hopped onto the elevator and pressed the button for the second floor.

Andrea could not believe how composed Leah appeared. She, on the other hand, was a ball of nerves. She still had her doubts about Leah following through with the childbirth classes. Her sister did not realize what she had gotten herself into. That was quite obvious from the placid look on her face.

When they entered the classroom, a few couples were already assembled. They smiled and nodded at the group. Andrea felt so uncomfortable amid all the smiling, happy couples. She did, however, notice a young lady who was accompanied by an older woman. She wondered what her plight was.

More people entered the room along with their instructor. Moments later, the teacher talked about the basics of pregnancy, the pain in pregnancy, and the labor and birth process. When it came time for them to view the childbirth video, Andrea eyed Leah suspiciously.

Leah caught her sister's gaze. "What?" she asked.

Andrea attempted a smile. "Nothing," she lied.

As the video played, the narrator explained the birth process:

As labor progresses, contractions become stronger, occurring more frequently. The contractions cause the mouth of the cervix to open. When the cervix has opened to a diameter of about four inches or ten centimeters, the woman begins to push with her abdominal muscles.

Andrea stole another peek at her sister, whose eyes were as big as saucers. *Oh, God, please don't let her pass out.* Disheartened, Andrea looked back at the television screen.

When the mother pushes, this action forces the baby through the cervix and out of the mother's . . .

Andrea didn't hear the rest. Neither did Leah, as she was out cold on the floor. Andrea saw heads turn in their direction. The instructor was by their side in a flash. "Is she all right?" she asked Andrea.

Andrea was down on her knees beside Leah, shaking her. "She'll be fine. She just has a weak stomach. Leah. Leah."

Leah slowly began to regain consciousness.

"I'll get her some water," the instructor offered.

Two of the men in the class assisted Leah in returning to her seat. The instructor handed Andrea the water, and Andrea held it up to Leah's mouth. Leah took a couple of small sips. After a few minutes, she seemed okay.

Andrea was quiet during the ride home as Leah apologized profusely for her fainting spell. "Andrea, I am so sorry. I know I let you down tonight, but I still want to do this."

The last thing Andrea wanted to do was hurt her sister's feelings, but she needed someone she knew she could count on to help her through this pregnancy. Right now, she did not feel Leah was that person.

Andrea looked at her sister with all the love she had for her in her heart. "Leah, I love you, and I know you want to help, but I need someone I can count on."

Leah felt horrible. After tonight, Andrea would probably never trust her again with anything important. Looking helplessly at her sister, she implored, "You can count on me, Andrea. You know you can. Sure I passed out tonight, but I tried, didn't I? Are you gonna give up on me just like that?"

All Andrea could say was, "I don't know. I'll think about it."

Leah felt like she was dying inside. The one time she could be there for her sister, she had failed miserably. She would try again, though. That is, if Andrea let her. Andrea would give her another opportunity. She was a pretty reasonable person. *After all, we're sisters.*

Chapter 11

On Wednesday, Andrea and Leah met for lunch. As they waited in line to pay for their meals, they overheard two women at a nearby table attempting to whisper.

The first woman asked her companion, "Isn't that Andrea Hamilton?"

The other lady answered, "I think so. Looks like she's pregnant."

"Yeah, looks like it," the first woman said. "Didn't her husband die a few months ago in an automobile accident?"

"Yeah, I think so," the second woman replied. "I wonder who the father is."

Leah shoved a twenty-dollar bill in her sister's hand. "Here. Pay for our lunch out of this."

Leah turned on her heels and strutted over to the women's table. With her hands on her hips, she snapped, "That's my sister you're talking about. Her husband did die. And if it's any of your business, it's *his* child she's carrying, so back off!"

The ladies were obviously embarrassed as all heads in the restaurant turned to stare at them, neither one responding to Leah's outburst. They just hung their heads as they fidgeted with the food on their plates. Leah turned around quickly and walked away.

Andrea was outside when her sister came out. As soon as she had paid their bill, she had fled the restaurant, but not before Leah had begun giving the two busybodies a piece of her mind.

As they made their way to the car, Andrea stated, "I can't believe you did that."

Leah huffed, "They need to mind their own business."

Andrea responded, "You don't even know them."

"Obviously they don't know you either. Otherwise, they wouldn't have been running their mouths. People just need to mind their own business." Leah unlocked the doors of the car. "Get in," she ordered.

Andrea started laughing. "Now wait a minute. Just 'cause you jumped bad at those women in there, don't think you're gonna start bossing me around."

Leah laughed. "Just get in the car." She added, "Please."

They climbed into the vehicle. Andrea could not get over what her sister had done. She realized Leah wanted to protect her, just as she wanted to be there with her for the birth of this baby. Leah could be trusted with a lot of things, but being in the delivery room with her wasn't one of them.

Andrea had called Ellen immediately on Monday night when she had gotten home from the childbirth class and asked her to be her Lamaze partner. Ellen was ecstatic and happily consented. Andrea had not told Leah yet and had no idea how she would do so. Leah would be hurt, but Andrea had to do what was best for her and the baby. Still, she felt profoundly guilty about her decision.

Leah didn't understand. It was Monday. She and Andrea were supposed to go to the childbirth class, but no one answered her knock at Andrea's door. Andrea's Cherokee Jeep was gone. Still standing on the front porch, Leah pulled her cellular phone from her purse and hastily dialed her sister's number. She could hear the telephone inside ringing. After four rings, the answering machine picked up, and she left a brief message.

"Hey. Andrea, it's Leah. It's six-thirty P.M., and I'm standing out-side on your front porch. Came to pick you up for our class. Did something change and you forget to tell me? Call me when you get this message." Leah ended her call and left.

When Andrea and Kayla returned home later that night around eight-thirty, there were several telephone messages from Leah. Andrea dreaded talking to her, but knew she had to sooner or later. More guilt washed over her. She should have been honest with Leah from the beginning. She felt as though she had betrayed her sister. Before she picked up the phone to call her, she practiced in her mind how she would explain her deception. Then she dialed Leah's number.

"Hey," Leah answered. "Where were you? Was the class can-celled?"

Andrea's voice was shallow as she attempted to explain. "No. I have something to tell you. I found someone else to be my Lamaze partner. She went with me tonight."

Leah could not believe what she was hearing. Without meaning to, she bellowed, "What? Are you serious?" She swiftly began to experience a range of emotions from anger to hurt. The fact that Andrea had gone behind her back agitated her more. The tears that pricked her eyelids felt like the needles of a cactus piercing skin.

"Yes. I'm sorry."

Leah didn't want Andrea's apologies. "So who's taking my place?"

"Ellen," Andrea answered. "Ellen Knight."

"So you would rather have someone who's not even related be with you during the birth of your baby, instead of your own flesh-and-blood sister?"

"Leah, you know that's not true. I told you I need someone I know I can depend on." Andrea felt the urge to remind her sister that she had told her she could fire her if she passed out, but she de-cided against it. "Why do you want to put yourself through this, when you know how hard it's gonna be for you?"

Leah did not hesitate to answer. "Because I love you, and you're my sister, and that's what sisters do for each other."

Andrea had no doubt that Leah loved her, but what she needed right now was someone she could count on not to pass out at the drop of a hat during the birth of this baby. She hadn't anticipated Leah being so upset. She figured her sister would have been relieved that she wouldn't have to go through with her pledge. "I'm sorry, Leah. I didn't mean to hurt you."

"Yes, you did," Leah snapped.

Andrea was startled by her sister's tone and response. "No, I didn't," she denied. "Why would you say that?"

"You snuck behind my back. You didn't even tell me. You let me think everything was okay and that I was still your partner. How did you think I would feel when I found out? And it's not that I don't like Ellen. She's a good friend to you, and she's our sister in Christ. Maybe she is more dependable in this situation than I am." The tears Leah had so successfully kept behind their prison walls were now breaking free.

"Andrea, you know I would go to the moon and back for you. I know I'm not as strong as you in the physical sense, and I get weak at the knees just thinking about pain, but I was willing to try to overlook that in order to help you. That's all I wanted. To try and help you through one of the most difficult times of your life."

Now Andrea was crying, too. She felt horrible about hurting her sister. "I'm sorry," she wailed. "I should have told you. Please forgive me. I'm so sorry. I didn't mean to hurt you."

After ending their telephone conversation on a good note, Leah rehashed in her mind what had transpired. Although she had been restored to her rightful position as Andrea's Lamaze partner, she was still angry at her sister for going behind her back and asking Ellen to be involved in the birth of *her* niece or nephew. She and Andrea had always been close. Now Leah felt as though their bond was starting to weaken.

The next day, Leah vented regarding Andrea's deception as she talked to her friend and coworker Yasmine Joyner during their lunch break at Zaxby's.

"You know, I can't believe she went behind my back like that."

Yasmine was sympathetic. "I know. She could have at least talked to you about it first."

Rambling on, Leah asserted, "I mean, she and I have been sisters all our lives. She's only known Ellen a few years, and Ellen's not even family. I just don't understand Andrea anymore. We used to be so close."

Yasmine reassured Leah, "Try not to think about it. It'll only upset you more. At least she changed her mind and you're her partner again."

Leah supposed her friend was right, but it would be mighty difficult not to continue calling to mind Andrea's betrayal.

Sunday afternoon, Leah and Devin ate dinner with Andrea and Kayla.

Leah placed a generous portion of baked macaroni and cheese in her mouth. Although she still felt somewhat irritated at her sister, it was good to be in her company. "Mmmm. Andrea, this macaroni and cheese is simply delicious. You really put your foot in it this time, girl."

Andrea smiled. "Thanks. I'm glad you like it."

Kayla frowned and asked, of no one in particular, "Mommy put her foot in the macaroni and cheese?"

The grown-ups burst into laughter. Kayla just stared at them with a serious expression on her face.

"No, sweetie," Leah explained. "I'm sure your Mommy didn't put her foot in the macaroni and cheese. That's just a figure of speech. You know, like when people say something is bad, but what they really mean is it's good."

"Oh, I see," Kayla said and placed another spoonful of the yummy cheesy dish in her mouth.

After dinner, Leah and Kayla played in the family room while Devin helped Andrea in the kitchen.

"So, Devin," Andrea said as she loaded the dishwasher. "How are you?"

Devin closed the refrigerator and turned his back to it. "I'm fine. What about you?"

"Okay. Just taking one day at a time."

"That's all you can do," Devin concurred. "Kayla seems fine."

Andrea smiled. "She is. Not having Clay around is hard for her, too, but she's okay."

Devin pulled out a chair and sat down. Andrea joined him. "She's something else, isn't she? Just makes you smile every time you're around her."

Andrea giggled. "She's so like Clay. He could make you laugh without even trying." She looked around, surveying the area. "I miss him so. I still don't feel normal, if there is such a thing anymore. Is that how you feel?"

"Yeah. Life just doesn't seem the same without him. It's gonna be so strange not having him at the wedding. He was there for all the other important events in my life, but he won't be here for this one."

Andrea smiled. "Speaking of the wedding, has my sister driven you crazy yet with all the planning?"

Devin leaned farther back in his chair. "We agreed we would have a small, inexpensive wedding. The dress she wants costs fifteen hundred dollars. So we came to another agreement—if she gets the dress, she'll cut down on the other expenses. However, a couple of weeks ago when we went to pick out the flowers, she went overboard again."

"Well, what can I say?" Andrea warmly expressed, "A wedding is a momentous event in a woman's life—one of the most important steps she'll ever take. Of course, it's a serious step for the men, too, but y'all don't get all giddy about it like we do. The day Clay and I got married, he was as cool as a cucumber. Me, on the other hand"—

she lowered her head, smiling sheepishly—"I was a total wreck. I was so nervous." Her revelations caused a shadow to spill over her like the setting of the sun after a sunshiny day.

Devin discerned Andrea's misery. He wished there was something he could do or say to make it disappear forever.

As she reawakened from her perfect day of long ago, Andrea smiled warmly. "Well, after eight more months of planning this wedding with Leah, you'll be an expert on weddings. Before we became teenagers, we couldn't stand boys. We thought they were the most disgusting creatures God had ever put on the face of the earth. By the time we were teenagers, we were already planning our weddings."

Devin chuckled.

Andrea continued, "Leah's ideas were more unconventional than mine, but she's always been her own person. She's never been one to follow trends. That's what makes her so unique."

Devin agreed. "That's one of the reasons I love her so."

Leah walked up behind Devin, leaned down and put her arms around him, and kissed his cheek. "That's one of the reasons you love who so?" she asked teasingly as though she didn't know to whom he was referring.

Devin reached up and grabbed Leah's hand. "You, of course, but you already know that. You just had to hear it," he said jokingly.

Andrea smiled at the two lovebirds. She was happy and excited for them. Yet, at the same time, their happiness made her loneliness even more painful. Her despondency had her feeling that she wouldn't be able to honor her sister's request to be her maid of honor—not without reliving the sensation of her heart being ripped apart. Andrea wanted with every fiber of her being to be there for Leah on her special day, but didn't know if she could.

Chapter 12

When Andrea woke up, she felt horribly depressed. In six more days it would be Sunday, May 15—her and Clayton's wedding anniversary. The date would be forever embedded in her memory. It was to be their eleventh year together as a married couple. They had always planned a special two- or three-day trip for just the two of them. Then they'd exchange gifts.

She managed to pull herself out of bed and get Kayla ready for school. She didn't feel like cooking, so she fixed Kayla a bowl of cereal. She called Glenn and advised him that she was not feeling well and would not be in the office. When she returned home from taking Kayla to day care, she climbed back into bed and finally cried herself to sleep. She stayed in bed all day until it was time for her to pick up Kayla.

Kayla was aware of her mother's gloomy condition. On the way home, she inquired, "Mommy, are you sick?"

Andrea didn't dare look at her daughter, for fear the tears would break forth. "I'm not feeling too good, but I'll be all right."

"What's wrong?"

"I just had a bad day, honey."

"Maybe you should go to the doctor."

"No, I'll be fine. Stop worrying."

Kayla didn't say anything else, but Andrea could see her little girl from her peripheral vision, watching her as she drove the remainder of the way home.

Once they were home, Andrea gave Kayla a snack before going to lie back down. She got up around five to heat some leftovers for her and Kayla to eat for supper. She found Kayla in the kitchen making peanut butter and jelly sandwiches.

Upon seeing her mother, Kayla smiled and said, "Look, Mommy, I made us something to eat. Come on."

As Andrea made her way over to the table, she stepped on something wet and mushy. She felt it gush between her toes. Stopping in her tracks, she looked down at her bare foot in the purple sticky substance. "Kayla!" she squealed. "You've got jelly all over the floor! How many times have I told you, when you make a mess to clean it up?"

"I'm sorry, Mommy. I didn't know I dropped it. I'll get it up." Kayla immediately sprang from her chair and darted to the kitchen counter, where she grabbed a paper towel from the upright holder and ran over to wipe up the floor. She smeared the jam over the tile.

"Stop!" Andrea yelled. "You're just making it worse. Let me have it," she demanded, snatching the towel from Kayla's hand.

Andrea hobbled over to the sink, turned the faucet on, then back off, and dabbed the napkin in the sink to soak up some of the water. As she bent over, she attempted to wipe the jam from between her toes with the damp towel. "Kayla, this is sticky. You have to wet the towel first."

Kayla had never seen her mother so angry. She cried, "I'm sorry, Mommy. I'll help you."

Andrea snapped, "I'll do it myself. Just go to your room."

The little girl ran away in tears. Andrea wet more napkins and wiped off the floor. She felt terrible. She hadn't meant to lose her temper like that. Kayla was her child, her baby. She went to Kayla's room where she found her lying on her bed and sobbing, her back to her mother.

Andrea sat beside her and gently placed her hand on her daughter's back. "I'm sorry, honey. I didn't mean to yell at you. I was wrong for doing that. Come here."

Kayla sat up, turned around, and threw her arms around her mother. "I'm sorry, Mommy. I didn't mean to make a mess. I was just trying to fix us something to eat."

"I know, baby, and I'm so sorry." Andrea held Kayla, gently rocking her back and forth. "I had a bad day, but that doesn't give me the right to take it out on you. Will you forgive me?"

Kayla answered earnestly, "I forgive you."

Andrea sat a few more minutes with Kayla and went to call Leah. She was in no mood to attend the childbirth class tonight. As she lay in bed later, all she could think about was her angry outburst at Kayla. She felt so guilty, for her child was the most humble creature she knew. Andrea cried until she fell asleep.

Andrea was gloomy the remainder of the week. In the office on Friday, Glenn asked her if she was okay. She choked back tears as she lied to him that she was fine. She still felt terrible for the way she'd treated Kayla earlier in the week and had told no one about it, not even Leah. She was too ashamed. She had never allowed anything to affect her in such a manner. She felt as though she was going insane.

That night, Leah and Devin stopped by to visit with Andrea and Kayla. While Devin watched television with Kayla on the family room floor, Leah chatted away about the wedding. Andrea was sick of hearing about her sister's upcoming nuptial. Everyone seemed to be happy, except for Andrea. Everybody else had everything they needed and wanted. Their lives hadn't been turned upside down like hers. She was tired of hearing about people's plans for the future. She no longer had a future.

Leah merrily pronounced, "Next month, we're going shopping for our rings. Then you and Kayla and I and the bridesmaids will have to select your dresses. My gown is gonna be off-white. For your dress, I was thinking of an A-line in lavender with an off-white, fold-over-cuff bodice. And for Kayla, a lavender dress with off-white lace. What d'you think?"

Andrea sat in stony silence.

Leah inclined her head slightly and gazed at her sister. "So what do you think?"

Andrea had tuned out most of what Leah had just said, but knew she had mentioned something about dresses for the wedding. Her words tumbled from her lips in a dry, bitter tone. "Sounds fine."

Leah asked, "Are you all right?"

"What?" Andrea asked.

Leah repeated, "Are you all right? You don't seem like yourself today. As a matter of fact, you've been acting strange all week. You didn't go to your class on Monday. Something's wrong. What is it?"

Andrea was fed up with her sister's observations. "I'm tired. Don't I have a right to be tired? Stop bugging me."

Andrea's cruel tone and harsh words offended Leah. "Well, excuse me for being concerned. You don't have to be so hateful."

"I'm not being hateful. I just wish you'd stop nagging me."

Leah jumped up. "Well, I didn't realize I was nagging you. Since I am, maybe I'd better leave. Devin, let's go. I'm afraid I've worn out my welcome here."

Devin and Kayla stopped watching television. Devin asked, "What's the matter?"

Not wanting to make more of a scene in Kayla's presence, Leah answered, "We just need to leave. I've got to work tomorrow."

Devin stood and rubbed Kayla's head. "Well, Lil Bit, I've got to go. Aunt Leah's got to get up early in the morning. I'll see you later. Okay?"

Kayla cheerily responded, "Okay, Uncle Devin."

Andrea remained on the couch while the threesome said their good-byes. She and Leah said nothing further to one another. Devin leaned down and hugged Andrea before bidding her farewell.

Once in the car, Devin asked, "What happened back there?"

Leah bitterly responded, "All I did was ask Andrea if she was all right, and she practically bit my head off. She's been acting strange all week. She told me I was nagging her."

As Devin drove, he stole a quick glance at Leah. He knew how much she wanted to help her sister. "Honey, don't take it so personally. You know she's under a lot of stress. She's still grieving over Clay, and she's pregnant."

"That doesn't give her the right to take it out on me. All I'm trying to do is help. She acts like because she's unhappy she wants everybody else to be miserable. I know she's going through a lot, but I've tried to be there for her."

"I know you have, and you've done a terrific job," Devin commended her. "Just try to be patient with her. She loves you."

"I know she does. I just want her to be like she used to be. I miss the old Andrea," Leah pouted.

"She probably misses the old Andrea, too. She's not the same person she was because her life was suddenly made different, and not by her own choice. She's hurt and angry and, because the two of you have been spending so much time together, you're the one who's always around for her to take her hostility out on. I'm not saying it's right. That's just how it is. Don't give up on her. She needs you."

Leah didn't say anything. She guessed Devin was right. She just didn't take too kindly to people's anger—not even that from her grieving sister—aimed at her for something that wasn't her fault.

Sunday afternoon when Leah answered her telephone, she heard her mother's distressed voice on the other end. They spoke briefly before Anna informed her that she had talked to Andrea earlier in the day and that she didn't sound well. Anna asked Leah how her sister had seemed to her lately.

Leah answered, "Mama, I don't know what's wrong with her.

She's been grumpy all week. She didn't go to her childbirth class Monday. She snapped at me Friday night when Devin and I were there. She told me I was nagging her just because I asked how she was."

Anna could hear the irritation in her daughter's voice. "Well, you know, today is her and Clay's wedding anniversary."

Leah's mouth fell open. She had forgotten. How could she have failed to remember? "Oh, Mama, I forgot. So that's why she's been so moody. I could kick myself. I got so angry at her Friday, and I walked out on her. If I'd known, I never would've done that. I need to go, Mama. I've got to go see her."

As soon as she hung up the telephone, Leah called Devin and told him of her plan. Thirty minutes later, he picked her up, and they drove to Andrea's house. It was about four o'clock, and Andrea and Kayla were outside planting flowers. When they got out of the car, Leah immediately raced over to her sister and gently grabbed her gloved hand, pulling her off to the side of the house while Devin entertained Kayla. Leah grasped Andrea's other hand as Andrea stared at her, wondering what was going on with her sister this time.

"I'm so sorry," Leah declared. "I totally forgot that today is your and Clay's wedding anniversary. Is that why you've been so down this week?"

Tears spilled down Andrea's cheeks. "Yes," she stated in an inaudible whisper.

The two sisters wrapped their arms around each other and wept. Then Leah advised Andrea that she was taking her out and that Devin was staying with Kayla. She had suspected that Andrea would give her a hard time, but she didn't.

After Andrea had showered and gotten dressed, the two sisters went to the Cultural Arts Center in Carrollton where they saw a fabulous play. Afterward, they went to Dairy Queen. As Andrea stood at the counter licking her lips, Leah knew what her sister was craving, and she had come prepared. Leah opened her pocketbook and pulled out a small bag of plain Lay's potato chips to go with Andrea's vanilla ice cream.

At their booth, Leah frowned, playfully complaining, "I don't see how you eat that. Your taste buds have gone haywire."

Andrea grinned. "It's good. Try it. You might like it."

Leah shook her head.

Andrea grabbed a generous spoonful of the ice cream and chips mixture and offered it to her sister.

Leah shook her head again. "No-o-o. I don't want it. Ugh."

"Come on," Andrea urged. "Just a little taste."

Leah could not believe she was actually letting her sister talk her into tasting the hideous concoction. She cautiously took a small bite and chewed slowly. Andrea popped the remainder of the creamy-crunchy mixture into her own mouth.

Leah swallowed, smiling. "Hey, that was pretty good."

Andrea extended another spoonful to her sister. "Here. Want some more?"

Leah grinned as she shook her head. "No, that's enough for now. I don't want to throw my stomach into spasms. You know I have a delicate digestive system," she teased. "Not like yours. You've always been able to put anything in your tin belly."

Andrea laughed. "You're awful."

After finishing their ice cream, the two sisters talked and laughed all the way back to Andrea's house. Andrea had had a wonderful afternoon, just the two of them. It had been like old times when one was feeling blue and was cheered up by the other. It didn't take the place of Clayton in her life, but it certainly helped to ease her sorrow.

Chapter 13

Summer was less than three weeks away. Hydrangeas, fully bloomed in shades of pink, blue, and white, hugged the front porch of the Hamilton home. Andrea and Kayla busily picked some juicy red tomatoes from the vines they had planted earlier in the year. Every year, they had a garden. This year, however, it was smaller than usual. If it hadn't been for Kayla begging Andrea to set out a few seeds and seedlings, they wouldn't even have what little they did.

Kayla yanked a plump green tomato from a vine and placed it in the wicker basket that hung from Andrea's arm. "Mommy, let's get some green ones, too. We can make fried green tomatoes for supper. We can have biscuits and squash and pork chops. Doesn't that sound good?" She looked up at her mother, grinning.

She certainly had stirred up Andrea's taste buds. "Yes, sweetie, it sounds delicious. But we'll cook the pork chops on the grill so we can cut down on some of the heat in the kitchen. It's hot enough as it is."

Andrea grabbed Kayla's hand as they proceeded to the front of the house. They cut some flowers and placed them in the basket with the vegetables. They were about to head inside when Leah and Devin drove up in Devin's truck. Leah jumped out excitedly and hurried to Andrea.

Grabbing the basket from her sister's arm, Leah set it on the table on the porch, and pulled Andrea and Kayla with her to the truck. "Come see what Devin and I got you. It's an early baby shower gift."

When they reached the back of the truck, Devin was already on the bed about to take down a beautiful cherry-oak rocking chair.

Andrea gasped. "Oh, it's gorgeous. Thank you both so much."

Kayla smiled, concurring, "It's pretty."

Devin took the chair inside and placed it in the nursery on the brown and beige, oval-shaped, braided rug next to the crib.

"Thanks again, guys," Andrea said. "This is so nice."

"You're welcome," Leah and Devin replied in unison.

"Hey," Andrea said. "Can the two of you come over for supper tonight? Kayla's already planned the menu."

Kayla pleaded, "Please come."

Leah and Devin looked at each other, grinning, and said, "Okay."

Later that night after supper, Andrea and Leah sat at the table on the patio watching Kayla and her uncle play the card game Uno. Andrea felt the need to express her heartfelt gratitude for all her sister had done thus far to help her.

Andrea stated solemnly, "Well, our last class is Monday. The baby's due in three weeks. We're almost there." She clutched Leah's hand. "I couldn't have done this without you, girl. You've really been there for me, and for that, I thank you. Sometimes I acted like I didn't appreciate it, and I'm sorry."

Leah quickly asserted, "There's no need to apologize and no need to thank me either. We're sisters. We've got to be there for each other."

Andrea stated earnestly, "Well, you're the best sister anybody could have, and I love you."

All the tension that existed previously between the sisters

seemed to have melted away. "I love you, too, girl." Leah's tone quickly turned refreshingly jubilant, and the smile on her face could have lit up the entire solar system. "Devin and I picked out our rings today. Oh, you should see them. They're beautiful. We're getting the matching gold and platinum set. I can't wait for you to see them."

Andrea was happy for Leah and Devin, but her sister just didn't understand how all her wedding details were propelling her into an abyss of even deeper sadness and loneliness.

The following Saturday, Leah picked up Yasmine, who was also to be one of her bridesmaids, along with Andrea and Kayla, and drove them over to My Chocolate Boutique in Carrollton where they would meet the other three bridesmaids.

As the ladies and Kayla sat around the table flipping through the assortment of catalogs, Leah exclaimed, "Oh, Andrea, look!" Pointing to a dress, she said, "This is what I had in mind for you. You will look so good in this. What do you think?" She pushed the book toward her sister so she could get a better view.

After catching a quick glimpse, Andrea simply nodded and stated, "It's nice." With Clayton gone and her life in such turmoil, her desire to be her sister's maid of honor was slowly fading away. It was hard for her to share anyone else's joy when hers had been taken away. Nevertheless, she would try to prevail, for she wanted to be there for Leah.

Leah discreetly cut her eyes at Yasmine, then quickly averted them back at Andrea. "You don't like it? You can pick out something else if you want to."

Andrea replied, "No, it's fine."

Leah was hurt by her sister's indifference regarding the dress and her big day. Every time she attempted to engage Andrea in conversation about the wedding, Andrea acted unconcerned. Leah realized that her sister was still grieving from the loss of her husband, but one of the most memorable days of her life was about to come, and she was feeling that Andrea was neither the least bit happy for her nor supportive. It had been eight months since Clayton had died, and she felt bad for Andrea, but how much longer was she going to mourn?

They selected the remaining dresses. Leah wanted to take everyone out to lunch, but Andrea said she was tired and wanted to go home. Leah steered her vehicle into Andrea's driveway and stopped for Andrea and Kayla to climb out of the backseat. Pressing the power button, she allowed her window to slide down halfway. As the beams of sunlight burst through the trees past Andrea and into her face, Leah squinted as she eyed her sister suspiciously. "Are you sure you're all right? You look pale."

Andrea's heart was weeping, yet she replied, "I'm fine. Just tired. I think I'm gonna lie down and take a nap."

Leah granted her sister an understanding nod of her head. "Okay. I'll call later to check on you. Kayla, gimme a kiss."

Kayla leaned her head forward and pecked her aunt on her left cheek. "Bye, Aunt Leah."

"Bye, sweetie."

"Bye, Ms. Yasmine," Kayla said, peeking past Leah at her aunt's friend beside her on the front seat.

Yasmine bent over slightly and waved at the little girl. "Bye, Kayla. You be good."

Kayla grinned. "Yes, ma'am."

Yasmine said, "Bye, Andrea. I hope you get to feeling better."

Andrea replied, "Thanks, Yasmine. I appreciate it."

After Andrea and Kayla had closed the door to the house behind them, Leah backed out of the driveway and took off down the road. She looked at her friend. "Was Andrea acting strangely to you?"

Yasmine had felt some negative vibes coming from Leah's sister, but she had no intention of voicing them, as she assumed that Andrea's world was still dark from the loss of her husband. "What do you mean?"

"Well, when we were at the boutique selecting the dresses for the wedding, she seemed so uninterested in the whole process. I've noticed that every time I try to talk to her about the wedding, she's unresponsive. Like yesterday when I told her about my and Devin's rings, she just sat there with this blank look on her face. You know, between her mood swings and Devin's unnecessary concern about how much we're spending on the wedding, I'm about to lose my mind. I feel like everything I say and do is wrong."

Yasmine's heart ached for her friend. She herself had just turned thirty-four three months ago, and she was still single of her own free will because Mr. Right had not yet come along. She, too, had her wedding already pictured and planned in her mind. She felt terrible that at a time when Leah was supposed to be so enraptured, she was experiencing dissension instead.

"Your wedding is a big deal to you even if it isn't to anyone else. Try not to let anyone steal your joy. And what's the harm in spending your money on something nice for yourself? I mean when we die, we can't take it with us. There's nothing wrong with having nice things, as long as we don't make them the main focus in our life."

Leah agreed, "You're right. But you know, it hurts so much when someone you've been close to all your life seems to turn against you. And the thing is, if we didn't love them so much, it wouldn't even matter what they said or did to us. But when it's someone we love and care about and thought they loved and cared about us, it just tears you up on the inside. I'm not saying Andrea doesn't love me. I know she does, but it seems to me that she's allowing *her* pain to take over every aspect of her life. Do you understand what I'm saying?"

"Yeah, that's how it is sometimes. When we hurt, we feel less compassionate toward other people because of what we ourselves are going through. It's not really that we mean to be that way, but that's how it is. Just give her some time. Things'll get better."

Things'll get better. How many times had Leah heard that, only to be reminded each time she saw Andrea that things were not getting better. She never would have guessed in a million years that anything would have broken their bond.

Three weeks later, Leah peeked her head into the master bedroom to check on her sister as she rested on a chair. "How y'all doing in here?"

Andrea gave Leah a dismal stare. "This baby's never coming," she moaned. "He's a week late. I'm tired of being pregnant. It's hot, and I feel miserable."

Leah walked over to her sister and gently ran her fingers through Andrea's hair. "I know you are, but it won't be long. Just be patient."

The telephone rang, and Leah went to the nightstand to answer it. It was Kayla. She was in Birmingham with Lizzie and Edward. Leah and Kayla spoke briefly. Then Kayla talked to her mother. When they were done, Andrea talked to the Hamiltons for a few minutes.

Afterward, Leah attempted to restart their conversation where she and Andrea had left off. "Dr. Murphy said walking will help. We did a lot of it today, so maybe something will happen soon."

"Maybe you're right. I just feel like I've been pregnant forever, and I'm so big."

Leah attempted to console her sister. "Well, you're pregnant. You're carrying a whole extra person inside you."

Andrea looked at her sister and smiled. She knew her twin was trying to make her feel better. "Thanks. I think I'm gonna take a shower and go to bed. Can you help me up?"

Leah ran over to assist Andrea. She took her sister by both hands and pulled, but Andrea didn't budge from the seat. "Wait a minute. This isn't working. Let's try it a different way."

Leah let go of Andrea's hands and leaned down with her legs out as far as she could get them, placing her arms underneath her sister's armpits. "On the count of three, I want you to push yourself up into my arms." Leah began rocking back and forth. "One. Two. Three."

Andrea pushed up and forward with all her might and fell into Leah's arms. They came close to crashing to the floor, but Leah managed to halt their fall. The two sisters were about to keel over from laughing so hard.

Later that night, Leah was awakened by someone shaking her. She glanced at the clock on the bedside table. It was a few minutes past ten.

"Leah!" Andrea screeched. "It's time. My water broke. My contractions are five minutes apart."

Leah jumped out of bed. "Okay. I've got this. Everything's under control. I'm coming. Just let me get dressed." As she dashed across the room to the chair where her clothes were, she stubbed her toe on something. "Ouch!" she screamed.

"What's wrong?" Andrea asked.

"I hurt my foot."

"Maybe we should turn on the light." Andrea flipped on the switch and went over to check on Leah. "Are you all right?"

"I'm fine," Leah assured Andrea. "You better get dressed. You need me to help you?"

Andrea stared at her sister who was grappling with her nightgown in an effort to pull it over her head. *Help me? You can't even dress yourself.* "No, thank you." She went to put on some clothes.

Andrea and Leah met at the front door where Andrea's weekender bag sat. Leah grabbed the carryall. "Let's go," she said, taking her sister by the arm and escorting her to the car.

By the time they made it to Leah's vehicle, Andrea had another contraction. Leah dropped the bag on the ground and ran to assist her sister. With Andrea securely strapped in her seat, Leah dashed around the front of the car and jumped into the driver's seat. As she began to speed out of the driveway, it felt as though one of the back wheels rolled over something.

Leah brought the car to an abrupt stop and asked, "What was that?"

"I don't know," Andrea said.

Leah got out and looked down at the rear tire on the driver's side. She spotted Andrea's bag underneath the car. Grabbing the carryall, she opened the back door, threw the bag onto the seat, shut the door, and reentered the vehicle.

"What was it?" Andrea asked.

Leah didn't want to alarm her sister. "Nothing."

"What did you open the door for?"

"I just wanted to make sure it was shut," Leah lied.

Leah quickly backed out of the driveway. When she turned the steering wheel, she saw an object fall past her window. She stopped the car in the road. "Now what?" She exited the vehicle a second time and found her small, black, spaghetti-strap purse lying on the ground. She grasped it and reentered the car again.

Andrea looked at her sister, not wanting to know what had happened this time.

Leah peeped at Andrea and grinned, letting out a fake chuckle. "Just had to get my pocketbook. I've got this," she reminded her sister. "Don't worry. I'll have you at the hospital in no time." She took off down the road.

Leah felt like she was in a Looney Tunes cartoon, the kind where Elmer Fudd kept getting outwitted by Bugs Bunny. It would have been funny if it weren't for the fact that she was scared to death.

She'd done it. Leah Nicole Washington had made it through one of the most challenging experiences of her entire life—her twin sister's delivery of the eight-pound, two-ounce Clayton David Hamilton II. Unbelievably, she hadn't even passed out. Not that she hadn't come close to it a time or two. She wanted very much to be there for Andrea, so she had put up a hard fight to remain calm and re- laxed. Leah had never personally witnessed anything as beautiful as seeing someone bringing another living, breathing human being into the world. It was, as her sister had told her, awesome.

Little Clayton was born on Saturday, July second, at twelve min- utes before midnight. After calling their family, Leah rejoined her sister in her room.

Leah glanced at the tire mark on Andrea's floral canvas bag, which was sitting on a chair in a corner. "Sorry about your bag," she apologized once again.

Andrea smiled. "Girl, don't worry about it. It could've been worse. That could've been me you ran over."

The two sisters held hands as Leah laughed and Andrea tried hard not to.

"I couldn't have done this without you. I know it wasn't easy, but you put aside your fears for me, and I'm so thankful that you did. It's so hard not having Clay here. I don't know what I'd do without you. I just love you so much," Andrea cried.

Leah leaned down and hugged her sister. "You're my sister, girl. I love you, too."

Devin walked in. "Hey, you two." He kissed Leah's cheek, and she stepped aside so he could hug Andrea. "Congratulations, Mommy. How are you?"

Andrea smiled. "I'm fine. Thanks to Leah."

Devin stood up straight and placed his arm around his wife-to- be. "My baby did good, huh? I knew she would."

Leah's face lit up like the moon. "It wasn't easy at first. The hard part was getting to the hospital. After I ran over her overnight bag and my purse fell off the roof of the car, it was smooth sailing. Andrea made it easy for me. She did so good."

"That's great," Devin said. "Well, I talked to Mama and Pop. They'll be here tomorrow with Kayla."

Leah said, "Oh, that's good. Mama and Daddy are taking a flight

out in the morning so they'll be here sometime tomorrow afternoon."

Andrea asked Leah, "Did you call Ellen and Alex?"

"Yes. They'll be by in the morning on their way to church."

Andrea was happy. With the birth of her son, her life was almost
complete, but it would never be whole again.

Chapter 14

Clayton II was eight days old and so adorable. To Andrea, he looked more like his father every day. He was the best baby. He slept the night through and only cried when he was hungry or wet. Andrea felt she should be bubbling over with glee. However, she wasn't.

Today, Leah had thrown her an elegant baby shower. All her family and friends attended. Andrea received more gifts than she knew what to do with. Everyone was lavishing her with love and attention. Yet, none of it replaced the one thing she needed most— the presence of her husband.

After putting Clayton down for a nap, Andrea had taken to heart some very good advice that all new mothers should live by—sleep when baby sleeps. When she awoke, she decided to take a nice warm bath. Anna offered to wash her back. As her mother gently made circular motions up and down her back with the warm, sudsy washcloth, Andrea rested her chin on her knees.

Anna inquired, "How's that feel?"

"Good," Andrea mumbled.

Anna was worried. When she and William had arrived last

Sunday, Andrea had appeared happy. Now she seemed so sedate. "Honey, what's the matter?"

Andrea didn't want to burden her mother, but she needed some consolation. "I'm so lonely without Clay. I miss him terribly. My life will never be the same."

Anna sympathized with her daughter, but Andrea had to get on with her life. How could she not see that? Especially now with the new baby.

"Andrea, you have two beautiful children and a family and friends who love you dearly. Count your blessings. You have to get on with your life and stop grieving so much over Clay."

Andrea could not believe what her mother had just said to her. How could she be so insensitive regarding her feelings and what she was going through?

Andrea raised her head and turned slightly in the direction of her mother. "Mama, how could you say something like that to me? How can you be so insensitive?"

"Honey, I wasn't trying to be insensitive. I was just trying to help you to see that life goes on, and you should be thankful for what you have."

Andrea began to cry. "Well, you're supposed to make me feel better, not worse. So if this is any indication of what your last week here is going to be like, maybe you should leave today and go home."

Anna was appalled that Andrea would speak to her that way. She'd never done it before. Andrea's words cut her to the quick.

"Honey, I'm sorry," Anna apologized. "I wasn't trying to make you feel bad."

"Well, you did," Andrea snapped. "Just leave me alone."

"Andrea . . ."

Andrea reached back and removed the washcloth from her mother's hand. "Mama, just go, please."

Anna got up and left without saying another word.

As she and William lay in bed that night, William queried,

"What's wrong? You've been quiet all afternoon. Are you feeling okay?"

Anna didn't think she could relay to him the scene between her and Andrea earlier that day. It brought tears to her eyes just thinking about it. "I'm fine," she lied.

"You're not fine. I can tell." William put his arm around his wife. "It's Andrea, isn't it? Something happened between the two of you." He'd noticed how distant the two of them had seemed toward one another all evening. "Now tell me. What is it?"

Anna buried her face in her husband's chest and sobbed as she told him what had transpired. "I'm worried about her. I was only trying to help."

William rubbed Anna's arm. "I know you were. Andrea knows it, too. She's just in too much pain to see it right now. Give her some time. This is a tough period for her. She just had a baby. She misses her husband. She's scared. Don't try to push her too hard. She'll be all right."

Anna looked up into her husband's face. "You really think so?"

"Sure," William answered. He kissed Anna's cheek. "Now go to sleep."

As Anna and William lay there, William prayed that their daughter would get beyond the loss of her husband, so that she could have joy and peace of mind once again.

On Wednesday afternoon, Leah sat with her mother in the family room while Kayla played outside with her grandfather William and Devin.

"Well, Mama," Leah was saying, "she did just have a baby. Maybe she's suffering from an attack of the baby blues. I read about it while she was pregnant."

Anna nodded. "Maybe you're right. I'm just worried about her."

Leah asked, "What do you think we should do?"

"I don't know," Anna answered. "Maybe I can talk her into getting some counseling."

All of a sudden, a voice seemed to come out of nowhere. "What is this? Some sort of conspiracy?" Andrea asked as she stood in the doorway.

"Andrea," Anna said, "I thought you were taking a nap."

"I can see that," Andrea vented. She gave her sister a cold, hard stare. "Leah, what's going on here? Mama telling you how crazy I am?"

Leah didn't know how to respond. She and her mother had been having an earnest conversation about Andrea due to their heartfelt concern for her. Leah felt that no matter what she said, her sister would not understand.

Leah said, "Andrea, you know Mama wouldn't do something like that. She's just worried about you is all. I am, too. Everybody is."

Andrea retorted, "Well, I don't need my family talking about me behind my back. If you've got something to say about me, say it to my face."

Anna stepped in. "Andrea, honey, nobody was talking about you behind your back—not in the way you're thinking. We weren't saying anything bad about you. Leah and I were just sharing our concern for you. I haven't said anything to you about counseling yet because I didn't want to upset you."

Andrea reminded her mother, "Mama, I already told you if you're going to say things to make me feel worse while you're here, maybe you need to go home."

Leah was not going to sit quietly by and allow her sister to talk to their mother that way, no matter what Andrea was going through. "Andrea, don't talk to Mama like that." Her voice was stern.

Andrea shot at her sister, "You don't tell me how to talk."

At that moment, William, Devin, and Kayla came in. Kayla stood between her grandfather and uncle, looking and listening.

William inquired, "What's going on?"

Sensing that more harsh words were about to fly, Devin took Kayla by her hand and headed for her room.

Leah responded, "Nothing, Daddy. Andrea just overheard me and Mama talking, and now she thinks everybody is against her, when all any of us want to do is help."

Andrea declared, "It's not nothing to me. How would any of you like it if you walked in on your family talking about how you need psychological help—when all you really need is for them to be supportive?"

Anna said, "Andrea, that's not at all what happened. Honey, you're upset. Come and sit down and let's talk about it."

"I don't want to talk to any of you," Andrea spat out.

Leah said sympathetically, "See, Andrea, that's part of the problem. You just said if we've got something to say to tell you to your face. We're not here to condemn you. We love you. We know you're hurting, and we want to help. But if you won't talk to us, how can we?"

Andrea replied, "You're all against me. Everybody's against me. Just because I'm having a hard time dealing with Clay's death, you think I'm weak."

William, who had been standing there all this time trying to figure out when to step in and what to say, finally said, "Sweetheart, nobody is against you, and we don't think you're weak. You're human. We hate to see you hurting, and perhaps we've been somewhat selfish in our efforts to help you get better. While we don't want you to suffer, neither do we want to feel the pain and agony of being witnesses to your misery.

"Right now, the most important thing in the world to us is that you're okay. But you've got to work through the grieving process in your time, not ours. Don't be angry at your mother and your sister. They love you. You know that. Your need and desire for your life to be back the way it was . . . is just clouding it out right now."

Her father had spoken all the right words. It was as though he had reached down into the depths of her soul and lifted out her innermost thoughts and feelings. "Oh, Daddy," Andrea cried and threw herself into her father's arms.

William held his daughter, allowing her to release her grief. When Andrea was through, she walked over to her mother and sister. "I'm sorry. Please forgive me."

Anna and Leah stood.

"It's okay," Anna said.

Mother and daughters wrapped their arms around each other, sobbing.

As William stood watching them, he thought back to a time when their lives were so uncomplicated. He prayed that they would find their way back there.

On Sunday afternoon as Anna put the last of her belongings in her suitcase, Andrea wandered into the bedroom. "Mama, you got a minute?"

Anna presented her daughter with a smile. "Sure, baby."

Andrea sat down on the bed. Anna pushed her luggage back so she could join her.

Andrea looked at her mother longingly. "I'm so sorry for the way I've been acting. I know I made your visit miserable. Please don't hate me."

Anna took Andrea's hands in hers. "Baby, I could never hate you. There's nothing in the world you could ever do to make me feel that way. I know you're going through a lot right now. You have a new baby, and you're still struggling with feelings of loneliness. Things aren't going to be easy, and I worry so much about you."

"I know you do, Mama, but I'll be okay. It's going to take some time. Even though you may not believe it, I'm gonna miss you. Thanks for coming. You've been a tremendous help. I really appreciate it."

"There's no need to thank me, but you're welcome. I'm your mama. What kind of mother would I be if I hadn't come?" Anna put her arms around Andrea's neck and hugged her tightly. "You stay strong. Things'll get better."

Andrea hugged her mother with all her might. "I will. I love you, Mama."

"I love you, too, baby."

On the airplane flight back to New York, Anna sat in a daze staring out the window at the puffy white clouds. She'd never felt as aged and weary as she did now. It seemed to her that during her latest visit with Andrea, she had said and done all the wrong things. The trip had not gone at all as she'd hoped. She wished her daughter would seek professional help in dealing with her grief. However, Andrea refused to even discuss it.

William interrupted Anna's thoughts. He knew his wife was feeling anxious about their daughter and was in deep contemplations about her. "She'll be okay."

Anna turned to face her husband. "Hmm?"

"I said she'll be okay."

Anna took William's hand in hers and pasted a fake smile on her face. "Sure she will."

William squeezed her hand. The scary part was that neither of them were too sure about what they'd just said. Their daughter had never gone through anything as traumatic as what she was undergoing now. However, they had to keep a positive attitude.

Chapter 15

Andrea couldn't believe it. She'd only been back at work less than two weeks, and she was already exhausted. The mental and physical fatigue were making it difficult for her to function. She found herself being irritable at work, although she tried not to let it show. The pleasure she once received from her job was gone. She felt miserable. Yet, in the office, she plastered a smile on her face and attempted to be pleasant with her patients and coworkers. However, once she made it home, the despondency was clearly evident.

Andrea picked up the children from day care, and Kayla proceeded to tell Andrea about her day. Not knowing her mother was in a world of her own, Kayla asked from the backseat, "Did you hear me, Mommy? Mommy?"

Andrea came out of her meditations, turning her head slightly to answer. "Hmm? What did you say, honey?"

"I said we're gonna have Career Day at school, and Ms. Johnson said we can invite our parents to come and tell what they do for a living. Will you come?"

Andrea didn't want to commit to anything. She had enough to do as it was. "Ah, when is it?"

"I brought a note home," Kayla replied cheerily. "It's in my book bag."

"Well, I'll read it when we get home, and we'll see. Okay?"

"Okay, Mommy."

When they got home, Andrea gave Kayla an apple to snack on while she changed Clayton's diaper and let him nurse for a few minutes. Then she warmed some leftover spaghetti for her and Kayla. After supper, Andrea bathed Clayton while his sister took her bath. When the baths were completed, Andrea and Kayla lay on a blanket on the floor of the family room and played with Clayton.

Kayla announced, "He's so sweet and cute. Was I this sweet when I was a baby?"

"You sure were. And you had the most beautiful smile," Andrea bragged. "You still do."

"Thank you, Mommy. I like your smile, too."

"Thank you."

There was a brief silence. Then Kayla asked, "Mommy, do you think you'll ever be happy again? I mean the way you used to be."

Andrea looked adoringly at her child. "I don't know, sweetie. I hope so."

"Me, too, because I miss the way you used to laugh."

Andrea rubbed Kayla's head. "So do I, baby."

Two days later, Andrea felt somewhat better. Perhaps because it was Friday, and she was looking forward to a weekend of rest and relaxation. Hopefully, Kayla and Clayton would allow her to get some. Life as a single parent was hard, especially now that she had two children, but she wouldn't trade her offspring for the world.

Andrea peeked her head in Glenn's office as she passed his door on her way out. "Bye, Glenn. Have a good weekend."

The man looked up. "You, too," he said, standing. Glenn was worried about Andrea. She did not seem at all like herself. Walking toward her, he offered, "Let me walk you to your car."

"Okay." Andrea prayed that he was not going to question how

she was doing. She feared she would lose control of her emotions if he did. Her desire was to continue what she'd been doing since she'd returned to work—put on her happy face around her patients and coworkers and replace it with her sad one when she got to the privacy of her home.

Andrea attempted to pay attention as Glenn chatted away on the walk to her car. When they reached her vehicle, they stopped.

As she inserted and turned her key in the lock, Andrea said, "Thanks for walking me to my car, Glenn."

"You're welcome."

She proceeded to get into her vehicle when he asked, "Andrea, are you okay?"

Andrea stared up at the doctor and answered, "I'm fine."

"Are you sure?"

"Yes." Andrea wanted to slam the door shut and speed away. *I'm gonna lose it if I don't get out of here.*

Glenn earnestly stated, "You know I'm your friend, and you can talk to me. Everyone here loves you. We want to help you. Whatever it is you need, we're here for you."

Andrea was close to tears. She was afraid to say anything, for fear the weeping would start. Before she spoke, she prayed that she would remain composed. "Thanks. I appreciate that, but I'm fine." She needed an excuse to make her exit. "I gotta go get my kids. I'll see you Monday."

Glenn stepped back so Andrea could close her door. "Okay. Bye."

As Glenn watched Andrea drive away, he thought, *I don't know who she thinks she's fooling, but she's not fine.* The wheels started turning in his head as he wished he could come up with an idea to help Andrea.

Devin was beginning to get more than a little agitated with his bride-to-be as he stood in front of the floor-length mirror in the tuxedo store at the mall. He had chosen an off-white suit with a lavender bow tie and cummerbund, and he liked the look and feel of the ensemble.

"Leah, I like this one. It's *my* suit. I'm the one who has to wear it. I've given in to you about everything else that has to do with this wedding. It's *my* wedding, too. You seem to keep forgetting that."

Leah suddenly looked embarrassed. How could she be so selfish? "You're absolutely right. I'm sorry. I got carried away again, huh?"

Without turning his attention away from his reflection in the mirror, Devin stated in a tone lacking savor, "Yeah, you did."

The store clerk appeared. "Do you like this one, sir?"

Devin grinned with pride. "Yes, I'll take it."

The clerk returned Devin's smile. "Excellent choice."

After Devin made his purchase, Leah declared, "Now it's off to order the invitations."

All Devin could think of on the way to the car was that by the time Leah finished selecting the invitations, every ounce of sanity he had left would be dissolved. It was a good thing his head was already bald, because if it wasn't, it'd sure be headed that way after this excursion.

Chapter 16

When Andrea walked into the office on Monday morning, she saw decorations everywhere. A huge colorful banner that read WE LOVE YOU, ANDREA! hung over the waiting room entrance. Not only were her coworkers present but also some of her patients and their families. Andrea took in the sight of each smiling face before her as she grinned back at them. That's when she spotted her sister, Devin, Ellen, Alexander, and some other members from her church. She couldn't believe her eyes.

Andrea went around hugging everyone and thanking them for their generosity. Then Alexander led them in prayer before they all sat down to the best brunch they'd ever tasted. She received many cards with kind expressions. She simply could not believe that all these people would go to this extent for her. She never would have imagined that she had made such a huge impact on anyone's life.

When she got up to thank them one last time, she could hardly speak through her tears. "No one's ever done anything like this for me before. It's the best surprise I've ever had. It's a good feeling to know that you all love me this much to plan something as nice as this. The past several months have been hard, but with friends like you, I believe I'll make it. Thank you so much. I love you all."

Everyone clapped, then hugged Andrea. When the party was over and things had quieted down, she peeked her head in Glenn's office. He looked busy as he scribbled something down on a piece of paper, so she turned to walk away.

"Andrea," Glenn said. "Come in. Did you want to see me?"

She turned around. "I'm sorry. I didn't mean to interrupt."

Glenn motioned for her to enter. "Nonsense. Have a seat."

Andrea sat down. "I know you were the mastermind behind the party you all threw for me. I just want you to know how much I appreciate it. You're a kind, wonderful person. I feel so blessed to be able to work for you and have you as a friend."

Glenn humbly stated, "You're a kind, wonderful person who doesn't deserve what happened to you. Yet, you come in here every day despite what you're going through, and you still do a good job. I appreciate that. So I should be thanking you, but you're welcome."

"Thank you, Glenn. Did I ever tell you that you're the one who brought me and Clay together?"

Glenn raised an eyebrow. "No. How's that?"

Andrea filled her boss in on how she and Clayton had met in his office when Clayton had come in to have his teeth cleaned.

Glenn smiled. "Well, you two were a match made in heaven, so I don't mind taking the credit."

Andrea stood, smiling. "Well, thanks again."

Glenn stood and walked around his desk to give her a hug. "Sure."

After she had gone, Glenn said a silent prayer that she would stand strong.

Wednesday morning, Andrea took the children to day care and hurried back home to get an extra hour and a half of sleep. She didn't have to go in to work today, but she was due to be at Kayla's school at ten o'clock for Career Day. Clayton was colicky, and Andrea had only gotten about three hours of sleep the night before. She hastily set the alarm for nine o'clock and climbed back into bed.

When Andrea awoke, she noticed how brilliant the sun was streaming through the windows. She stared groggily at the clock and bolted up out of bed when she saw that it was after one. She began whirling around in circles, not knowing exactly what to do. Should she get dressed and head for the school, or should she call first to explain what had happened? She couldn't think straight. Kayla must be devastated. Since the day she'd told Andrea about Career Day, Kayla had asked her every day if she was still coming. Andrea had assured her that she would be there. She had let her child down.

Andrea decided to call the school. They could probably squeeze her in. Everything would be fine, and Kayla wouldn't be disappointed. However, much to Andrea's dismay, there were no more time slots available. Not unless some of the other parents had let their kids down, too. She felt terrible. Would Kayla ever forgive her?

Andrea wanted to get the inevitable out of the way. She thought about stopping by the school to check Kayla out early. She was a nervous wreck. She changed her mind. She would just pick her up from day care when she got Clayton. No matter what explanation she gave, she was certain Kayla would not understand.

When Andrea picked up the children later that afternoon, it was obvious that Kayla had been crying.

As soon as the child saw her mother, she asked, "Mommy, where were you?"

Grabbing up Clayton's diaper bag, with Clayton in his carryall in the other hand, Andrea said, "Honey, I'm so sorry. I was tired, and I overslept. You know I would have been there otherwise."

Andrea didn't want Kayla making a scene in front of everyone, so she attempted to get them all outside. "Come on. We'll talk about it in the car," she said, gently pressing her hand on her daughter's back to give her a nudge.

Kayla tagged along, but not without voicing her feelings. "Mommy, I was embarrassed. Everybody was staring at me. I told everybody you were coming."

Andrea repeated, "Honey, I'm sorry. I told you I overslept. I didn't mean to make you look bad. Come on. Get in the car."

Kayla was quiet on the ride home. Andrea attempted to engage her in conversation by asking her what she wanted to do over the weekend. All she got from Kayla was an *I don't know.*

Kayla was closemouthed during supper as well. Andrea realized she had let her daughter down and didn't know how she could ever make it up to her.

After Andrea had put Clayton to bed, she went to Kayla's room where she found her reading one of her books.

She sat down on the side of the bed. "Want me to read to you?"

Kayla kept her eyes focused on her book. "No, I can read it myself," she answered, without displaying any type of emotion.

Andrea felt her heart drop. "Okay."

She waited on Kayla to say something else. When she didn't, Andrea said, "Sweetie, I know you're angry at me because I missed Career Day. It's hard for me right now trying to do everything without Daddy. I didn't get much sleep last night, and I overslept."

Kayla didn't take her eyes away from her storybook when she asked, "Didn't you set the alarm?"

"Yes, but I set it on P.M. by mistake, instead of A.M. You remember the difference between P.M. and A.M.?"

Kayla looked at her mother this time. "Yes, Mommy. P.M. is nighttime. A.M. is morning time."

Andrea smiled as she nodded. "Right."

"Mommy?"

"Yes, sweetie."

"Next time, can you just check to make sure you're setting the clock right 'cause I don't ever wanna go through what I went through today again."

"I will," Andrea said.

"Mommy?"

"Yes."

"Since I had such a rough day, I think I need some ice cream to cheer me up."

Andrea snickered, "You do?"

Kayla grinned. "Yes."

How could Andrea resist such a reasonable plea? She tickled Kayla, saying, "Come on. Let's go get some ice cream." On their way to the kitchen, she reminded her daughter, "We have to be quiet. We don't want to wake Clayton."

Kayla whispered as she tiptoed behind her mother. "Okay."

They made it to the kitchen where they pulled the chocolate ripple ice cream from the freezer and filled their bowls with it. They talked and giggled while they ate.

Andrea would give anything to be able to bounce back from a tragedy as quickly as Kayla. Sometimes she wished she could go back to her childhood, when her parents could make everything all right.

Chapter 17

Two more weeks went by. Andrea had now missed her third Sunday in a row of worship services, plus all of the midweek Bible study classes. Today, she was so tired that she decided to stay in bed before Clayton arose. She was in a deep slumber when she felt someone shaking her, yet she refused to move.

Kayla attempted once more to rouse her mother from sleep, shaking her a little harder this time. "Mommy, wake up."

Andrea peeked her head from underneath the covers, glancing at the clock. It was a few minutes past eight. She asked sleepily, "What is it, honey?"

"Mommy, it's time to get up," Kayla reminded her. "We're gonna be late for church."

"Baby, we're not going today. Mommy's tired. Let me sleep for a little bit. Then I'll get up and fix you breakfast."

Kayla responded, "I already ate some cereal. I wanna go to church."

Andrea did not feel up to debating the subject. After all, she was the parent. She replied in a stern voice, "Kayla, I told you that I'm tired. Now let me get some rest. Later today, I'll take you to the park or something."

Kayla said nothing more as she turned around and left her mother alone.

An hour and a half later, Andrea woke up when she heard Clayton's cries over the baby monitor. After changing his diaper and nursing him, she put him back to bed and went to check on her vibrant daughter.

Their church family was a huge part of their lives, and Kayla missed the fellowship. Andrea felt horrible for not fulfilling her daughter's wishes to attend services. Every week, she intended for them to go. However, when the time came, she reasoned that she was too tired and that they would be present the following week. But it was always easier to just stay home.

Andrea found Kayla in her room playing. When Kayla saw her mother, she inquired, "Mommy, why don't we go to church anymore?"

Andrea sat down on the bed beside her daughter. "Mommy's not feeling well. We'll go back soon. Okay?"

"Okay."

Andrea felt guilty for getting Kayla's hopes up about them returning to church in a short time. She honestly didn't know when they would go back. Working, raising two kids, and taking care of home had just about taken their toll on her, plus she was still grieving over Clayton's death. She needed some time to rest. Surely God understood that.

Weary as she was, Andrea managed to put together a decent meal of burgers and oven-baked fries for her and Kayla. Andrea ate lunch in her robe and still had it on later when the doorbell rang. She wondered who it was. She really did not feel like having any visitors today. Kayla started running for the door, but Andrea stopped her.

Andrea asked who it was. It was Ellen and Alexander. Andrea loved them dearly, but she didn't feel like having company. She was tired. She opened the door just enough to speak to the couple through a crack.

"Hi," Andrea said. She could see the bewildered look on the Knights' faces, as she had always been hospitable to them.

Alexander said, "Andrea, we just stopped by to see how you're doing. We've missed you."

Andrea responded, "I'm okay. Just tired."

Ellen offered, "Well, maybe there's something we can help you with while we're here."

"No, thank you," Andrea said. "But thanks for stopping by. I just need to get some rest." She didn't want to hurt their feelings. She was too tired for company. Why couldn't people understand that?

Ellen had also wanted to see if Andrea felt up to meeting at Ellen's house with her and some of the other sisters from their congregation to discuss the details of Leah's bridal shower, which would be coming up in less than two months. They'd had to rent a hall for the occasion to accommodate everyone on the guest list. After Ellen saw how distressed Andrea appeared, she refused to even bring up the subject.

"Okay," Alexander said. "We'll check on you later."

The Knights told Andrea good-bye and were soon gone.

A few minutes later, Leah stopped by. Andrea wondered, *Why can't people just leave me alone for a few minutes?* She thought seriously about turning her sister away at the door also, but didn't.

Leah was very much concerned about Andrea. It was unusual for her to miss so many meetings, especially since she had always been such a spiritual person. Leah didn't want to upset her, so she kept silent about her worries. Besides, Andrea would return to the congregation before long. She was having a difficult time at the moment, but she would keep afloat.

Yet, when Andrea made an earnest plea for Leah to allow Kayla to accompany her to church, Leah's heart dropped. Was this a sign that Andrea would be missing services indefinitely? Leah was not quite sure how to reply. She desired to help her sister in any way she could. Nevertheless, she didn't want Andrea not to take her own spirituality seriously, and Leah certainly had no desire to enable her in the process.

Leah answered, "Sure . . ." However, she had to set some boundaries. "For how long? A week or two?"

"Yeah," Andrea replied, not having a clue regarding the longevity of their agreement.

What Andrea did know was that she had never felt so physically, mentally, and spiritually drained of energy. It seemed as though her life was withering away.

Devin couldn't believe he was spending this Sunday afternoon sitting with Leah in her living room addressing wedding invitations. This was the one thing he didn't mind paying someone to do, but his future bride had insisted that they do the invitations themselves. He also couldn't believe that they were doing two hundred of these things—another one of Leah's ideas. He said a quick silent prayer of thanks that he had finally been able to get her to narrow the invitation list down from three hundred.

Without looking up from her task, Leah asked, "Do you know it's been three weeks since Andrea's been to church? That's not a good sign. I'm worried about her. Maybe she needs some encouragement."

Devin realized Leah's concern for her sister went deep. However, he felt that Andrea was at a very vulnerable stage in her life; therefore, people needed to be cautious about how they approached her. "If you say anything, just be careful about what you say and how you say it. She's still not over losing Clay, and the least little thing can probably throw her over the edge."

Somewhat frustrated, Leah replied, "Devin, it's been almost a year. She should be better by now. People die all the time, and it doesn't take their family this long to get over them."

Devin was shocked that Leah was being so insensitive to her sister's unfortunate situation. He stopped writing and looked at her with fire blazing in his eyes. "How do you know how long it takes them to get over losing a loved one? Do you climb inside their heads and feel every painful memory? Are you there when they go to bed at night and get up the next morning, if they get up at all, to see the agony they go through each day and night without their loved one? It doesn't matter how long it's been—one year, ten, twenty, the rest of their lives. *You* can't feel her pain, so stop judging and criticizing. It wasn't your husband who was killed. As her sister, I'd think you'd be more sensitive toward her and what she's going through."

Leah ceased addressing an invitation and stared at Devin. Never before had she seen the look of anguish he'd just given her or heard the pain he'd just revealed. Sometimes it was as though she forgot that Clayton had been his brother and that he was still hurting, too. "Baby, I'm sorry."

Blinking hard in an effort to contain his tears, Devin leaned back on the sofa with his head against the cushion.

Leah's heart raced. Moving swiftly to Devin's side, she said, "I'm so sorry." She gently reached up, put her hand on the back of his head, and pulled him into her arms.

As Devin's tears splattered onto his face and his sobs filled the air, all Leah knew to do was hold him and let him cry.

Two and a half weeks later, the one-year anniversary of Clayton's death arrived. Andrea still had not returned to church, and she was very despondent. She had been relying very heavily on her sister to pick up her slack as far as Kayla's spirituality was concerned. Leah had been a pillar of support.

It was Wednesday, Andrea's day off. She took the children to day care and went back home, where she climbed into bed and wept into her pillow. It felt like she was reliving Clayton's death all over again. She kept replaying the scene in her head when she had received the phone call to go to the hospital—how when she got there, Clayton was already gone. They didn't even get to say goodbye. The last kiss and embrace she had given her husband was after he had breathed his last breath. No life left in him, he had been unable to return her tender sentiments.

Andrea stayed in bed until midday, at which time she got up to get a glass of water. On her way back to the bedroom, she felt the urge to stop by the family room. She slowly glided herself to the entertainment center. She stood there for a brief moment, simply gazing at the stack of music CD's. She slowly removed a CD from the stand, opened the plastic case, and popped the disk into the CD player. The music played, and soon the soft, mellow voices of Eric Benét and Tamia filled the atmosphere as they sang "Spend My Life With You."

This had been Andrea and Clayton's favorite song. Andrea threw herself down onto a corner of the sofa and hugged a pillow, as she listened to the beautiful lyrics. As the song played, tears spilled down her cheeks. By the time it had ended, she was sobbing profusely. Hearing the verses hurt so much, but she had to hear them one more time. The words expressed what she and Clayton had felt for one another.

Before she knew what was happening, Andrea threw her head back and cried out, "Why?! Oh, Lord, why did you let this happen? Of all the things in the world that could've happened, why this? I can't take it. I wanna die!"

Andrea was still sobbing when the telephone rang. She allowed the answering machine to pick up. It was her mother. Andrea wanted to talk to her. Needed to talk to her. However, she was in no condition to do so now. She would call her mother back later.

Deciding that a bubble bath would do her good, Andrea ran some water. When she was done with her bath, she put on a long blue jean skirt and a white, long-sleeved, button-front, cotton shirt.

Sitting on the side of her bed, she pulled on a pair of white ankle socks and her white Keds. She needed to go somewhere. Where, she didn't know.

She had slung open the front door when Devin was about to ring the doorbell. Andrea jumped.

"Hi, Andrea." Devin apologized, "Sorry I scared you. Were you going out?"

"Hi, Devin. Yes, but come on in."

Devin stepped inside. "I just came by to see if you wanna grab some lunch."

It would be nice to have some company, especially someone who could sympathize with how she was feeling. "Sure," Andrea said.

They decided to go to Chili's in Douglasville. As they sat at their table eating, they could see the sadness in each other's eyes. On the drive to the restaurant, they had attempted to discuss happy things, not the sorrow they both felt. However, they had to talk about it, for it was a common bond they shared.

Devin hung his head. "It's hard to believe it's been a year today since Clayton died. I didn't sleep at all last night. I had to call the office and ask for the day off. It's like reliving his death all over again."

Andrea looked at her brother-in-law. "That's exactly how I feel. I lay in bed this morning reliving it over and over in my head. Then I put on our favorite CD and cried while I listened to it. You know, the strange thing is, I don't know why I did it, because hearing it was pure torture. But it somehow made me feel closer to him despite all the hurt."

"I know what you mean. I spent the morning looking through old photo albums of us when we were kids. You know, he used to really bug me when we were little. Always wanting to follow me around and do everything I did." Devin choked back a smile as he said, "He was every big brother's nightmare."

Andrea giggled as she listened to Devin reminisce concerning his little brother.

Devin went on. "The next thing I knew, we were buddies. I miss him so much," he said as he choked back tears. "It's gonna be so hard not having him at the wedding."

Andrea put her hand on Devin's. "Yes, it'll be hard. He loved you. We all loved him, and he knew it. Right now, that's the only good thing I can think about—he died knowing he was truly loved."

"Yeah," Devin agreed.

Andrea and Devin talked as they finished eating. Yet, in the back of their minds, they were thinking about the man who had meant the world to them.

Andrea knew her mother was worried and called as soon as she had put the children to bed.

"I'm okay, Mama. Today was rough, but I made it through. Devin and I went to lunch and consoled each other."

"That's good," Anna said. Against her better judgement, she decided to mention the support group for bereaving spouses. "I'm glad Devin was there for you. I've been doing some research on support groups for people who have lost their spouses. I've got some phone numbers and Web addresses I wanted to give you."

Andrea wished her mother would stop trying to force her to go to counseling and join some group. She didn't need any of that. She was capable of handling her grief on her own.

"Mama, please don't start that again. Why do you keep insisting that I go and talk to a bunch of strangers about my personal business?"

"You don't have to tell them anything you don't want them to know. It might help to talk to people who know what you're going through."

Andrea firmly stated, "They can't possibly know what I'm going through. Just because their wife or husband died, they're supposed to know how *I* feel?"

Why did her daughter have to be so argumentative? Every time Anna tried to offer Andrea a solution to her problem, she took offense. "Andrea, that's not what I meant, and you know it. All I'm saying is that since you would all be in similar situations, you would be able to relate to each other's feelings and concerns. You don't even have to say anything if you don't want to. Just listen to them."

Andrea knew her mother meant well. She just wished she'd let her deal with this her own way. "I'm sorry. Can we talk about something else?"

Andrea and Anna managed to end their conversation on a positive note.

Andrea decided to call her in-laws. She wondered how their day had gone. Lizzie answered the phone. It had been a difficult day for her and Edward as well. Andrea spoke briefly with both of them.

Leah called a few minutes later. "Devin told me you and he had lunch this afternoon. I'm sorry today was hard for you. How are you?"

Andrea answered, "Thanks to Devin, I'm okay." Hoping it didn't sound as though she was throwing hints, she added, "It was nice to talk to someone who could relate to what I'm going through."

Andrea and Leah talked briefly before ending their call. Andrea thought about what she'd told her sister. *It was nice to talk to someone who could relate to what I'm going through.*

It had been nice, but Devin was family. She couldn't talk to a bunch of strangers about her personal life. Her family and her faith were supposed to help her get over her grief. But were they helping? It had already been a year, and she felt she was at the lowest point in her life. In addition, she no longer had the desire for spiritual things. Was her faith wavering?

Chapter 18

Leah and Devin had just left Andrea's. They had visited for a few minutes after taking Kayla home after church.

Leah was quiet as Devin drove. She simply did not understand her sister. How could Andrea not see that her spirituality was an important part of the healing process to her recovery? Andrea had asked her to help out with taking Kayla to church for a couple of weeks. That was a month ago. Every Saturday night, Andrea would call and ask Leah if she'd pick up Kayla for church the next morning. It had been almost two months since Andrea had set foot in church herself. Leah could see that the more her sister neglected her spirituality, the more withdrawn she became.

Devin gazed at his fiancée. "What's wrong?"

As if he doesn't know. She didn't want to fight with him again regarding her sister, especially after what had transpired the day they were addressing the wedding invitations. Just last week, she had threatened to have it out with Andrea and stop being her enabler. Devin had expressed how disappointed he was that she would abandon her sister in her time of need. He'd even asked her if that was what she planned to do to him after they were married—bail out at the first sign of trouble.

Leah refused to look at him and replied, "Nothing."

Devin reckoned that Leah was still feeling as though her bond with Andrea was weakening. "Just give her a little more time," he humbly requested.

Leah said nothing as she breathed a heavy sigh.

Devin went on. "I know you want her back the way she was, but this has been hard on her."

Leah wished he would stop making excuses for her sister. Andrea wasn't the first person whose husband had died, and she certainly wouldn't be the last. How could a person let one incident turn her away from all she'd ever believed? She was so angry at Andrea that she could scream. How could the sister she'd always admired and looked up to turn her back on God? Not only that, she couldn't believe how selfish Andrea was being concerning the wedding. This was supposed to be one of the happiest times of Leah's life, and her sister was taking all the joy out of it. Most sisters would be excited and eager to help the other sister with planning the wedding and getting everything in order, but no, not Andrea.

Devin was still talking. Leah wished he would hush. She didn't care to hear anymore about poor Andrea and what she was going through. She needed to get up off her behind and stop feeling sorry for herself.

Devin said, "You know, she needs you to be there for her."

Leah had heard enough of her fiancé's sentiments. She glared at him as she responded, "Devin, I'm sick and tired of you making excuses for Andrea. Maybe since you're so worried about her, you should marry *her* and take care of her." As soon as the words were out of her mouth, Leah felt a deep sense of regret, but she was not going to admit it.

Stunned, Devin stared momentarily at his wife-to-be. "What is that supposed to mean?"

"Just what I said," Leah snapped.

"Leah, how could you let something that disgusting even come out of your mouth. Andrea's your sister. She was married to my brother."

Leah snapped again, "Well, that's what they used to do back in Bible times. Maybe that's what you wanna do, too."

Devin responded, "That's what they were required to do under God's Law if the brother died without a son. I can't believe you would even think something like that. I can't believe we're having this conversation." Feeling the need to settle the matter here and now, he added, "I love Andrea like a sister—nothing more. You're the one I want to marry. I just worry about her. I'm sorry if I made it seem like more than that."

Leah felt horrible. "You didn't. I'm sorry. I'm just so mad at her. It's like I don't know who she is anymore. I miss the person she used to be, and I just want her back. I can't even talk to her about the wedding. Every time I try to share some of the details with her or get her more involved, she just clams up."

Devin quickly responded, "Andrea's happy for us. I know she is. I think our happiness and all the fuss about the wedding are just making her situation more unbearable for her. Try to be patient with her."

"I'm trying, but it's so hard. I want to do right by her, but I feel like if I keep taking Kayla to church, she'll never come back. And that's a feeling I can't live with. Do you understand what I'm saying?"

Devin gazed adoringly at Leah. "Yes. I know I've been pressuring you a lot to help her. I just don't want her to give up in her fight to go on without Clay."

Leah looked at Devin, tears about to bubble forth from the corners of her eyes. "But Devin, don't you see? She's already given up. And I can't continue to help her bury herself deeper."

Devin supposed Leah was right. However, he did not want her to do anything that would push Andrea over the edge.

* * *

Later that evening, Leah telephoned Yasmine to see if she was home, as she desperately needed to talk to someone other than her family and Devin. They were all too personally involved where Andrea was concerned.

As the two friends sat in Yasmine's living room, Leah said, "I'm so tired of everybody making excuses for Andrea. I know she's still hurting over losing Clay, but she's got to get on with her life. She hasn't been to church in almost two months. A month ago, she asked me to take Kayla to church just for a couple of weeks, but now she calls me up every Saturday night asking me to pick her up. I've been doing it because I feel obligated, but it's not right. She needs to be there, too, no matter how bad she feels."

Yasmine's heart went out to her friend. She could only imagine what an unpleasant position Leah was in having to choose between lending her sister a helping hand and trying to get her sister to help herself. "Have you tried talking to her about it?"

"No. Every time I even breathe about how I feel, Devin tells me I need to give her some time and that she needs me. What she needs is God, but she seems oblivious to that."

"She still refuses to get counseling?"

"Umph. She already bit my and Mama's heads off about that right after Clayton was born. No way am I bringing it up again. I don't have any control over that, but I can call the shots as far as me continuing to take Kayla to church while she sits around feeling sorry for herself."

Yasmine felt the urge to tell Leah to simply stop picking up Kayla for church. Perhaps Andrea would get the picture then, and Leah could avoid an unsavory confrontation with her sister, unless Andrea eventually brought up the matter. Sometimes a person needed to let another stand on his own two feet. As long as Leah was doing Andrea's work for her, Andrea would never recover from her loss.

Yasmine found herself saying, "Talk to her. I'm sure she'll understand."

Leah prayed her friend was right. The last thing she wanted to do was increase the gap between her and Andrea any further.

Friday afternoon, Leah pulled her vehicle into her sister's driveway. She was somewhat nervous, for she was about to approach a subject she knew Andrea cared not to discuss. After their conversation the previous Sunday, Leah and Devin had sat down and considered the situation. Devin had wanted to be by Leah's side when she talked with Andrea, but Leah felt she should do it alone. Now, as she exited her car and walked up to the front door, she wished she'd allowed him to accompany her.

Andrea opened the door, cradling Clayton in one arm. Leah tickled the bottom of his bare feet. "Hey there, sport. How ya doing?"

Clayton awarded his aunt one of his many smiles.

"You're so cute," Leah bragged. "Yes, you are."

It was unusual not to see Kayla running about. On the way to the family room, Leah asked, "Where's Kayla?"

Andrea responded, "Ellen and Alex took her out to eat and to a movie."

They sat on the sofa.

Leah attempted to smile, despite her uneasiness. "That's nice." She considered it a blessing that Kayla was out, especially since she didn't know how things would go with her and Andrea. "So how are you?"

"Okay," Andrea answered. "Just trying to take one day at a time."

"Yeah," was all Leah could manage to get out. Her palms were sweaty—a sure sign of her nervousness. She dreaded what she was about to do, but she had to do it. *Lord, please help me find the right words. I don't want to hurt my sister, but I have to do this. For her sake.* She was about to speak, when Andrea asked her to hold Clayton while she went to get a blanket to put on the floor for him to lie on.

As Leah sat holding the baby and playing with him, she couldn't help but think how sweet and innocent he was. How he had come into the world fatherless. How he might not come to have faith in a higher power if his mother didn't get her act together.

Andrea interrupted Leah's thoughts when she returned with the blanket and began spreading it out on the floor. After placing little Clayton on it, Andrea rejoined her sister on the sofa.

Leah felt a lump well up inside her throat. "Andrea, we need to talk."

Andrea looked at her sister. "What about?"

Leah couldn't believe what she was about to do. "Remember last month when you asked me if I would take Kayla to church with me?"

Andrea was staring at her, which only made Leah more nervous.

Leah continued, "Well, you said it would only be for a week or two. You know I love you, and I don't mind helping. But it's been almost two months now. Kayla's still coming to church with me, but you haven't returned. I'm concerned. So I was wondering when you're coming back." Though frightened about how her sister might react, Leah looked at Andrea, waiting for an answer.

Andrea should have known that sooner or later Leah would say something like this. She figured it was just a matter of time, since her sister could be annoyingly aggressive. Still, she didn't appreciate it. Leah knew she was under a lot of stress. She didn't need this pressure about church.

"I don't know," was Andrea's curt reply.

"Well, why don't you and Clayton come Sunday when I pick up Kayla?"

Andrea shook her head. "No, maybe another time." She wasn't promising Leah anything because she didn't know how she'd feel when Sunday came.

Leah knew she would be pushing it, but she had to ask, "If not Sunday, when?"

Andrea felt a headache coming on. "I told you I don't know," she replied sternly.

Leah knew her sister was getting angry, but she had no intention of backing down. "Andrea, don't you miss the fellowship and the spiritual aspect?"

"Yes," Andrea honestly admitted, "but I've got too many other things I'm trying to deal with right now."

"I know you're still hurting over losing Clay. Then you found out you were pregnant and had the baby. You're a single parent now, and you have a full-time job on top of everything else. But Andrea, church is where you need to be in order to help you deal with your pain. How else do you think you're going to get through it?"

Andrea's head was throbbing now. "Leah, please. The last thing I need is to be preached to."

"I'm not preaching. I'm worried about you. I know you feel overwhelmed, but neglecting your spirituality is only going to make things worse. If you lose your faith, you will have nothing to fall back on. Is that what you want? I know it's not. Please come to church Sunday," Leah begged.

What made Leah think she could just waltz into her home and demand that she go to church? Andrea jumped up and glared down at her sister.

She was angry. However, she attempted to keep her voice low, so as not to startle Clayton. "I told you I don't know when I'll be back. I don't wanna talk about this anymore."

"Andrea . . ."

Andrea threw up her hand to silence her sister. "No, Leah, I don't wanna hear anymore. Just go."

Shocked that her sister had just ordered her to leave her house, Leah asked, "What? Are you serious?"

"Yes. I want you to go. Now."

It was obvious to Leah that Andrea was not kidding, so she stood up to make her departure—but not before having her final say.

"Okay, Andrea, if you want me to leave, I'll leave. But I've got one more thing to say to you."

"You've said enough. I told you I don't want to hear anything else."

"Well, you're gonna hear it whether you want to or not. I won't be taking Kayla to church anymore. When you start taking your own spirituality more seriously, I'll reconsider. I love Kayla, you, and Clayton, but I'm not gonna keep enabling you. *You're* Kayla's mother. *You* should take her to church. *You* should be there with both of your children, but all you wanna do is sit at home feeling sorry for yourself. I never thought I'd see the day when you'd give up on yourself or God."

Andrea wasn't expecting this. She needed Leah to be there for Kayla. Though Andrea was not ready herself to go back to church, it was important to her that Kayla maintain her spirituality, as it was a part of the life Kayla had grown accustomed to. Immediately, Andrea thought of a way that would keep her sister involved.

Andrea threatened, "If you want to continue being a part of Kayla and Clayton's lives, you'll keep taking Kayla to church with you."

Leah was aghast that her sister would suggest such a ridiculous notion. She assumed Andrea was joking and let out a quiescent laugh. When Andrea didn't say anything, Leah stared at her. "What? Are you serious?"

"You heard me. If you won't help me out with this one small thing, I won't allow you to see Kayla or Clayton."

"Andrea, that's the craziest thing I ever heard. And I won't agree to something so ridiculous."

Andrea hadn't planned on her sister not backing down, for she knew how much Leah loved the children. But neither was she going to cower. Leah would come around after she'd thought about what she was losing. "Well, you may as well leave."

Without uttering another word, Leah stormed out of the house.

She had tried her best to be there for her sister out of the goodness of her heart, and this was the thanks she got. Well, Andrea could just handle her business by herself for all she cared, but Leah would never give in to her.

Andrea was fuming. How dare Leah think she could force her to do something she wasn't ready to do. However, she was confident that once Leah realized how wrong she was, that her sister would apologize and recant her refusal to take Kayla to church.

When the telephone rang later that night, Andrea's heart skipped a beat. She knew her sister would come around. However, when she checked the caller ID, her heart dropped when she saw her parents' names.

Anna wasted no time in relaying what Leah had told her. "Honey, don't you think you're being unreasonable?"

"Mama, why are you taking sides with Leah?"

"I'm not taking sides. I just want you to think about what you've done. How are you going to explain to Kayla why she can't see Leah?"

"I'll think of something. Mama, they're my children. Leah should have thought about the consequences before she came over here running her mouth."

Anna's tone was firm but loving. "Andrea, do you hear yourself? The 'consequences'? You're talking like your sister has done something deserving of punishment. I'm not saying she was right to try to force you back to church, but, honey, you've taken this too far. Don't do this. Don't take your pain out on the people you love, especially not your children."

"I'm not taking anything out on anybody," Andrea vehemently denied. "I don't wanna talk about it anymore."

"Andrea . . ."

Andrea gently replaced the phone in its cradle. She realized she'd never hung up on her mother before, and she wasn't trying to be disrespectful. She just wished everyone would stop telling her what to do.

When the telephone rang immediately after Andrea had hung it up, she refused to answer. She heard her father leaving a message on the machine. She could always talk to her father, but she didn't want to speak to anyone else tonight. Everyone was turning against her. Perhaps he, too, was calling to chastise her, and she didn't care to hear it. She had to get away. She called her in-laws to see if they would be home for the weekend. She informed Lizzie that she and the kids would be in Birmingham around eleven o'clock the following day.

As she lay in bed, Andrea felt very lonely and afraid. She so desperately needed some companionship. Someone to talk to. Someone who understood her as no one else did. Clayton. She'd always been so in control of her life. Now she felt as though there was no hope for her.

Chapter 19

As Andrea maneuvered her vehicle up the gravel entrance to the Hamiltons' ranch-style brick home, Kayla jumped up and down in the backseat at the sight of the ducks swimming along the lake's rippling water. They hadn't been here since her father's death, and she was extremely excited.

Kayla squealed, "Mommy, can I feed the ducks?"

"After a while," Andrea reminded her daughter. "First, we have to visit with Nanna and Poppy for a few minutes."

Andrea heard Kayla telling her baby brother, "Clayton, you're gonna like it here. I'll show you how to feed the ducks, and . . ."

Andrea's mind wandered off as she thought about her and Leah's argument the night before. She felt as though no one understood what she was going through, except for Lizzie, Edward, and Devin. Her parents and her sister could not possibly fathom the pain she was still experiencing over Clayton's death, even one year later. They had promised they would be there for her. Now, when she needed them the most, they had turned their backs on her. She felt she could no longer confide in them. That was why she had left this morning without telling them of her whereabouts. Why should she? They didn't care.

When she finally pulled up in front of the Hamilton home, Andrea didn't even remember the short journey she'd taken up the driveway. Lizzie and Edward ran out to greet her and the children. After everybody was inside, they sat down to a delicious meal of home-cooked fried chicken, biscuits, mashed potatoes, and gravy.

Andrea asked, "That restaurant in Waldo that serves the fried pickles, are they still in business?"

Edward queried, "The Old Mill Restaurant? They sure are. How 'bout we go there for supper tonight?" He knew how much Andrea and Kayla loved the food.

Andrea smiled. Her favorite dish was the pickles. "Can we?"

Edward answered, "Sure, if you want to." He looked at Kayla. "What about it, Pooh Bear? You wanna go?"

Kayla nodded her head as she bit off a huge piece of chicken.

Edward smiled. The only time his vivacious granddaughter didn't talk was when she was eating or sleeping. She was a joy to be around.

Upon seeing that Kayla had cleaned her plate, Lizzie asked, "Kayla, would you like to help me feed the ducks? They've missed you."

Kayla's entire face lit up as she wiped her hands and mouth with her napkin. "Yes." She was out of her chair in a flash. "Can we go now?"

"Sure," Lizzie answered.

Kayla asked, "Mommy, are you coming?"

Andrea wasn't sure a stroll to the lake was what she needed right now. It was where they had scattered Clayton's ashes. Her pain would be that much more unbearable. "No, I'm gonna stay here. You go ahead."

Kayla said, "Okay. Can Clayton come? I wanna show him how to feed the ducks."

Andrea was proud that Kayla had a desire to have her baby brother tag along, so to speak, and teach him some of the pleasures of life. Her heart ached. Oh, how she wished Clayton were here. "Sure, honey."

While Lizzie and the children were at the lake, Andrea and Edward talked in the den.

Edward leaned back against the sofa. "Liz and I were thrilled when you called last night and told us you were coming. Are you okay?" He sensed something was wrong.

Pushing her hair back behind her left ear, Andrea let out a heavy sigh. "I'm tired."

Edward nodded. "You need to get some rest. Why don't you go lie down and take a nap. Lizzie and I will watch the kids. We may even go into town, so if you wake up and we're not here, that's probably where we'll be."

A nice, long nap did sound good. The suggestion was music to Andrea's ears. After all, including the stops she'd made along the way, she had driven two and a half hours to get there.

She responded, "I think I'll take you up on it."

Edward smiled. "Good. We'll try to leave around five o'clock for the restaurant. Think you'll be up and ready by then?"

Andrea managed a smile. "I think so." She stood. When Edward got up, she gave him a hug and whispered, "Thank you."

"Sure," Edward said.

In the bedroom, tired as she was, sleep did not come quickly for Andrea. All she could think about was how, ever since Clayton's death, her life had gone downhill. No one understood her. Sometimes she didn't understand herself.

Devin had called Andrea all morning, but kept getting her answering machine. Leah had been livid last night after she'd talked to Andrea. No matter how angry the two sisters were at each other, he could not believe Andrea had forbade Leah to see the children. He knew he should have gone with Leah. Perhaps he could have said something to smooth things over between them. Both sisters were headstrong. However, he wondered if Leah had said something to instigate the situation. He loved her, but she was too outspoken at times.

Devin decided to go by Andrea's house. When he saw no trace of her vehicle and no one answered the door, he became increasingly alarmed. He called Leah at the salon.

"No," Leah answered. "She didn't tell me she was going anywhere. Why don't you call your folks and see if they've heard from her, and I'll call mine?"

As soon as Leah finished talking to Devin, she dialed her parents' number. Their mother hadn't talked to Andrea since last night. When their father called after that, he had left a message on her machine, but hadn't heard from her. They'd called several times this morning and not gotten her on the phone either. They figured she was home, but just not answering.

Leah was scared. What if something terrible had happened to Andrea and the children? She was about to call Devin when he called her instead and told her that Andrea and the kids were at his parents' house. Leah called and gave her parents the news.

Leah was thankful that they were all right. However, she grew furious at her sister for needlessly putting the family through such an ordeal. All she had to do was pick up the phone and let someone know where she'd be. That's what the old Andrea would have done.

The children were exhausted. As soon as everyone had left the restaurant and gotten into the Hamilton's car, Kayla and Clayton went out like lights. When they got back to Birmingham around nine o'clock, the two were still asleep. Andrea hated to wake them for baths, so she and Lizzie carefully slipped their pajamas on them and put them to bed.

Andrea decided to nibble on some of the leftover pickles and catfish nuggets she'd brought back with her. She and the Hamiltons sat talking at the kitchen table.

Edward had shared with Lizzie earlier that the rest of the family had been worried about Andrea and that Devin had called inquiring about her.

Lizzie sensed that something was amiss. She gave Andrea a solemn look. "Andrea, is everything back home okay?"

Andrea was taken aback by her mother-in-law's direct question. Had her parents or Leah called Lizzie and Edward? "Why do you ask?"

Edward spoke. "Devin called today. Everyone was worried. They didn't know where you were."

Andrea felt like reminding her in-laws that she was a grown woman and didn't have to check in with anybody. Instead, she confessed, "Leah and I had an argument last night. I needed to get away."

Lizzie inquired, "Do you wanna talk about it?"

Andrea needed some sympathy. She felt confident that the Hamiltons would take her side in the matter. She began, "All I heard from my family after Clay died was, 'We'll be here for you. You're not alone.' Leah was taking Kayla to church with her because I just haven't felt like going. She told me last night that she's not taking her anymore." She purposely left out the part about her forbidding Leah to see the children.

Lizzie gasped. "That's terrible. Why in the world did she tell you that?"

"She's upset with me because I haven't been to church in a while."

Lizzie briefly recalled advising Andrea that she not isolate herself too much from her church family, but Leah had no right to impose her views on Andrea. "Well, that's the most ridiculous thing I've ever heard. No one has the right to try to force someone to go to church." Her voice grew louder. "Who does Leah think she is? God?"

Edward gently placed his hand on his wife's. "Honey, calm down. You'll wake the children."

Lizzie lowered her voice. "Edward, don't tell me you're not upset about this."

Frankly, Edward was shocked, also, at what Andrea had just related to them. He agreed that she should not neglect her spiritual well-being, but he couldn't believe that Leah would turn her back on her sister in her time of need.

He said, "I think she meant well. Maybe she'll change her mind."

Lizzie asked her husband, "Is that all you have to say?"

Edward gave his wife a stern look. "For the time being, yes."

"Edward . . ."

Edward's voice was firm. "Liz, not now."

Andrea was thankful that Lizzie had backed down. She didn't want her in-laws arguing. However, she was pleased that they were on her side.

The next morning, Clayton woke up around six o'clock. Andrea put a dry Pamper on him, nursed him, and put him back to bed in one of the spare bedrooms the Hamiltons had made into a partial nursery. The baby shower gifts they had received at their grandparents' shower, given by their church members, certainly were coming in handy. It was nice to visit her in-laws without having to lug all the baby's things with her.

Andrea sluggishly strolled back to the room she was sharing with Kayla. She climbed back into the twin bed and eyed her daughter, still sleeping, across from her in the other bed. Yesterday had been exhilarating for Kayla. However, Andrea was sure she'd be up and about in a bit.

Her eyelids grew increasingly heavy, and Andrea was soon fast asleep. When she awoke two hours later, everyone was preparing for church. She found all four in the nursery. Edward dressed Clayton while Lizzie did Kayla's hair.

When Lizzie spied Andrea, she announced, "Good morning. Did we wake you up?"

Andrea leaned against the doorjamb, taking in the sight of her family getting ready for Sunday morning worship. She missed these times with Clayton. "No."

"Mornin', Mommy," Kayla said cheerily.

"Good morning," Andrea greeted her daughter as she strolled over to kiss her cheek.

Edward said, "Good morning, Andrea. How'd you sleep?"

Andrea answered, "Good morning, Edward. Okay."

Lizzie said, "We're going to church."

Andrea simply nodded.

Lizzie wasn't sure whether or not to extend an invitation to Andrea. "Do you wanna come?"

"No, I think I'll stay here."

Lizzie didn't want to give her daughter-in-law the impression that she was trying to pressure her, so she quickly changed the subject. "We left you some breakfast in the oven."

"Thanks, but I'm not hungry."

After everyone was ready to go, Andrea kissed her children good-bye. Then she was all alone. She felt no motivation to do anything except go back to bed. Sleep would not come, for she had so much on her mind. She felt the need to pray but couldn't. Supplication used to come so easily. What was happening to her?

Chapter 20

Silence filled the Hamilton home. With Andrea and the children now gone, Lizzie's heart grew heavier. She was glad Edward had to make a trip to the store. She couldn't wait to call Leah and Anna. She knew Edward wouldn't approve; therefore, she would take advantage of his absence to call the two women. First, she called her future daughter-in-law.

Lizzie didn't beat around the bush regarding the purpose for her call. "Leah, I've liked you ever since the day I met you. And when you and Devin started dating, I couldn't have been happier, but I'm more than a little upset with you right now. Andrea told us what you did."

It was obvious to Leah that her sister had gone to Birmingham and only told her own side of the story, blaming everything that had happened between them on Leah.

Leah didn't appreciate her future mother-in-law's tone or insinuation that she was in the wrong. If it had been anyone other than Devin's mother, she would have given as good as she'd just gotten. She respectfully replied, "Liz, I don't know what Andrea told you, and I don't care to know. I've done nothing but bend over backward trying to help her."

Lizzie vented, "If you were trying to help her, why'd you tell her you're not taking Kayla to church anymore? She needs you to be there for her. You know that. Doesn't your religion teach you to help people when they're in need? You've turned your back on your own sister. How could you do that?"

Leah and Lizzie had always gotten along until now. If Lizzie kept running off at the mouth, Leah was bound to say something she'd later regret. She was Devin's mother, but she was not going to talk to her in this manner.

Leah warned, "Lizzie, I don't want to disrespect you, so I'm letting you know I'm hanging up the phone now." She felt like slamming it down. Instead, she gently placed it back on the receiver.

Leah was furious at Andrea and Lizzie. She called Andrea and left a message on her machine, asking that she call her as soon as she got home. Then she dialed Devin's cell phone number. He was visiting a friend of his. She hated to bother him, but she needed to talk to him immediately.

As soon as Devin answered, Leah began ranting. "Your Mama just called accusing me of not being a Christian because of a bunch of mess Andrea told her while she was there."

On the other end, Devin attempted to calm her down. "Honey, slow down. You're talking too fast. What happened?"

Leah went into a spill regarding the telephone conversation between her and his mother.

"Calm down," Devin urged. "I'm sure she didn't mean it the way it sounded. She's just worried about Andrea."

Leah threw her free hand up in the air and quickly pulled it back down. "Andrea!" she shouted. "I'm so tired of everybody moaning and groaning about Andrea. The world does not revolve around her. She's not the only one with feelings."

"Baby, will you just try to calm down?"

"No, I will not try to calm down. All I've tried to do is help Andrea. And this is the thanks I get? To have her fill your parents' heads with her side of what happened and then have your Mama call me up saying horrible things to me. Devin, I don't deserve this," Leah cried into the phone.

"Listen to me. I'll come by later tonight, and we'll talk. Right now, you just need to calm down."

"Stop telling me that!" Leah shouted. "You need to call your Mama and tell her to calm down. She's the one who called me fussing and carrying on."

"Leah, I said I'll come by later. We'll talk about this then."

"Just forget it. If you can't talk to me now, don't worry about coming by later." Leah slammed down the phone.

Leah was fired up at Andrea, Devin, and Lizzie. She dialed her parents' number.

When Anna heard her daughter's voice, she said, "Hi, honey. I was just about to call you." She decided not to waste any time, for she knew Leah was upset. "Lizzie called me a few minutes ago. She said she called you."

Leah interrupted, "Did she tell you what she said and how she talked to me?"

Anna spoke slowly. "Leah, don't let what she said get to you."

"Mama, that's easier said than done."

"I know, but I have a few questions for you."

Leah moaned, "Oh, Mama, I don't feel like answering a bunch of questions."

"Not questions you have to outright answer. Rhetorical ones." Anna went on. "Who, despite her weak stomach and fear of blood, volunteered to be her sister's Lamaze partner? Who went to every class, and when the baby was being born, stayed with her the whole time? Who's always been by her sister's side trying to help out in any way she can?"

There was silence on Leah's part.

Anna continued. "You've been an angel of mercy trying to help your sister in whatever way you could, regardless of what anyone says. Try to patch things up with her. Life is too short. We all know that from what happened to Clay and what happens to so many other people every single day."

Her mother was right. Yet, Leah still refused to enable Andrea. "I can't talk to her anymore. She needs some spiritual encouragement, but she doesn't want to hear it."

"You can't force her. Just be patient with her. The way you would want someone to be with you if it were you in her situation. Remember the Golden Rule."

Leah began to get defensive. "Mama, I'm not taking Kayla to church. If that's what it's going to take for us to patch things up, then I guess we'll be feuding from here 'til Armageddon."

"I didn't ask you to take Kayla to church. You've already made up your mind about that."

Leah reminded her mother, "Well, Mama, I already told you she said I can't see the kids as long as I don't do what she wants. So what's the point of trying to talk to her? Her mind's made up, too."

"Just try to talk to her. If you don't want to go over there, call her up on the phone."

Leah called her sister several more times later that evening. She was certain Andrea was back from Birmingham. Maybe she was tired. *Or maybe she just doesn't want to talk to me.*

Devin dropped by Leah's house as he said he would.

"I can't believe any of this is happening," Leah said. "I feel as though my whole life has been turned upside down. Andrea and I have always been close. We've never been this upset with each other. Maybe I should have just kept my mouth shut and continued taking Kayla to church."

Even though she'd just made that statement, Leah knew in her heart that she had made the right decision. She felt very strongly that her sister needed to be spiritually active in order to help herself deal with the changes in her life. She wasn't trying to force Andrea back to church, but Leah supposed that was how it appeared to Andrea and everybody else.

Leah was much calmer now after having talked to her mother, and felt the urge to apologize to Devin for her outburst on the telephone earlier.

She held his hand in hers as they sat on the sofa. "Baby, I'm so sorry for the way I acted this afternoon."

Devin squeezed Leah's hand. "It's okay. I'm sorry if you felt I wasn't there for you. You were so upset. I was just trying to get you to calm down."

"Don't worry about it. Thanks for stopping by like you said you would. I know I can always count on you to be there for me. I guess I kinda see now how it must be for Andrea. You were just a phone call away when I needed you. She doesn't have that anymore with Clay." Leah sighed. "She must be so lonely without him."

"Yes," Devin agreed, "I can only imagine." He decided not to say more than that, since Leah felt that everyone was constantly sticking up for Andrea. He started to stand. "Well, I've got to go." He pulled Leah up with him.

The couple held hands as they made their way to the front door. "I love you," Devin said.

"I love you, too," Leah spoke softly. She felt so tired and drained of energy from all the drama of the past few days. "Good night."

"Good night," Devin said as his lips brushed gently up against her cheek.

After Devin had gone, Leah made up her mind that she would go by her sister's house the next afternoon to talk with her. She prayed things would go better than the last time.

Chapter 21

Monday afternoon, Leah went by Andrea's. Andrea opened the door just enough to reveal a small crack.

"Hi," Leah greeted her. "Can we talk?"

Andrea stated flatly, "I don't have anything else to say to you."

"Listen. I don't want to argue. I just want to talk."

Andrea gave Leah a stern reminder. "I meant what I said about you seeing the children."

Leah sighed. "Can't you just let me in for a few minutes so we can talk?"

"The kids are inside," Andrea spoke in a low tone.

Of course, the kids are inside. They live here. "Andrea . . ."

Andrea cut her sister short. "Have you changed your mind about what you said?"

"About me not taking Kayla to church?"

"Yes."

"No, I haven't."

Andrea's response was abrupt. "Then you can't come in. I've got to go. I have things to do." She proceeded to close the door.

Pushing the door slightly with her hand, Leah inquired, "Andrea, can't we just talk a minute?" Although she felt like an intruder that her sister was trying to keep out of her home, she suggested, "We can stay on the porch if you want to."

Andrea's response cut Leah to the quick. "Until you can be the sister you should be, I've got nothing more to say to you." Andrea slammed the door shut.

Leah stood there for a moment, dumbfounded. *What just happened here?* Her bewilderment quickly turned to anger as she turned and stormed away. She was not going to beg her sister to speak to her. If that was what Andrea was hoping for, she could forget it.

She could not believe the nerve of her sister. Leah had come to try to make amends, and this was the reception she got? She was fed up with Andrea and her pitiful self. Andrea was mad at the world because of what she was going through, and she was taking her frustration out on everyone, mainly Leah.

When Leah got home, she called their mother to tell her how Andrea had treated her.

Anna was not pleased that things had gotten to this point with her daughters. She relayed to William what Leah had told her. Likewise, he felt worried. He decided it was time for him to call Andrea. Perhaps she would answer the telephone this time.

Kayla answered. "Paw Paw!" she squealed. She proceeded to tell her grandfather about their trip to Birmingham.

William listened intently. When Kayla was done, he asked, "Where's your Mommy?"

"She's taking a bath," Kayla answered.

In walked Andrea. She thought she'd heard the phone ring. She didn't feel like being bothered by anyone and demanded, "Kayla, who are you talking to?"

"It's Paw Paw. He wants to talk to you."

Andrea reckoned her sister had called whining to their parents because she hadn't been allowed entrance into the house that afternoon. She didn't care to discuss it with anyone—not even her father. However, she had to keep up appearances for Kayla's sake, as her daughter stood holding out the receiver to her. Andrea gently removed the telephone from Kayla's hand and held it to her left ear.

"Hey, Daddy."

"Hey, sweetheart."

Desiring to get her father's reproof over with, Andrea sent Kayla off to her room to select her outfit for school the next day. She waited until she felt the child was out of earshot. Then she uttered into the receiver, "Daddy, I know why you're calling, and I really don't want to talk about it."

"Andrea, I know you're in a lot of emotional and mental pain, but your sister is worried about you. We all are. What if your mother and I come down this weekend and stay about a week and help you out?"

It would be nice to have her parents here, but Andrea certainly didn't need them breathing down her neck, too. Therefore, she decided it wasn't a good idea.

She quickly tried to think of an excuse for her parents not to come. "You'll be coming down in December for Leah's wedding. It's a little over a month away. That's too much traveling for you and Mama. That's okay. I'll be fine."

William was adamant. "It's no problem. We'll try to get a flight out Saturday. We'll probably rent a car this time and book a room at a hotel, but I'll call you back with the flight information." Anna was not pleased that they would be putting up residence at a hotel this trip. William had insisted on them not smothering Andrea. When Anna had suggested that the two of them stay with Leah instead, William reminded his wife that perhaps Leah needed her space as well.

When her father mentioned that he and her mother would be staying at a hotel, Andrea felt guilt combined with a huge sense of relief.

* * *

By Friday, Andrea was in a worse mood than previously. Her parents would arrive the next day. Although they would be staying at a hotel, she still was not looking forward to their visit. She had already received calls all week from the Knights and other members of her congregation expressing their concern for her and wanting to stop by. She knew they meant well, but she didn't want to risk having people come over and saying things, whether intentionally or unintentionally, that would make her feel lower than she already felt.

It was lunchtime. She'd had a bad morning. For the first time in Andrea's career in dental hygiene, she'd snapped at a young child to sit still. It wasn't the fact that she'd instructed her young patient to remain still during the cleaning, but it was her tone. So impolite and inconsiderate. She felt horrible. She was constantly feeling as though she were going to lose control of her emotions at any given moment. She hoped Glenn hadn't heard her rude behavior this morning. He cared so much about their patients and people in general. She was positive he wouldn't appreciate her temperament.

Andrea wished she didn't have to pass Glenn's office on her way to lunch. She prayed he'd already left for lunch himself. As she passed his door, she didn't dare look for him through her peripheral vision. She made it to the side entrance and had her hand on the doorknob. She'd made it by undetected. Or so she thought. Just as she swung open the door, she heard her name.

She begrudgingly turned around. "Yes?"

Glenn met her at the door. "I need to see you when you get back from lunch. What time is your next appointment?"

Andrea responded, "One-thirty."

Glenn looked at his wristwatch. "It's twelve now. You take an hour, right?"

"Yes."

"I'm eating in today. So as soon as you return, just stop by my office. Okay?"

Andrea didn't like this one bit. Now she'd have to suffer through lunch, contemplating exactly what Glenn wanted to say to her. "Sure."

"Okay. Enjoy your lunch."

"Thanks. You, too," Andrea managed to say before going out the door.

When she returned promptly at one o'clock, she reluctantly strolled to Glenn's office and stopped in the doorway. She lightly tapped before making her entrance.

Glancing up from the file before him, Glenn motioned for her to enter, saying, "Come in, Andrea. Close the door."

He wants the door shut. This is worse than I thought. Andrea closed the door and geared up her defensive mode as she made her way over to sit down. *He better not start with me. I've had just about all I can take of everyone's demands.*

Glenn closed the file and pushed it to the side of his desk. Focusing his full attention on Andrea, he spoke sympathetically. "Andrea, you and I have been friends and co-workers for a really long time."

This is not going to be good, Andrea surmised. Glenn's mood was much too pleasant. Something bad was sure to follow.

Glenn continued, "I know how hard this past year has been for you, and I've noticed how withdrawn you've been lately."

Andrea wished Glenn would quit stalling, lay everything on the line, and just let her have it. Then she could give him a piece of her mind. She was still in a fighting mood. One more person to duke it out with wouldn't bother her one bit. She was tired of everybody trying to counsel her because they thought their lives were so much better than hers.

She was on the verge of telling Glenn exactly how she felt, when he said, "Do you need a little more time off work? You know, you came back a week earlier than you were supposed to. I can only imagine how hard it must be being a single parent and working a full-time job as well." Glenn ceased talking and looked at Andrea, waiting for her reply.

Andrea wasn't quite sure if she should feel relieved or insulted. Was he trying to get rid of her because of her attitude this morning, or was he genuinely concerned for her? She'd never been asked to take time off from work. Was he trying to fire her and replace her with someone else?

She was finally able to say, "What brought this on? Are you trying to fire me?"

Glenn shook his head. "No, of course not. It's like I told you. It's obvious you're still having a hard time coping with Clay's death. I just thought you might like to take a leave of absence for a short while."

Tears began to well up in Andrea's eyes. All the while she and Glenn had known each other, she had thought he liked her and cared about her. Now here he was trying to boot her out the door. "Are you sure that's what it is? I'm getting the feeling you're trying to get rid of me."

Glenn was shocked and somewhat hurt that Andrea would think such a thing. "Andrea, you know how much I care about you. Do you think I *want* you to leave? I don't, but I know you well enough to realize that you're not okay. I believe you want us to think that you are. Have you thought about counseling?"

Well, that question was the straw that broke the camel's back. Andrea wondered if Glenn had been talking to her mother. Why else would he mention counseling—something her mother had been bugging her about? She had heard enough. She stood.

Andrea held up her hand as she spoke. "Glenn, I really don't know where all this is coming from. But I don't need time off from work, and I don't need counseling. If you don't mind, I need to get ready for my appointment." She didn't even give him an opportunity to respond. She was out the door.

Andrea had never responded toward Glenn in such a manner.

He reasoned that she'd taken his offer the wrong way because of the emotional suffering she was undergoing, so he tried not to take her reaction personally. However, his conclusions did nothing to ease his concern for her. He wouldn't attempt to discuss the subject with her anymore today. Perhaps she needed time to think it over.

Chapter 22

Monday morning, Andrea dreaded going to work. She was still thinking about her and Glenn's conversation on Friday, and she was still a little upset with him. No, she wasn't going to voluntarily take a leave of absence. If he didn't want her around, he'd have to fire her.

Since she was feeling especially blue, Andrea was glad that her parents were in town. She wouldn't have to rush this week getting herself *and* the children ready for work and school, since her parents would be coming over early in the mornings to help her out. Anna and William would be keeping Clayton with them at her house all week during the days Andrea was at work. Since they lived so far away and didn't get to see their grandchildren often, they were looking forward to bonding more with Clayton during this visit.

Anna cooked a big breakfast, and everyone sat down to eat. When William passed the blessing, Andrea held hands with Kayla, but refused to bow her head, close her eyes, or say *Amen.* She barely talked as she put down a small portion of food.

After breakfast, Anna and Kayla prepared to leave for day care. Andrea kissed her little one good-bye before the two were out the door. She desired to spend a few minutes with her son, so she headed to his room. She hoped he wasn't asleep, for she needed to see his bright eyes and cheerful smile. He and Kayla were the reason she'd made it this far. They put the icing on the cake. However, with Clayton gone, the cake wasn't as sweet.

Andrea's heart skipped a beat when she saw that her baby was wide awake as he lay in his crib gurgling away. She reached down to lift Clayton's soft body from his bed. She kissed both his cheeks. He smelled of baby lotion and powder, and his breath was sweet. She loved a baby's scent.

Andrea went to the rocking chair and sat down. As she nursed Clayton, she sang "Hickory Dickory Dock" in a low whisper. Clayton stared up at his mother with big, brown eyes. He looked more and more like his father every day. It wasn't long before he'd fallen asleep. Andrea kissed his cheek before gently laying him back in his bed. She tiptoed away and closed the door slightly. She met her father in the hallway.

William whispered, "Is he asleep?"

Andrea grinned and spoke in a low tone. "Yes. As soon as he got his little belly full, he was out like a light."

William stifled a snicker. "He's got it honest. As soon as your mother eats, she's ready for a nap. It's like there were tranquilizers in her food."

Andrea let out a quiescent giggle.

William could still sense his daughter's pain. They'd always been so close. Now she wasn't opening up to him like she used to. He yearned to reach out to her, yet he didn't wish to push her farther from him than he felt she already was. When he and Anna had returned home after Clayton's birth, they had sought counsel from their minister regarding how to best help their daughter. They had been told to be there for her as they'd always been and show her empathy. They were trying so hard not to do or say the wrong thing, for they didn't want to increase her misery.

William asked, "Are you leaving for work now?"

Andrea glanced at her watch. It was a few minutes past seven-thirty. It only took her about ten minutes to get to the office, but she liked to arrive early so she could get settled in before seeing her patients. She didn't need her father pressuring her about Leah. He and her mother hadn't attempted to bring up the subject so far. However, Andrea knew it was bound to come up before their departure on Sunday.

"Yes," Andrea answered. That is, if she still had a job after the scene with Glenn on Friday, which she cared not to discuss with anyone, not even her father. Glenn's suggestion that she take some time off was a hard blow to her ego. She'd always taken pride in being a loyal, dedicated worker. "I have to get my things." She stepped into her room and came out with her pocketbook, a satchel, and a jacket, which was thrown over her arm.

Andrea and her father walked to the front door as William made light conversation along the way. When they stopped, he took her coat and held it for her to put on, as she switched her bags from one hand to the other.

Andrea looked at her father, granting him a brief smile. He was so kind and sweet. She hoped he knew that despite her demeanor she still loved and adored him. "Thank you," she said.

"You're welcome. Have a good day."

"I'll try." Andrea kissed his cheek.

William opened the door for her. He followed her onto the porch and observed her as she walked down the steps to her car. As she drove away, he was still watching her. He and Anna used to be able to make everything all right for their girls. Now they were women who had to make things right for themselves.

Andrea was relieved that Glenn wasn't in the office when she arrived. She didn't want another confrontation with him. She just wanted to be left alone so she could do the job he was paying her to do.

She was preparing for her first appointment when she heard a noise behind her. She turned and stared right into Glenn's face. She didn't know what to say except, "Good morning." What did he want this time? Had he come to finish what he'd started Friday? She wasn't in the mood for it.

Glenn's face showed anxiety. "Good morning. Andrea, if I upset you Friday, I just want to say I'm sorry. That was not my intention. I'm just worried about you."

Andrea continued placing the shiny, silver cleaning utensils on a tray. Without looking away from her task, she replied dryly, "Thank you, but I'm fine."

Glenn stood there for a brief moment as though he expected her to say something more. When she didn't, he said, "All right," then turned and walked away.

Andrea felt a tinge of remorse for her coldness toward Glenn. However, she was still hurt that he no longer wanted her around. She went to call back her patient.

The day dragged by at a snail's pace. Andrea was relieved when it was finally time to go home. It was nice to be able to go straight home and not have to stop by the day care center to pick up the children. It was pure heaven to step inside a clean house with dinner already cooked on the stove. Her parents were a godsend. She could get used to this.

When supper was over, William and Anna cleaned up the kitchen before departing to their room at the hotel for the night. Andrea played with the children and gave Clayton his bath. After putting him to bed, she and Kayla prepared to read a bedtime story. Kayla wanted to read tonight.

When Andrea selected a nursery rhyme book, Kayla implored, "Mommy, let's read this one," as she grabbed her Bible storybook from the shelf.

Andrea was in no mood to talk about God, but she did not express her apathy. Andrea and Clayton had read the book so many times to Kayla that she practically knew the stories by heart. As

Kayla read the story about the faithful man Job, Andrea couldn't help but wonder how he lived through all the atrocities that befell him without losing his faith. Why couldn't she be like him?

When Kayla was done, she asked, "Mommy, are you ever coming back to church?"

The question caught Andrea quite by surprise. She wasn't sure how to respond. The truth was, she didn't know the answer, but she couldn't tell Kayla that. No matter how little faith she now had, she had no desire to shatter her daughter's. So she said, "Right now, honey, Mommy just has to take one day at a time, so we'll see. Okay?"

"Okay," Kayla replied.

Andrea was glad Kayla seemed content with her response for now. Planting a kiss on her daughter's cheek, she said, "Good night, sweetie."

"Mommy, I have to say my prayer. You forgot again," Kayla reminded her mother.

Yes, it seemed that Andrea had been neglectful in that area lately as well, especially with herself. "Okay. Come on." Andrea pulled back the covers so Kayla could climb out of bed.

When Andrea failed again to kneel beside her daughter, Kayla asked, "Are you gonna get on your knees, too?"

Still sitting on the side of the bed, Andrea responded, "Not this time. You go ahead. I'm listening."

Kayla implored, "God, thank you for my family and everything you give us we need. I love my family, 'specially my baby brother, Clayton." A giggle escaped her lips. "He's so cute. Thank you for sending him to us. Please bless everyone, 'specially my Mommy. She's sad and lonely 'cause she still misses my Daddy. Please make her strong like Job. I love you. In Jesus' name. Amen."

Kayla jumped up and climbed back into bed. "Good night, Mommy."

"Night, sweetie," Andrea managed to say as she quickly gave

Kayla another peck on her cheek. Then she turned off the lamp and dashed for the door as her tears were about to break free.

On Wednesday evening, William and Kayla attended Bible study. Anna decided to visit with Andrea and Clayton. Anna had been trying her best to be more sympathetic of her daughter's feelings. As a result, this visit seemed to be going better than the last one. Anna did not want to mess it up, but she was still concerned that Andrea was not saying her blessing at mealtime, something she'd always taken very seriously in the past. Was she praying at all anymore? Anna would attempt to approach her in an empathetic manner.

Anna had just finished giving Clayton his bath and putting him to bed. Andrea had disappeared. Her bedroom door was closed. Anna knocked. "Andrea, are you awake?"

Andrea had a good mind to pretend she was asleep and not answer. She didn't want to be bothered. She loved her mother, but she was tired of people pressuring her. Her parents' visit was going smoothly so far. She wanted nothing to happen to change that.

Against her better judgement, Andrea answered, "Yes."

"Can I come in a minute?"

Maybe it was nothing. "Yes," Andrea said.

Anna slowly opened the door. Andrea looked at her mother from the chair where she sat. Anna walked over and sat on an adjacent chair. "Clayton's sound asleep."

Andrea awarded her mother a fleeting smile. "Good. I'll look in on him in a minute."

Anna felt like she was walking on eggshells. "Can we talk?"

I knew it. "What is it, Mama?"

Anna wasn't quite sure how or where to begin. "I just want to ask you something." There was a pause.

Andrea simply stared at her mother, dreading what she was about to say.

Anna continued, "Have you been having problems praying lately?"

Andrea chose this moment to look away, for fear that her mother would see the answer in her eyes. "Mama, please," she begged, "don't start."

"Baby, I don't want to upset you. It's just that sometimes when we're experiencing hard times, we can't think clearly, and it can interfere with our prayers. It's happened to me before. There have been many times I tried to pray and couldn't. Times when I wanted to pour my heart out to God and couldn't come up with the words. Is that how you're feeling?"

Her mother would never understand the problem she was having with prayer. If Andrea told her, she would be shocked and probably disappointed that her daughter could have such feelings. God didn't care about her. If He did, Clayton never would have been killed. She just didn't understand. Of all the people in the world to die, why did He allow it to be *her* husband. She'd always been taught that God cared, but considering her circumstances, how could that be? She couldn't share these feelings with anyone. She didn't even talk to God about them. She no longer talked to Him about anything, but she wasn't going to admit that to her mother.

Andrea closed her eyes in an effort to numb the headache she felt coming on. "Mama, I don't wanna talk about this right now."

Andrea expected a fight from her mother, but thankfully, it didn't come. The next thing she heard was her mother getting up, walking across the room, and closing the door behind her.

As she sat thinking about what her mother had said, tears streamed down Andrea's face. She honestly did not know how much longer she could go on this way.

Chapter 23

By Saturday, Andrea was even more depressed. She hadn't seen or talked to her sister in almost two weeks. She missed Leah, but Andrea was not going to back down. Although she longed for Leah's companionship, she was still very much perturbed at her.

Another reason for Andrea's despondency was that her parents would be going back home the next day. Initially, she had really been dreading their visit. However, this time, things were going quite well. Her mother hadn't attempted again to speak to her about the matter of prayer. It was so nice to have them in town to help out, even though her parents would never replace the one person she so desperately needed.

As Andrea rested on her chair in her room, she looked out her window admiring the rustic colors of autumn. Next month would bring Leah and Devin's nuptials—December third. Andrea was in no mood for a wedding ceremony. She had no desire to witness anyone else's happy moments when her own life had been shattered into a million pieces. She was still angry at Leah and didn't expect things to get any better between them before the wedding. Perhaps their quarrel would provide the escape she needed to get out of being in the wedding. Andrea was still deep in thought when she heard a knock on the door.

Andrea turned around slightly as she answered, "Come in."

Her father entered. Walking toward his daughter, he asked, "You okay?"

For an instant, Andrea thought she would come up out of the chair and throw herself into the safety of his arms. She wanted to tell him everything she was feeling, but he wouldn't understand. No one would.

Andrea replied, "I'm fine."

William didn't believe her. She was not fine. If she were, she wouldn't stay cooped up in her room so much. For the first time in a long while, he felt himself getting angry at her. He realized losing Clayton was a devastating blow, but she still had two beautiful children and a family who loved her very much. She was acting as if she were giving up.

William heard himself saying what he had sworn he'd never tell her. "Andrea, regardless of how you feel, you have a lot to be thankful for. Count your blessings. So many people in your situation don't have a family who loves them like we all love you."

Andrea stared at her father as tears welled up in her eyes. This was the kind of talk she expected from her mother, but never her father. He always seemed to know the right thing to say.

Andrea's voice was louder than she anticipated as she yelled, "Blessings! I have no blessings! A year ago, my husband was taken from me and our daughter. The day after his funeral, I found out I was pregnant with the child that he and I both wanted. What did I do to deserve this?" Andrea pounded her fist against her chest. "What did Clay do? We always tried to live a good life, and what did it get us?" Tears streamed down her face.

William had never seen his daughter in this state. The empathy he felt for her caused his heart to jolt. The pain that had just emanated from Andrea had struck him like the charge from a live battery flowing through jumper cables and igniting the lifeless one.

He'd said all the wrong things. He hadn't meant to upset her. It was just that he couldn't bear to see her giving up on herself. He got down on one knee, grabbed Andrea, and pulled her into his arms.

Andrea held tightly to her father as she attempted to speak through her tears. "I'm tired and lonely. I miss him so much, Daddy."

William whispered, "I know you do, baby. I'm so sorry. I never meant to upset you."

Anna and Kayla thought they'd heard some sort of commotion. Anna ordered her granddaughter to stay in the kitchen. However, Kayla was right on her grandmother's heels as Anna ran toward Andrea's room. Anna stopped abruptly in the doorway, attempting to block Kayla's view. Andrea and her father were clinging to one another. Anna knew something terrible had happened. When William looked at his wife, his own face was soaked with tears. Anna quickly shut the door, grabbed Kayla by her hand, and walked away. Whatever had transpired, it appeared that her husband had it under control.

On the way back to the kitchen, Kayla was full of questions. "Mee Maw, what's wrong with Mommy?"

Anna attempted to reassure her young granddaughter. "Your Mommy will be all right."

"Are you sure?" Kayla wanted to know.

Anna put her hand on top of Kayla's head and smiled. "She'll be fine."

Kayla seemed satisfied with the answers given for the moment. As she and her grandmother finished preparing lunch, Anna prayed that God would rescue her child from her abyss of heartache and sadness.

Yasmine's magical fingers seemed to be helping some of Leah's tension to dissipate as she shampooed Leah's hair during some down time at the salon.

"Oh, Yasmine, that feels so good. Girlfriend, you give the best shampoo in town."

Yasmine grinned. All her clients complimented her on her shampoo method. "So have you decided how you're getting your hair done for the wedding?"

"No, I haven't decided yet. When it was longer, I used to wear it pinned up a lot. Devin likes it up, but I think it's too short to wear it up now."

Yasmine started the rinsing process. "Well, you've still got a month before the wedding. Your hair grows fast. If you stop getting it cut and let it grow out, I think by next month, it'll be long enough for you to wear it up. You know, I really don't mind fixing your hair for the wedding."

"I know, and I appreciate it, but I'll just let one of the other stylists here do it. We're gonna have so much to do that day, and I don't want you stressing over my hair. I'll make our appointments as early as possible so we can get in and get out. I'm gonna be nervous enough as it is."

Yasmine giggled. "Are you nervous now?"

"Not really, but I don't think it's gonna hit me until the actual moment. Besides, I've got so many other things going on in my life right now, it's a little hard for me to focus."

Yasmine finished rinsing Leah's hair and patted it with a towel. Then the two made their way over to the styling chair, where Yasmine began putting rollers in Leah's hair.

Yasmine knew Leah was referring to her troubles with Andrea. Some of the other stylists had customers, so she spoke low when she asked, "Things aren't any better between you and Andrea?"

Leah attempted to keep her tone at a minimum level as well. "She's still not talking to me and won't let me see the kids."

Yasmine shook her head from side to side. "That's so sad. Sounds like she's pretty angry."

Leah agreed, "She is, and she's taking all her frustration out on me."

"You think so?"

"Of course. I'm the only one she's banned from her life. Mama and Daddy are here now. As a matter of fact, they're probably at her house right now pampering her." Leah rolled her eyes.

Without meaning to, Leah rose her voice an octave. "I've barely had any time with them—they're always over there. Can you believe they're staying at a hotel? Now does that make any sense? They said they wanted to give us some space. Humph. Doesn't look to me like they're giving Andrea any space. Yeah, they got a room at a hotel, but they're still practically living at Andrea's.

"All anybody can do is talk about poor, sweet Andrea. What about me? One of the happiest days of my life is coming up next month, but nobody seems to care about that. My own sister acts like she's not even happy for me. She's acting so selfish. Even Devin's mama and I aren't close like we used to be. We haven't talked since she called fussing at me about all this nonsense with Andrea."

Yasmine asked, "What about Devin's father? How are things with him?"

"We're okay. The few times I've talked to Edward on the phone since all this chaos began, he's been very pleasant with me as he's always been. I mean, it's not like I talked to him and Liz all the time before this happened. Every now and then, we'd have a brief conversation over the telephone. Sometimes Devin would ride out to see them, and I'd go with him. We always had a nice visit. Of course, I've gotten to know them better since Devin and I have been dating.

"They seemed to really like me. Liz and I got along great until recently. Sometimes I think about picking up the phone and calling her, just to let her know I'm not holding a grudge against her, but she's the one who started it. I just feel like the people I love the most are the ones who've turned against me, and all because I wouldn't keep doing for Andrea what she needs to be doing herself."

Yasmine felt sorry for her friend. She couldn't believe how Leah's family, and especially Andrea, were treating her. Perhaps after the two of them got off work, she could take Leah out, but then she remembered that her friend was probably going out with her fiancé, so Yasmine attempted to offer some words of encouragement instead. "I know it's hard, Leah, but try not to keep harping on it. It'll just make things worse. Remember what I told you. Don't let anyone steal your joy—not even your sister. Your wedding is a big deal to you, even if it isn't to anyone else. You deserve to be happy about it."

"Thanks, Yasmine. I'll try to remember that." Leah would strive to have a more positive attitude, but it would be extremely difficult, considering everything she was up against.

Later that evening, Andrea was quiet as everyone else ate their dinner at the Olive Garden. Her parents had finally been able to get her out of the house. She had released emotions that afternoon to her father which she had wished to keep hidden. She was trying to be strong for herself and her family, but she couldn't.

William was beginning to think his wife was right. Their daughter needed professional help, but she would never agree to it. Every time Anna attempted to discuss the subject, Andrea would get upset. Nothing could have prepared William for what had taken place that afternoon when Andrea had unleashed her feelings.

Anna had been praying all afternoon. She was at her wit's end. *How do you make someone do something they're not willing to do? You can't. Andrea's a grown woman. She's choosing to live this way. Maybe without Clay, she doesn't want to ever be happy again. Oh, Lord, what do we do?*

Upon hearing Clayton make a playful sound as she held him in her arms, Anna reached down and gently stroked his cheek. "What did you say, Clayton? What are you talking about?"

The baby kicked his legs and wiggled his arms as he looked up at his grandmother and smiled.

Andrea looked forlornly at her baby. "Mama, do you want me to take him so you can finish eating?"

"No, I've got him. I'm full anyway. I'm gonna get a to-go box." Anna looked at Andrea's plate which was still piled with food. She hated to be a pest, but Andrea needed to keep up her strength. "You haven't touched your food. You need to eat. You're gonna waste away." Andrea was already looking thinner than usual.

Andrea replied, "I'm not hungry. I'll take mine with me, too."

When their waitress returned to their table, everyone got to-go boxes for their food.

The next morning, the dreaded time for her parents' departure had finally arrived. They stopped by one last time after checking out of the hotel. Since it was early November, it was a little chilly outside, but Andrea and Kayla insisted on bundling up themselves and Clayton and going outside with Anna and William.

After good-byes had been said to the children, Andrea hugged her mother while her father held Clayton. Then Anna took the baby so Andrea could say good-bye to her father.

With Clayton now back in her arms, Andrea told her parents, "I'm so glad you came. Thank you so much. Daddy, I'm sorry about yesterday."

William smiled. "You don't have anything to apologize for. I'm the one who's sorry."

Andrea wanted to ask if they would be back for the Thanksgiving holiday. However, it was less than three weeks away, and the wedding was less than two weeks after that. So she simply stated earnestly, "I'm gonna miss you."

Anna said, "We're gonna miss you, too."

Kayla asked, "Are you gonna miss me, too? I'm gonna miss *you*."

William replied as he tickled Kayla, "Of course, we're gonna miss you, you little jelly bean."

Kayla giggled. She still loved the nicknames her family called her. Her daddy had had a lot of funny names for her. She especially missed those.

Anna and William finally climbed into their rental car. Everyone waved their last good-bye as they backed out of the driveway.

Once inside the house, it felt cold and lonely again. Andrea felt more alone now than she had in a while.

Anna and William stopped by to see Leah before they headed for the airport. They had called earlier in the morning to say good-bye. When they learned she would not be attending church services because she wasn't feeling well, they decided to stop by.

Sitting in her living room, Leah told her parents, "She acts like she hates me. She won't let me in her house. She won't even let me see the kids. I can't talk to her about the wedding. When I try, she acts like she's not interested. This is supposed to be the happiest time of my life, and she's ruining it."

The Washingtons were shocked at their daughter's presumption. Andrea hating Leah was the farthest thing from the truth. It was obvious that Andrea was angry, but how could Leah think something so horrible about her sister?

Anna looked sympathetically at her daughter. "Leah, Andrea doesn't hate you."

Leah said, "She's acting like it. Why else would she be so cruel to me? She's not treating the rest of you the way she's treating me."

William stated, "She's just angry."

Leah bolted from her seat. "She's not just angry. Daddy, you and Mama have been here over a week. And for the first time ever, I wasn't even allowed to go to my own sister's house and spend time with anyone. I feel like an outcast. And the two of you even condoned it by telling me not to come over."

Anna protested, "Leah, we only told you that because we knew how upset Andrea would get if you came."

Leah began pacing. "I'm so tired of everybody talking about Andrea like she's the only one who has feelings. I've done nothing but bend over backward for her from day one, and all I get is everybody coming down on me like I'm doing something wrong. I'm tired of it."

William stood, walked over to his daughter, and took her in his arms. "Honey, nobody's saying you're doing anything wrong."

Leah cried as she buried her face in her father's chest. She sniffed, "That's how everybody's acting."

William felt empathy for his daughter. "Well, that probably is how it seems, but it's not so. Come on. Come sit down." He took Leah over to the sofa and sat her down between him and his wife.

Anna took Leah's hands in hers. "Honey, we know you're upset because you feel that Andrea has turned her back on her faith, but she isn't going to do anything about it unless and until she's ready. None of us have the right to try to make her do it. God doesn't even try to force us to serve Him. And as humans, we don't have the power either. But God does. You have got to let go and let God. Let Him do what we can't—bring your sister back to Him."

Leah stared at her mother. "I refuse to believe that there's nothing we can say or do to get through to her. It sounds to me like you've all given up."

William said, "Leah, all we can do is be there for her and leave the rest to God."

Leah turned to look at her father. "Daddy, I *am* there for her. She knows that. But ever since I refused to keep taking Kayla to church, she's been acting all crazy. I've already told you I'm not going to start taking Kayla back to church just so Andrea will speak to me and grant me the privilege of seeing my niece and nephew."

Anna said, "And we've told you that we're not asking you to change your mind."

Leah stated, "Well, I don't understand what else I'm supposed to do. Andrea thinks because she's the grieving widow that everyone is going to cater to her. Well, *I'm* not."

It was becoming very clear to Anna and William that this feud between their daughters might go on indefinitely. Both of the girls were headstrong, and it seemed that neither one was going to back down.

William said, "Honey, calm down. You're getting yourself more upset. We wanted to see you before we left. Let's try to make it a pleasant ending."

Leah said nothing. Her father was right. She'd hardly gotten to spend any time with them. She shouldn't spend what little bit they had complaining about Andrea.

Chapter 24

Much to her surprise, Andrea made it through the first week after her parents' departure. It had been tough, though. Today was Saturday. She and Clayton had only been home a few minutes. Kayla had gone with LeaAnn and her parents to see a movie.

Andrea was putting away her groceries when she heard the door-bell. When she asked who it was, she was surprised to hear Devin's voice. They hadn't talked since her bout with Leah. Andrea thought he was upset with her and was steering clear. After all, everyone else seemed to be.

Telephone calls and visits from church members had gotten sparse. Just because she had hinted to a few people that she needed some space, she supposed they had relayed it to everyone else, and so they all stayed away. Ellen and Alexander still called often. Several times, they had wanted to stop by for a visit, but Andrea would always decline. She imagined that soon they'd abandon her, too. She was lonelier than she'd ever been in her entire life. It was so strange how one part of her craved companionship while an-other fragment of herself yearned for solitude.

"Hi, Devin." Before inviting her brother-in-law inside, Andrea took a quick look to see if her sister was with him. He was alone. "Come in."

Devin stepped inside. "Hey. I hope it's okay that I stopped by."

Andrea felt guilty. She liked Devin—loved him like a brother. Just because she and her sister were having problems, that didn't mean she was going to take them out on him.

Andrea said, "It's fine. Come on in."

Devin followed Andrea into the kitchen and helped her finish putting away her groceries while they talked.

He eyed her suspiciously as he placed a can of corn in the cupboard. "So are you okay?"

Andrea refused to look at him as she made her way to the refrigerator. "Yeah."

Devin went to the table, reached his hand in a plastic bag, and pulled out a head of lettuce. Handing the lettuce to Andrea, he asked, "Is there anything I can do for you while I'm here?"

Andrea took the lettuce from Devin, pulled out the crisper, and dropped it into the plastic storage space. "No, I can't think of anything."

"You sure?"

She nodded as she closed the bin and stood up straight, shutting the refrigerator door. "Yeah."

They put the remainder of items away in silence.

As they made their way from the kitchen, Devin observed, "It sure is quiet."

Andrea responded, "Yeah, it is. Kayla went to the movies with LeaAnn. Clayton's sleeping. Do you wanna see him?"

Devin smiled weakly. He wished Leah could be here. She missed spending time with the children. "Of course."

Andrea and Devin walked quietly into the baby's room. As they stared down into the innocent face of the sleeping child, they grinned as he snored softly. They watched as his little belly rose gently up and down with each breath. They were careful not to make any noise as they made their way to the family room.

"He sure has grown," Devin said. "Won't be long before he's crawling all over the house."

Andrea smiled. "I know. Then walking, talking, and getting into everything."

Devin attempted another smile. He never dreamed that things would get this bad between the two sisters. He had made a silent oath that he would not get himself caught in the middle, but he was already there, whether he liked it or not. Andrea had been the twinkling star in his brother's life, and Leah was the star that lit up his world. "Andrea, I told myself that I wouldn't get involved in what's going on between you and Leah," he began.

Andrea studied Devin's face as she formed a condemnation for what she was sure he was about to say.

Devin went on, "I know you two love each other, and what's happening between you is tearing her apart."

Andrea felt the urge to remind Devin that it was up to her sister to make amends, but she allowed him to continue speaking.

"I know you're still grieving over losing Clay. It still hurts me, too, but please don't shut Leah out of your life or the children's. Won't you please reconsider your decision not to allow her to see them? She misses them. She misses you, too."

Andrea's heart toward her sister remained as cold as a block of ice. "Did she send you over here to speak for her?"

"No," Devin truthfully denied. "She doesn't know I'm here. I came because I'm worried about her. I love her."

Andrea refused to divulge her tender affections for the sister who'd betrayed her in her time of need.

"Devin, I really don't wanna talk about this. I can't deal with it right now. I've got too many other things on my mind."

Devin looked thoughtful. "I'm sorry." Rising, he added, "See you at the shower tomorrow."

"I'm not going." Actually, Andrea had planned to send her gift with Ellen and stay home. She didn't feel like socializing.

Devin was disappointed. Leah would be devastated. "Is it because of what's going on between you and Leah?"

"I really don't feel like being around a bunch of people. We planned the shower months ago. Everything's taken care of. Ellen and the other sisters will handle it. Ellen's coming by this afternoon to get my gift."

"Leah's not worried about the gift. She really wants you to be there. Won't you please try to come?"

Andrea and Devin had never passed any unpleasant words with each other, and she didn't want to now. But Leah and Devin had to accept that she would not be at the shower.

"Devin, please don't pressure me on this. Everyone is pressuring me to do stuff. I can't take anymore. Try to explain it to Leah. Surely she'll understand." Andrea didn't believe for one minute that her sister's view of the situation would harmonize with hers, but there was nothing she could do about it.

Devin certainly didn't want to add to Andrea's stress, so he let the matter rest. He dreaded giving the news to Leah.

Leah took it harder than he had expected. She grabbed her purse and headed out the door. When Devin attempted to stop her, she yelled at him.

"Let me go! Devin, stop! Let go of me!"

"Leah," Devin said. "If you go over there now, you'll only make things worse. She's not going to change her mind. Let it go."

"Don't you start with that. I'm tired of everybody telling me to let go. She's my sister. I can't just give up on her. I love her."

Devin pulled Leah into his arms. "Nobody's asking you to give up on her."

Leah cried, "I love her. I don't understand why this is happening. This is supposed to be one of the happiest times of my life, and I feel like I'm being tortured alive. Why does she hate me? Why is she doing this?"

"She doesn't hate you. Give her some time. Pray for her. That's all we can do."

Devin held Leah as she sobbed uncontrollably. As long as he'd known her, he had never seen her so emotional. The strife between her and her sister was tearing her apart.

Ellen looked sympathetically at Andrea. "I'm sorry you won't be at the shower tomorrow."

Andrea hoped her friend wasn't going to start hassling her, too. She wished everybody would just give her a break. Her simple reply was, "Me, too."

Ellen had heard that things were not good between the two sisters. However, she was not there to judge. She had even talked to her husband about the two of them taking Kayla to church with them. Alexander felt it was a family situation that they should not get involved in. He loved Andrea, but he didn't want his wife in the middle, like when she had stepped in as Andrea's Lamaze partner.

Ellen and Alexander missed Andrea and the kids. Everyone did. Ellen wanted Andrea to know that she and Alexander were there for her, no matter what. Ellen remembered what she had gone through years ago, and how people got upset with her when she didn't handle her situation the way they felt she should. She was trying not to display that kind of attitude with Andrea.

Of course, trying not to force your feelings and opinions on someone was more difficult to do when it was your own family member. Because you loved that person, you did and said everything you could think of to help—when in all actuality, perhaps you were making matters worse. Ellen imagined that was why the situation was putting a strain on Andrea's relationship with her sister.

Ellen reached over and gently touched Andrea's hand. "Do you want to talk? I'll listen if you need to. If not, it's okay."

Andrea looked tenderly at her friend. *Do I want to talk?* No one had asked her in a very long time what she wanted. All everyone else seemed to be doing was demanding things of her. When she did talk, she didn't feel that they were really listening. What she needed was for someone to listen and not necessarily provide a so-lution—because in her eyes, the only remedy was to have Clayton back. And that was something that none of them could do.

Without even thinking of what she would say, Andrea began, "It's been over a year since Clay died, but it still feels like yesterday. I never knew a person could hurt so much. My family doesn't un-derstand. I don't think they mean to be impatient, but they are. They want me to do things at their pace. They don't know how much I want to be the person I once was. I miss that Andrea. Perhaps more than they miss her. Because I'm the one who has to live with this day in and day out. The truth is, I no longer like my-self any more than they do."

Ellen was shocked that Andrea thought her family didn't like her. But then she remembered it had been the same way she'd felt herself. Whether or not it was true made no difference to Andrea—if that was how she felt in her heart.

Andrea went on, "The woman you told me about who lost her husband and children in the accident—what happened to her?" She looked into Ellen's eyes.

Ellen blinked once as she answered, "She eventually got on with her life and married a wonderful man."

"Did she have more children?"

"No, but she's still happy."

"I can't see myself being married to anyone else. I'm so lonely for Clay. I'll never remarry. If I can't have him, I don't want anyone else."

Ellen looked fondly at Andrea. Clayton still held a piece of her heart that Andrea felt no other man could ever have. She might feel differently one day, though.

Once Andrea started unleashing her feelings, she couldn't stop. Ellen was such a good listener. Every now and then, she would nod, smile when Andrea said something slightly funny, or ask a simple question related to something Andrea said.

When it was time for Ellen to leave, Andrea hugged her and said, "Thank you, Ellen. I know I probably talked your head off. It felt good to get all that off my chest."

Ellen smiled as she and Andrea stood at arm's length holding hands. "You didn't talk my head off. I love talking to you. That's one of the things I miss most—us getting together and talking like we used to."

Andrea said, "I know. I miss it, too. Just give me some time. Okay?"

Ellen grinned. "Okay."

After Ellen had gone, Andrea thought about how she had been dreading her friend's visit, believing that she would deliver a sermon to her while she was there. Instead, Ellen had proven to be a true friend in a time of distress.

"Where's Andrea?" Lizzie asked her son as they stood in line to fix their plates.

"She didn't feel like socializing. She's not coming." Devin hoped his explanation would suffice, as he was holding Leah's spot in line and didn't want them to be discussing the topic when Leah returned.

Lizzie attempted to whisper. "Devin, you think I was born yesterday? You know as well as I do that Andrea's not here because of your stubborn fiancée. Why can't Leah just take Kayla to church and stop making a big deal out of it?"

Devin appeared chagrined, hoping none of their guests had overheard his mother's dialogue. He answered her in an undertone. "Mama, this is not the time or place to be discussing this."

Lizzie had plenty more to say. Ignoring her son, she began, "Devin . . ."

Before Lizzie could finish her statement, Leah popped back into the line in front of Devin. Spying her future mother-in-law, she decided here was her opportunity to try to bridge the gap that had ob-viously occurred between them. Someone had to make the first move. She would put her pride aside in an effort to rectify matters.

Leah greeted Lizzie. "Hi, Liz. How are you?"

Lizzie quickly averted her attention to a lady who was standing in front of her and began engrossing the woman in conversation.

Leah couldn't believe Devin's mother had just disregarded her as though she hadn't even spoken. She felt like cutting in on Lizzie's communication with the woman and giving her a piece of her mind. However, she decided against it when she attempted to give her the benefit of the doubt. Perhaps Lizzie hadn't heard her greet-ing.

Devin was also shocked at his mother's attitude. If they weren't at a public gathering, he would quickly pull her aside and respect-fully express his displeasure. Andrea and Leah's disagreement was between the two of them, and his mother had no right to treat Leah as she just had.

After eating and playing an assortment of games, Leah and Devin opened their gifts. It was a wonderful event for Leah, except for the fact that her sister wasn't there. Leah had asked her parents not to make another trip just for the shower, since they'd recently visited and would have to return next month for the wedding. That was the affair that she wanted no one to miss.

After all the gifts had been opened, Leah and Devin thanked everyone for coming. Leah had made several more attempts during the course of the shower to talk to Lizzie and had gotten brushed off every time. She was certain now that she was purposely being ignored. However, she was determined to give it one more try.

When Leah approached Lizzie, she was talking her head off to one of the other guests. Leah waited a brief moment before cutting in on their discussion. Not desiring to make anyone feel left out or unimportant, she declared, "Excuse me. I'm sorry for interrupting your conversation, but I just wanted to thank you both for coming and for your gifts."

The other woman smiled, hugged Leah's neck, and said, "You're welcome, Leah. I wish you and Devin the best."

"Thank you," Leah expressed. She hoped she and her future mother-in-law could revert back to a more pleasant relationship. She glanced at Lizzie, hoping that she would say something in reply to her heartfelt sentiment. When she didn't, Leah turned and walked away with tears in her eyes.

Devin had had enough of his mother's repugnant attitude. He had observed all afternoon her infantile behavior toward Leah. After he escorted Leah to his vehicle, he approached his mother as she was heading toward her car.

Lizzie smiled when she saw her son. "Did you come to say good-bye?"

Devin stopped to stand beside his mother. "Actually, I came to tell you how disappointed I am at your attitude toward Leah today."

Lizzie denied any wrongdoing on her part. "Devin, I don't know what you're talking about."

"Mama, yes you do. Please don't stand here and look in my face and tell me that, because you know it's not true. I love you, and I also love Leah. She's going to be my wife. You hurt her, you hurt me. The same is true of you. If anybody hurts you, they hurt me, too. If Pop knew about how you acted today, he'd be pretty unhappy. I won't tell him, but please don't do it again."

Lizzie suddenly appeared embarrassed. She couldn't look at her son. She turned her head and gazed off into the distance.

Devin kissed his mother's cheek. "Bye. Drive safely." Then he was gone.

Leah had observed Devin talking to his mother. Alone in the car, Leah felt like a child being disciplined. The hurt she experienced from Lizzie quickly changed to exasperation, though. She would not continue to tolerate being shut out of everyone's life.

As soon as Devin got in the car, she turned on him. "Did you see how your Mama was acting toward me? Every time I tried to talk to her, she'd walk off or just plain ignore me. And I didn't appreciate you leaving me to sit in the car while you went over to talk to her—especially after the way she treated me."

Devin started the engine and pulled the vehicle out of the parking lot. Hoping his impatience with Leah would not be evident, he responded, "She's my mother. Just because there's some tension between the two of you right now, don't expect me not to talk to her or to ask your permission before I do." He attempted to soften his tone. "I went over to tell her I didn't like how she treated you today."

Leah was tired of everybody treating her as if she were their enemy. She didn't care what Devin had said to his mama. She had some things on her mind, and she was going to get them off right now. "You know, if she was gonna act like that, I wish she'd just stayed at home. I've got enough to deal with already with Andrea acting all crazy and only thinking about herself."

Devin was fed up with all the bickering. He suddenly blurted, "Mama was acting childish this afternoon, and you're acting childish right now."

Leah snapped, "Look, Devin, she's the one who started it."

Her juvenile response irritated Devin, and he gave the steering wheel one quick tap with his hand. "See? There you go. You sound just like a child talking about who started it."

Leah didn't like Devin's tone. She was tired of always being blamed for everything. "You know, as my future husband, I'd think you'd be more supportive of me."

"Leah," Devin said, "Right is right, and wrong is wrong. You're saying I'm supposed to support you even when you're wrong?"

"What d'you mean, *I'm* wrong? What about your Mama?"

"You're both wrong. Didn't I just tell you I told Mama I didn't like how she treated you? But you ignored that. You just wanna fuss. You're so angry at Andrea for the way she's treating you that you wanna have it out with everybody. Why do you always have to be so argumentative? Maybe if you hadn't given Andrea such a hard time, she'd still be speaking to you and none of this would even be happening."

Devin hadn't meant to say all that. Leah's bickering and complaining had pushed him to his limit. She was a wonderful sister. She was hurting enough as it was. Now he'd made it worse.

"I'm sorry," he said. "I didn't mean that."

Leah's eyes shot daggers at Devin. "Yes, you did. Maybe you didn't mean to say it, but you meant it. So how long have you been feeling this way?"

"I don't feel like that," Devin denied. "It's just that you've got so much fight in you. I admire your strength, but when you make up your mind about something, you just don't let up."

Leah felt hurt at her heart. "Sounds like you're complaining. Like it's a turnoff."

"I didn't say that."

"Then what are you saying? Maybe you don't want to marry someone like me with my personality. Maybe you want a wife who never speaks up or says anything, one who just lets you be the king of your castle."

"Leah, that's not at all what I want. We both know the marriage arrangement is not supposed to be like that." Devin recalled the counsel Alexander had given them when they'd announced their engagement. "Being the head won't give me the right to lord it over you. We will complement each other. You know I love you, and I want to marry you—no one else. Listen—we're all under a lot of stress right now. When we're stressed, sometimes we say things we don't mean, or we say things the wrong way. I'm sorry. I never meant to hurt you."

Leah looked away as she choked back tears. She believed Devin. She knew in her heart he hadn't meant to cause her pain. Nevertheless, his words had hurt and still rang in her ears.

Chapter 25

"Mommy?" Kayla stopped coloring long enough to tap her mother's leg as Andrea nursed the baby on the family room sofa.

Andrea looked down at her daughter, who was sprawled out on the floor with her crayons and Barbie doll coloring book. "What is it, honey?"

"Aunt Leah hasn't been by in a long time. She hasn't called, and she didn't even pick me up this morning to go to church. Why hasn't she been coming by?"

Andrea should have known Kayla would inquire about Leah's absence sooner or later. "Well, honey, she's busy planning her wedding. She can't come over like she used to." She felt a bit guilty for lying.

"Oh." A wide grin lit up Kayla's face as she leaped from the floor. "Can I call her?"

Andrea quickly thought of an escape. The shower was probably over by now. It was after seven o'clock, but she said anyway, "I don't think she's home right now. Let's wait."

"Okay." Kayla returned to her coloring.

Andrea wondered how the shower had gone and what Leah

thought of her gift. She had purchased it several months ago after her sister had mentioned that she didn't want her wedding pictures stuffed in a picture album—she wanted them someplace where she could always see them at a glance. Andrea had found the perfect reversible folding photograph screen at an antique store. It was one of a kind—unique—just like Leah.

Andrea missed Leah so much. If her sister wasn't so obstinate, they'd still be the happy siblings they once were. After everything that had happened, things between them would never be the same again.

About an hour later, Andrea gave Clayton his bath while Kayla took hers.

When the doorbell rang later, Kayla shouted as she ran toward the front door, "Maybe it's Aunt Leah."

Kayla had her hand on the doorknob just as Andrea made it to the door. "Kayla, wait. I'll get it. You know you're not supposed to open the door unless you ask who it is and you know the person."

Andrea asked who was at the door. It was Devin. Kayla almost knocked her mother down in an effort to get to him. Devin lifted her as she jumped up into his arms.

"Hi, Uncle Devin. I've missed you. Where've you been? Where's Aunt Leah? Is she with you?"

Devin laughed as he held Kayla in one arm and used his free hand to close the door. "Slow down, Lil Bit. Only one question at a time. I came by yesterday, but you were gone to the movies with LeaAnn. Aunt Leah's at home."

Kayla asked, "Why didn't she come? Doesn't she wanna see me?"

Andrea knew she looked uncomfortable, because she certainly felt it.

Devin answered, "Of course she wants to see you. She's a little busy with the wedding right now. You'll get to see her at in a couple of weeks when we get married." He didn't dare look at Andrea.

Andrea was glad Devin had given Kayla the same excuse she had.

Kayla was disappointed. "A couple of weeks? That's a long time," she pouted.

Devin assured his niece, "It'll go by fast."

"I hope so," Kayla replied.

While the two played, Andrea hoped Devin had taken Kayla's mind off calling Leah. In between her giggles, however, Kayla asked her mother again if she could call her aunt.

Andrea wanted to say no, but the sad expression on Devin's face forced her to say otherwise. However, Andrea didn't want her sister to get the wrong idea and think by her allowing Kayla to telephone that things were okay between them, because they definitely were not.

Andrea said, "Go ahead, but only for a few minutes. You've got to go to bed."

"Okay, Mommy."

Andrea and Devin watched Kayla skip over to the phone and dial Leah's number. They were quiet during her conversation.

Kayla asked, "Are you excited about your wedding?"

She listened intently, then giggled. "When I get married, I'm gonna have a big wedding. And Uncle Devin's gonna give me away."

Hearing Kayla conversing about her wedding day touched the hearts of Andrea and Devin. Devin felt honored that his niece wanted him to present her to her future husband. Andrea choked up at the thought of Clayton not being around for the big event.

Kayla and Leah talked a few more minutes before saying good-bye. When Kayla got off the phone, her mother reminded her that it was her bedtime.

The little girl asked excitedly, "Can Uncle Devin read me a story and tuck me in?"

Andrea answered, "You'll have to ask him."

Kayla looked at her uncle as she grinned from ear to ear. "Will you, Uncle Devin?"

"You bet I will," Devin cheerfully replied.

The two left the room, holding hands and talking. Andrea went to check on Clayton. As she was leaving his room, she could hear Kayla and Devin chatting away.

Andrea heard Kayla ask, "Are you and Aunt Leah gonna have children when you get married?"

Devin answered, "We'd like to."

"How many?" Kayla wanted to know.

Andrea grinned. The child was full of questions.

"Oh, I don't know. I'd love to have a little girl and a little boy just like you and Clayton. Wouldn't that be neat?"

"Yeah," Kayla giggled. "You know what?"

"No. What?" Devin asked.

"Besides my Mommy and Daddy, I think you and Aunt Leah will be the best mommy and daddy ever."

"You do?"

"Yes."

"Well, thank you, Lil Bit. Would you mind if I call my little girl Lil Bit—like I do you?"

Kayla stated seriously, "Oh, no, that's my nickname. I'll help you come up with another name for her."

Devin snickered. "Okay."

Andrea could hear them laughing.

Then Devin said, "Lil Bit."

"Yes," Kayla answered.

"You're too much."

"That's the same thing my Daddy used to say."

Andrea half-smiled as she walked away. Kayla had such fond memories of her father.

After Kayla was snug as a bug in bed, Devin rejoined Andrea in the family room. He sat on the sofa and smiled, and shook his head. "Your daughter is something else. She's like a precious gem."

Andrea grinned. "She *is* something. She helps keep me on my toes."

They grew quiet.

Then Andrea confessed, "Sometimes I wish I were a child again. The only bad part is, if I were, I wouldn't have Kayla and Clayton. If it weren't for them, I think I would have given up a long time ago."

Devin nodded. "Kids seem to add a joy to your life unlike any other you can experience." He grew quiet again, staring off into space.

He didn't seem like himself. Andrea sensed something was wrong, so she asked, "Devin, are you all right?"

Devin didn't look at her when he inquired, "Did you and Clay argue a lot right before you got married?"

Andrea half-smiled. "Yeah. We had our share." She waited for him to go on. When he didn't, she asked, "What's wrong, Devin?" Remembering how Ellen had given her a listening ear the day before, she asked, "I mean, do you want to talk about it?"

This time Devin looked at Andrea. "This afternoon I said something to Leah that I didn't mean to say. It hurt her, and she suggested that maybe she's not the person I want to marry. I just feel so bad. I love her. I don't want her thinking something like that. I don't want us going into our marriage with her feeling that way."

Andrea knew how she felt sometimes when people gave her advice she hadn't asked for, but she had to give Devin some reassurance. Even though she envied him and Leah, she felt the urge to try to put his mind at ease.

She said, "What you're feeling is normal. You want your marriage to last forever. I used to get scared when I thought about all the things that could go wrong. But that's just it—they're things that *can* go wrong. Just like everything else in life, anything can happen, but that doesn't mean it will."

Before she realized it, Andrea found herself quoting the Bible. "Is it Matthew 6:34 that says not to worry about tomorrow, because there will always be something to make us anxious?"

Devin nodded. Andrea was right. Not worrying wasn't always an easy thing to do, but she was correct in her statement. Devin knew, because it came from God's Word, the Bible.

"Yeah. Maybe I'm just nervous."

Andrea grinned. "Well, that's a natural feeling, too. Marriage is a serious step, one not to be taken lightly. I think you and Leah will be okay."

The two talked for a few more minutes. Devin expressed his and Leah's appreciation for the shower gift before he left.

Andrea found herself perplexed as to how she could so readily share scriptural counsel with someone else, yet she was having such a difficult time applying it in her own life.

On Monday evening when the doorbell rang, Andrea opened the door without inquiring or considering who it might be. When she saw her sister, she almost slammed the door in her face.

All she could say was, "Leah."

When Andrea failed to invite her inside, Leah asked, "Can I come in?" After Kayla had called her last night, Leah thought surely their family feud was over. Now she realized it clearly was not.

Andrea reluctantly allowed her sister to enter. She should have known Leah would mistake Kayla's call as a truce. *Well, it wasn't!*

Andrea wouldn't let Leah get past the foyer. "What is it?"

Leah answered, "I need you and Kayla to go by the boutique Saturday for your last dress fitting."

Irritated, Andrea asked, "You couldn't just call me on the phone and tell me that?"

Leah didn't know what to say. "Well . . . I figured since you let Kayla call me last night that it'd be okay to come by."

"Well, you're wrong. My letting Kayla call you doesn't change anything." Andrea was so angry, she decided to spring the news on her sister. "Besides, I'm not even sure I'll be at the wedding, let alone be in it."

Leah was not believing what she was hearing. Her mouth fell open. "Andrea, I know you're not serious. You would actually not come to my wedding just because I won't do what you want me to do?"

Andrea didn't say anything.

Leah stated matter-of-factly, "You are so selfish. You have turned into one of the most hateful, spiteful people I know. Why do you hate me? What have I done to make you hate me? All I've tried to do is be there for you. You're so angry at everybody. Me. Mama and Daddy. God."

Andrea flinched at the last word out of her sister's mouth. "How dare you say something like that to me. You get out of here right now!" she screamed.

Leah didn't move. "You're so angry and bitter because everybody else isn't miserable like you. You know what? I don't care if you don't come to my wedding. I don't want you there. But if you have an ounce of decency left in that cold organ in your chest you call a heart, I'd appreciate it if you'd let my niece come and be my flower girl. I hope she doesn't grow up to be the cold, heartless person you've become."

Andrea felt hurt at her heart at her sister's words. All she could say was, "I told you to leave."

Kayla had heard loud talking and had come to investigate. "Mommy? Aunt Leah? Why are you yelling at each other? What's wrong?" Tears streamed down the child's face.

"Nothing's wrong, baby." Andrea hastily put her hand on Kayla's back, grabbed her hand, and escorted her back to her room.

After Kayla was in bed, Andrea immediately went back to finish dealing with her sister, but Leah was gone. She locked the door, turned around with her back against it, and covered her face with her hands.

What have I done? By the time she made it to her room, Andrea was in tears. She shut the door, locked it behind her, and flung herself across her bed.

She kept playing the scene between her and Leah over and over in her head, recalling her sister's words. *You're a hateful, spiteful per-*

184

son. Angry and bitter. Why do you hate me? She didn't hate Leah. She loved her. Of course, she supposed she hadn't been showing it lately.

Leah said she hoped Kayla didn't grow up to be cold and heartless like her. Her sister didn't want her at her wedding. Was that really how Leah felt? She said Andrea was angry at everyone, including God. She wasn't angry with God. Or was she?

Leah was extremely upset when she left Andrea's house. She needed to talk to Devin. On the thirty-minute drive to his apartment, all she could think about was the harsh words she had thrown at her sister. She had not meant to say any of those terrible things. But when Andrea had implied that she might not be at the wedding, Leah had lost her temper. She thought she had handled things pretty well between them up to that point. She was disappointed in her behavior and knew God was equally not pleased, if not more so.

Leah raced up the stairs to Devin's apartment. She almost tore down the door banging on it.

When Devin opened the door, she dived into his arms, crying, "Oh, Devin, I've really messed up this time."

He led Leah over to the sofa where they sat down. She was obviously very upset, so he refused to let go of her hand. "What happened?"

"Andrea!" Leah blurted out. "I went to her house to tell her that she and Kayla need to go try on their dresses Saturday."

Devin listened intently as Leah explained what had happened, all the while wondering how things had gotten to this point.

"Okay. Try to calm down," he told his fiancée. "We'll figure something out. Don't worry."

Devin didn't want Leah driving, so he called up a friend who lived nearby and asked if he would meet him at Leah's house and bring him back home. Devin drove Leah home in her car with her crying all the way there.

When he got back home, he called the Washingtons and advised them of what had transpired between their daughters.

William did not want to believe what Devin had just told him. Anna sat beside her husband, trying to ascertain what had taken place. She gathered something terrible had happened between Andrea and Leah.

When William finished talking to Devin, he filled his wife in on the details. They tried several times to call Andrea. As expected, they got her answering machine. They called Devin back and asked him if he would go check on Andrea. Then they called Leah.

When Andrea heard the doorbell, she immediately decided to let it go unanswered. She wasn't in the mood to see or talk to anyone. Whoever it was, they were persistent. Not only were they ringing the doorbell, but it sounded like they were about to knock down the door. She'd finally been able to get Kayla back to sleep and didn't want Clayton awakened, so she made her way toward the front door. However, no matter who it was, she was not letting anyone in.

When she discovered it was Devin, Andrea answered from behind the closed door, "Devin, I really don't feel like talking right now."

Devin responded sympathetically, "All right. Your folks called, and you didn't answer. They just want to know you're okay."

"I'm all right. Will you call and tell them?"

"Sure."

"Thanks. Good night."

Devin wasn't ready to leave. "Andrea?"

"Yeah."

"For what it's worth, Leah really feels bad about what happened."

"Okay. Thanks. Good night."

"Good night."

Andrea had been doing a lot of soul-searching since Leah had gone. She had begun to realize things about herself that she had been too ashamed to admit. Things about her sister and God. She was jealous of what Leah and Devin shared, because they reminded her so much of her and Clayton and the love they had. Worse than that, she was angry at God because He had allowed her husband to be taken from her.

Chapter 26

The next morning, Andrea gently tapped on Glenn's office door. When he looked up and saw her, he smiled.

"Andrea, come in. Sit down."

Andrea closed the door behind her and took a seat.

Whatever she wanted to discuss with him, Glenn figured from the look on her face that it was something of a serious nature. She didn't look well.

"Well, how are you this morning?" he asked.

Andrea was finding it difficult to speak.

Glenn asked, "Andrea are you okay?"

Finally, she said, "I'd like to know if I can still take you up on your offer."

Confused, Glenn asked, "What offer?"

"The one to take a leave of absence. I need some time off . . . to sort out my life . . . to try to put things back in order."

Glenn was shocked that Andrea had come to him with her request, for he had sensed her displeasure when he had initially extended the offer. She obviously did need the time off or she wouldn't have asked.

"Sure, Andrea. No problem. You take as much time as you need. Your job will be waiting for you when you come back."

"Thank you, Glenn. I appreciate it."

"Did you want to finish out the week?"

"No. I'm sorry—I know it's short notice, but I'd like today to be my last day. Hopefully, you won't have too much trouble reassigning my appointments."

"Don't worry about it. I'll call the temp agency. I'm sure they can find someone for us."

"Okay." Andrea stood. "Well, that's all."

Glenn got up, walked around his desk, and gave her a hug. "You take care of yourself and those precious children."

Tears streamed down Andrea's face as she embraced Glenn with all her might. Leaving the job and people she loved was one of the hardest things she'd ever had to do. "Okay. You take care, too."

When they let go of each other and stood face to face, Andrea said through her tears, "One other thing. I'm so sorry about the way I acted before when you asked me if I needed time off. Please forgive me."

Glenn smiled. "You're forgiven. Don't worry about it. Stay in touch."

"I will."

Later that afternoon, everyone cried as they said their farewells to their friend and coworker. Andrea felt like a failure at everything—as a mother, a sister, a daughter, an employee, a friend, and a servant of God. However, she had made some decisions about her life, and this was just one of the things she had to do.

She cried off and on all the way to the day care center. Kayla asked if she was all right. Andrea lied and said yes.

That night, after she'd read Kayla a bedtime story, Andrea told her daughter she would be taking some time off work.

Kayla looked curiously into her mother's eyes. "Why, Mommy? Are you sick?"

Andrea tried to blink away her tears. "Yes, in a way."

"Well, what's the matter?" Kayla placed her tiny hand on her mother's stomach. "Do you have a tummy ache? Maybe you can take something and make it better."

Andrea shook her head. "No, baby, it's not a tummy ache. I have another kind of sickness." It hurt, but she had to say it. "It's in my brain and my heart."

"Can the doctor make you better?"

"Yes, there are things the doctor can do to help."

Kayla smiled. "That's good. And I'll help take care of you, too, Mommy."

Andrea smiled as she gently ran her fingers through Kayla's hair. "That's sweet. You're so good to me and your brother. We love you, you know."

"I know. I love you, too."

This time when Kayla said her prayers, Andrea joined her on the floor, also on her knees. Maybe hearing her little girl's heartfelt prayers would help rekindle her own.

When the telephone rang later, Andrea answered it. She saw Devin's name and number on the caller ID. However, the voice she heard was not Devin's.

Leah. Andrea's heart began to pound in her chest. She wasn't ready to talk to her sister yet. The way she had treated Leah had consumed her with shame, and the guilt was unbearable. Her sister had been there for her through the good and the bad times. She saw no way they could ever revive their friendship and be as close as they once were. Simply to say she was sorry would never be enough. How could she ever face Leah again after the way she'd treated her?

Leah pleaded, "Andrea, please don't hang up. I'm so sorry for all the terrible things I said to you last night. I do want you at my wedding, but I'll try to understand if you're not there. Please don't hate me," she cried.

Andrea began to cry. "I don't hate you. I know I act like I do, but I don't. I'm sorry, too. Can you ever find it in your heart to forgive me? I love you. I love you so much. Please forgive me."

"I forgive you. Will you forgive me?"

"Yes, I will." Leah had stated that she would try to understand if Andrea wasn't at the wedding. Now would be the perfect time to free herself of the commitment she'd made to her sister to be her maid of honor. Instead, Andrea found herself saying, "I'll be at your wedding. I want to be your maid of honor."

Leah was ecstatic. She was still holding on to Devin's hand as she and Andrea talked. It felt like she was about to squeeze the life out of it, and he now had no feeling left in it. Leah had wanted him there by her side when she called her sister. He was about to go to his knees on the floor, though, from the pain he felt in his hand.

Suddenly, Leah glanced at her fiancé. When she realized what was going on, she let go of Devin's hand, saying, "Oh, baby, I'm sorry. Are you okay?"

Devin stood up, smiling, and shaking his hand as he made his way to the kitchen. "I'll be fine."

It sounded like the two sisters had finally made up. He was thrilled. If he and Leah ever did have children, he hoped he remembered not to let her get too tight a grip on his hand during labor.

Three days later on Friday, Andrea and Leah were both quiet as they walked from the medical office complex to Leah's car. During Andrea's doctor's visit, Leah had learned just how depressed her sister was. She felt horribly guilty for any part her actions might have played in her sister's depression. She thought highly of Andrea for finally seeking the help she needed. In her opinion, it took a strong person to take that step.

Andrea didn't think she was strong because of everything that had happened in the past year. She felt like such a weakling. Her doctor had diagnosed her with chronic depression and had assured her that it did not indicate a weak personality or character flaw. However, she still had a very low opinion of herself. She was also feeling blue because, once she started taking her antidepressant, she would no longer be able to nurse Clayton. But she realized that she needed to stabilize her mental and emotional health so she could take care of her children and herself. She knew the road to recovery would be long and hard.

Leah unlocked her door and pressed the button to unlock the other doors. She and Andrea climbed into the vehicle.

Leah started up the car, asking, "You wanna grab some lunch after we get your prescription filled?"

Andrea just stared straight ahead. "No. Just take me home."

Leah didn't think her sister should be alone. Andrea was also feeling depressed about not working. However, after all that had transpired, Leah was trying to be extremely cautious about what she said and how she said it. "Okay."

After they left the drugstore, Leah took Andrea home. When she got to her house, Leah called their parents.

Anna and William had been waiting on Leah's call. Anna answered on the first ring. When she heard her daughter's voice, she said, "Hi, honey. How is she?"

Leah filled her mother in on Andrea's visit to the doctor. "Mama, I feel so guilty. All that time I was so angry at her, I never knew what she was really going through. We're twins. I should have known. I should have been there for her."

"Leah," Anna stated flatly. "Don't do that to yourself. You girls have been through a lot together. Sure you're twins, but you're also individuals." Leah still expected her and Andrea's emotions to intertwine. "You're not a mind reader. We can't change the past. Just try to use what time you have with your sister to the full."

"Well, that's what I'm trying to do, but even though we made up, she's still distant."

"Well, honey, you can't expect everything to go back the way it was just like that. And besides, she just got her medication today, and it'll take a couple of weeks for it to get into her system and take effect. But just remember, even then, she may not go completely back to the same person she was. She's been through a lot. I know you don't want to hear this, but I just want you to be prepared, just in case."

Her mother was right. Leah didn't want to hear that. She and Andrea had a bond that would never be broken, despite all they'd been through.

Andrea sat at the computer in the kitchen typing in the Web address of one of the support groups the doctor had given her. After finally finding one that appealed to her, she joined the online discussion.

She typed in her thoughts.

I am now thirty-six years old. In October of last year, my husband of ten years was killed by a drunk driver. Our daughter was five when it happened. The day after his funeral, I found out I was pregnant with our second child.

Andrea clicked the left mouse button to send her message. Another participant asked how her children were doing.

Four months ago, I gave birth to our son. He's a lovable, healthy little boy. My little girl remembers her father. However, my son will never have that. I'm hurt, angry, and lonely.

She next received reassurance that she had made a wise decision in seeking a way to cope with her feelings.

For the past year, I've taken my frustration out on all the wrong people—my family—the ones who were there for me and tried to help me through this nightmare. To admit that I needed help seemed to shout to the world that I'm weak because I can't handle this on my own.

Someone else shared with Andrea that asking for help when needed was not a sign of weakness, but a symbol of courage and humility.

I've never had to do anything like this. I've always been able to handle whatever life threw my way, but this time, life threw me a curveball that put me out of the game. I'm still not crazy about having to seek outside assistance, but if it'll help, I think it'll be well worth me putting aside my pride so I can move on with my life.

Andrea received several heartfelt responses to her experience. She also read other discussions from people who had lost children, parents, siblings, and others. She soon began to realize that she was not alone in her plight, as she oftentimes felt. For the first time in a long while, she didn't feel so alone. She stayed online a few more minutes and located a group in Atlanta that she could meet with in person if she ever wanted to. Since she liked face-to-face contact, she felt she might want to attend from time to time.

Andrea shut down the computer, wondering what she should do next. She missed her job, but she wasn't ready to go back yet. She recalled some of the self-help techniques the doctor mentioned, like exercise. She quickly dismissed the idea, as she simply could not summon up enough energy to do it today. Even a simple walk in the neighborhood seemed too much for her.

Andrea went to the family room, pulled out one of Kayla's Disney DVD's, *The Little Mermaid*, and popped it into the DVD player. She ran to the hall closet, grabbed a flannel blanket, and dashed back to the sofa. As she lay down, she pulled the blanket up over her, and began to watch the movie. When the cartoon ended, she got up and went to pick up the children from day care.

The next day, Andrea and Kayla went to the boutique for their dress fittings. As they and Leah left the store, Kayla chatted away, swinging her hand back and forth in Leah's.

Kayla climbed into the backseat. Leah helped buckle her in while Andrea fastened Clayton in his seat. After everyone was buckled in, they went to Pizza Hut.

While they ate, Leah filled Andrea in on the wedding details. "Now, the rehearsal dinner is the night before the wedding on Friday, December second. We need to be at the church at six o'clock. When we finish rehearsing, we'll meet at Sam and Roscoe's restaurant in Douglasville. I made our reservations for seven-thirty."

Andrea was listening, but not saying anything. Her head was spinning. She still didn't know if she would be able to go through with the wedding. She didn't think she could make it through the ceremony without falling apart. However, she would endeavor to compel herself to follow through with the commitment she'd made. She couldn't disappoint Leah.

Leah noticed the flustered look on her sister's face. "Andrea, are you all right?"

"I'm fine."

Even Kayla could tell something was wrong. "Mommy, what's wrong?"

"Nothing, honey. I'm fine." Andrea attempted to fight the attacks of anxiety she was starting to feel again about the wedding.

When Leah dropped Andrea and the kids off at home, she asked Andrea, "Do you want me to pick Kayla up in the morning for church?"

Andrea looked at her sister. She certainly had not been expecting this. She wasn't sure what to say. "Yeah.... Sure. If you don't mind."

"Okay." Leah told Kayla, "Lil Bit, I'll see you in the morning at nine-thirty. You're coming to church with me, right?"

"Yes, I'm coming," Kayla answered gleefully.

When Leah drove away, she was wondering how long it would take Andrea to overcome her depression. She prayed for patience in dealing with her sister.

Chapter 27

Everyone had just finished eating Thanksgiving dinner at the Hamilton home. Since the day Devin had expressed to his mother his displeasure of the way she had treated Leah at the shower, Lizzie had been putting forth greater effort to rebuild their relationship. Devin, Edward, Leah, and Kayla had retired to the den to watch the football game on television. Andrea was not into sports like her sister. Neither was Kayla, but she'd sit through anything just for the chance to be with her uncle, grandfather, and aunt. Andrea took Clayton with her to the sunroom on the back of the house. Lizzie decided to join them.

Lizzie cheerily said, "Let me hold my grandson," as she gently lifted the baby from his mother's arms. She sat down on the floral love seat opposite her daughter-in-law. She talked to Clayton a few minutes before focusing her attention on Andrea.

Lizzie had noticed how uncommunicative she had been during dinner. "You've been so quiet all day. What's wrong?"

Andrea was too ashamed to admit her feelings to anyone, especially her family. If they knew the truth, she would not be able to look them in the face ever again.

Andrea forced a smile on her face. "Just tired. That's all," she half-lied. After all, she was exhausted.

"Are you having problems sleeping?"

"Not really."

Lizzie supposed that coping with depression was a constant everyday battle. She felt guilty that, instead of encouraging Andrea to seek help, she had turned on everyone the night she had made the phone calls to Leah and Anna. "You've only been taking your medication a week, right?"

Andrea nodded. She was still trying to get used to the fact that she was on medication for depression. Hopefully, with time and the support and encouragement of her family, friends, and support group, she would be able to get past her feelings of inadequacy.

"Once you get it in your system, you'll start to feel better," Lizzie assured her.

"I hope so."

On the ride back home, from the backseat of Devin's Maxima, Andrea tried not to pay any attention to the happy couple as they chatted away about their wedding, which was now a little over a week away. The pair had attempted to engage her in conversation. Since she hadn't been very talkative, they had obviously given up. With Kayla and Clayton asleep in the back with her, Andrea attempted to get some rest herself.

The more she tried not to focus on Leah and Devin's chatter, the harder it was not to listen. They reminded her so much of her and Clayton. It hurt just to think about it. Andrea loved her sister and Devin, yet she was so jealous of what they shared. She felt extremely guilty. What kind of sister was she to feel this way about her own sibling? She hated herself. Her anger and jealousy had caused her to be so unkind toward Leah, who had stuck by her through thick and thin.

Finally, Andrea dozed off. When she opened her eyes, they had turned off the main highway and onto her street. She began to yawn as she stretched.

Leah turned around. "You awake, sleepyhead?"

Andrea managed a grin. "Yeah."

Leah asked, "You're really tired, aren't you?"

"Yeah. That nap helped."

"That's good," Leah said and turned back around in her seat.

When they got to Andrea's house, everyone exited the vehicle. Once inside, they made microwave s'mores and lounged around in front of the fireplace. While Devin played on the floor with the children, Andrea and Leah sat on the sofa.

Leah lightly touched her sister's hand. "You sure you're okay? You're awfully quiet." She wished Andrea would hurry up and get over her depression. *Patience, Lord. I gotta be patient.*

"I'm fine." Andrea could barely look Leah in the face as she spoke.

Leah attempted to cheer up her sister. "Your dress looks so good on you. Lavender's your color."

Andrea attempted a smile. "Thanks."

Leah threw back her head, grinning from ear to ear. "I'm so excited. I can't wait to walk down that aisle. I'm kind of nervous, too, though. I didn't think that would happen until the last minute. I hope I don't trip and fall. Wouldn't that be embarrassing?" she asked, looking at Andrea.

Andrea half-smiled. Trying with every fiber of her being to sound encouraging, she said, "That won't happen."

"I hope not. I just want everything to be perfect."

"It will be," Andrea assured her. She wanted Leah and Devin's wedding to be the best it could be, too, but each time she witnessed their joy, the pain in her heart grew more unbearable.

The next day was pleasant with the temperature in the mid-sixties and the sun beaming through the clouds. Andrea decided not to take the children to day care. She needed to spend some time with them. She couldn't remember the last time they'd done anything fun together, just the three of them. She decided to take advantage of the beautiful weather and take Kayla and Clayton to the zoo. She knew Clayton wouldn't remember the trip, but she believed he would enjoy the moment.

The children thoroughly enjoyed the zoo outing. The giraffes were Kayla's favorite, while Clayton seemed to like the polar bears best. Seeing the various animals made Andrea think about God and how His love, wisdom, and power were evident in the things He had created. He had been so good to her. Only she was in so much mental and emotional pain that she hadn't been able to see it. Without Clayton, she had felt as though she no longer had anything to be thankful for.

On the way home, they dropped off some film to be developed. Then they stopped at the mall. At Sears, Andrea bought some cute little outfits for Clayton, as though he needed more clothes. For Kayla, she found a pair of pretty, black, patent-leather shoes and a red, crush-velvet dress. Kayla also selected a pair of white tights, which she playfully called her pantyhose.

Afterwards, they went to the women's department. Andrea hadn't bought anything for herself in a while. She loved lingerie, but with Clayton gone, what was the point? However, she felt the need to buy something pretty for herself. She chose a flowing pink satin gown with a lacy bodice and matching bed jacket.

"Mommy, get these, too," Kayla insisted, pointing to a matching pair of pink slippers. "They're pretty. You like 'em?"

Andrea dropped her items into the cart and looked at the slippers. She picked them up. "Yes, I do. They're lovely."

Kayla smiled. "Get 'em, Mommy," she urged.

Andrea smiled as she dropped the shoes into the buggy.

After a couple of hours at the mall, they picked up their pictures and headed home. They went by the drive-through at McDonald's and got burgers and fries for supper.

Andrea pulled the jeep up close to the mailbox when they got home and let Kayla grab the mail. In the house, they sat down at the kitchen table to eat. When they were done, they retired to the family room to look at the pictures so they could put them in the scrapbook.

As Andrea and Kayla looked through the photos, they laughed and made comments. The ones they'd taken at the zoo had turned out well. When they got to the ones they had taken in January in the snow, Kayla showed them to Clayton.

"Look, Clayton," Kayla encouraged. "Me and Mommy took these before you were born." In his mother's lap, Clayton kicked his feet frantically as he squealed with glee.

They continued looking at the pictures. When they got to the last one, what Andrea and Kayla saw caught them by complete surprise. It was a picture of Andrea's husband acting silly as he made a face. Andrea had forgotten about the photo. Now she remembered. It was September—about a month before the accident. She had just inserted a fresh roll of film into the camera. She always liked to snap a picture when she put in new film.

Clayton had been in the family room watching television when Andrea had come in with the camera. When he had seen her, he'd put on one of his dramatic poses. She recalled she was laughing so hard she could barely snap the picture. She hadn't thought it had even taken.

Holding the photograph for her mother to see, Kayla announced, "Look, Mommy, it's Daddy."

Andrea gently withdrew the picture from her daughter's hand and held it directly in front of her face, looking at it longingly. She felt her heart pounding against her chest. "Yes. I had forgotten about this." Now they had a picture of Clayton during one of his silly moments that they could share with little Clayton. This was priceless indeed. Andrea managed to keep her tears at bay, although she had no idea how.

She handed the picture back to Kayla who proceeded to share it with her brother. "Look, Clayton, here's Daddy acting goofy. He was so funny."

"Yes, he was," Andrea agreed. "He always made us laugh."

After the children had been bathed and tucked into bed, Andrea looked through the day's mail, finding the usual bills and junk mail. One envelope, though, stood out among the others. It was addressed to her in a bright yellow envelope. The name and return address were those of her church. She opened it quickly. As she read it, tears of happiness washed over her face.

Someone Who Cares

When you feel lost and alone,
When you feel all hope is gone,
There is someone who cares for you,
Someone who is a friend forever true.

Someone who'll share a kind word or two,
Someone you can count on to be there for you,
Through the good and the bad, the sun and the rain,
To share your smiles of joy and hurt when you feel pain.

Though they can never know exactly how you feel,
Remember there is one who can your sorrow heal,
He's our Father, our Creator, who knows us inside out,
So remember that He cares for you beyond the shadow of a doubt.

The card was filled with the signatures of her church members. She had shut most of these people out of her life. Yet, they had thought enough of her to send this card. Words from the heart contained huge amounts of healing power.

Andrea decided to take a nice, long bubble bath. She placed some candles on the side of the tub, lit them, and plugged in the simmering pot of peach-scented liquid potpourri that sat on the counter.

Her doctor had told her about some relaxation techniques that would help ease stress, muscle tension, and anxiety. In the tub, Andrea lay back with her eyes shut and took slow breaths in and out, allowing her nostrils to take in the peachy scent of the potpourri as it filled the air. By the time she climbed out of the tub, she felt much more relaxed.

After slipping on her new lingerie ensemble, Andrea stared at herself in the oval-shaped, floor-length mirror in her bedroom. She was glad she'd treated herself. She felt pretty, even though her eyes were the only ones beholding her. She strolled back into the bathroom, pulled open a drawer, and removed a pearl barrette, which she used to pull her hair up on top of her head. Now she felt even prettier.

After unplugging the potpourri pot and blowing out the candles, Andrea went to her room. She flipped off the switch to the ceiling light and turned on the bedside lamp. She pulled off her robe and slid her feet out of her slippers. After neatly draping the garment across her chair, she climbed into bed. Then she leaned over, pulled open the top nightstand drawer, and took out her journal and a pen. She'd only made a few entries, but had found it to be extremely therapeutic, along with her support group.

She opened the book to a fresh page and jotted the date and a quick entry before falling asleep.

On Saturday, it rained all day. The temperature had plummeted overnight to the thirties, a big difference from the day before when Andrea and the children had gone to the zoo. She was glad they'd gotten the opportunity to enjoy their outing before the weather had turned cold again.

It was five o'clock, and Andrea was awaiting Alexander and

Ellen's arrival in an hour. She had called them earlier in the day and asked if they could come over. She had managed to throw together a huge pot of vegetable beef soup for them to eat with pimento cheese sandwiches and Kayla's favorite sandwich, peanut butter and jelly.

Making the call to the Knights had been hard. Andrea hated to tell them about her negative feelings, but she needed some spiritual direction. She hoped they wouldn't appear shocked when she told them or think badly of her. They were dear friends, and she wanted nothing to destroy their relationship.

When Alexander and Ellen arrived, everyone went to the dining room to eat. Andrea and the children had been eating a lot in the kitchen lately. Andrea felt the change of atmosphere would do them good.

When Alexander said the blessing, for the first time in three months, Andrea joined in prayer as she held his hand and bowed her head. However, when she said, "Amen," she only mumbled it almost under her breath.

Everyone enjoyed the meal. Afterwards, Andrea and Ellen cleaned up the kitchen while Alexander played with the children. Then Ellen gave Clayton his bath while Andrea helped Kayla with hers.

Later, with the kids snugly tucked away in their beds, the adults retired to the family room.

Ellen said, "Andrea, dinner was delicious. There's nothing like a good bowl of hot soup to warm you up on a cold day. Yours is the best. It warmed up my tired ol' bones."

Andrea smiled. "Thanks, Ellen. I'm glad you liked it."

Alexander added, "Yes, we really enjoyed it. Thank you for inviting us."

"You're welcome," Andrea said. "Please tell everyone I said thank you for the lovely card. I got it yesterday. It was the perfect end to a perfect day." *Almost perfect.* Things would never be the same without Clayton.

Alexander assured Andrea, "We'll tell them. We all love you."

Andrea blinked. "I know you do. I love you all, too." Without thinking about what to say next, she began, "Losing Clay is the hardest thing I've ever been faced with. I thought my faith was strong. I never guessed anything would cause me to turn my back on God. I've been angry with Him ever since it happened, but I was so afraid to admit it and talk to Him about it, that I just stopped talking to Him at all.

"I was afraid I'd say something awful to Him. Several times, I found myself questioning Him in my mind. That was bad enough. Even though He knew what I was thinking and feeling, I just didn't think I could talk to Him about any of it. Have I lost his favor?" Andrea looked sorrowfully at her friends, hoping the answer would be no.

Alexander spoke. "Andrea, there's a phrase on the card we sent you that says God knows us inside out. Tell me, what does that mean to you?"

Andrea was not expecting Alexander to answer her question with a question. But then, she remembered that asking thought-provoking questions was one of his teaching techniques—just like Jesus.

Andrea replied, "To me, it means that He knows everything there is to know about me. He knows me better than anyone else, even better than I know myself."

Alexander nodded. "You know, the one hundred and third Psalm in verse thirteen says God knows our frame and remembers that we're dust. So as you said, He knows everything about us because He made us. Even though you're experiencing some negative feelings, God knows your heart. He knows that is not how you *want* to feel.

"Being bothered by it is an indication that you want to please God, but don't keep beating yourself up over it. Pray to Him. Ask Him to help you deal with your feelings and, hopefully, overcome them. Ask Him for patience with yourself, because sometimes we're harder on ourselves than He is. He knows you've suffered a tremendous loss, and He'll help you through it."

Andrea was feeling a sense of relief. She had half expected Alexander and Ellen to express their displeasure—and God's—at what she'd just told them. She recalled how nonjudgmental they were. She wished she'd talked to them about her feelings sooner. However, she wasn't through yet. She still had a couple more things to share with them.

Andrea confessed, "I haven't prayed in so long, I don't know if I can. I feel that God and I are two friends who were once close but have grown apart, and I just don't know what to say to Him. And if I try to talk to Him, will He even listen?"

Alexander said, "Believe it or not, we all feel that same way many times. And when I say *we*, I'm including myself."

Andrea was shocked. "You're a minister. I find that very hard to believe."

Alexander humbly replied, "Ministers aren't God. We're human and imperfect just like everybody else. We have our low moments, too. You know, Andrea, there have been times I couldn't pray and times I thought God wasn't listening, but I still tried to pour my heart out to Him. Sometimes I couldn't even find the right words, and at times, I may have only said a sentence or two.

"And when I was done, I'd say to myself, 'That was pitiful. Why would God listen to such a pathetic prayer?' But not long after that, I saw indications that He had listened. You see, even though I couldn't express myself to Him, He saw what was in my heart. So even when we find it difficult to pray, God knows what we want to say but can't."

Andrea nodded. She could easily recall similar experiences of God answering her pleas, even when she felt she had not quite gotten through to Him with words. She was beginning to feel a healing within her that she had not felt in quite a while. However, the worst was yet to come. She wanted to get it over with, so she blurted, "I have another confession."

Andrea couldn't bear to look at Alexander and Ellen this time. As she spoke, she looked down at her hands as they lay on her lap. "I'm jealous of Leah and Devin." She still refused to look up. "I mean, I love them, but they remind me so much of me and Clay. It's so hard seeing them—any happy couple—together . . . but especially them. I'm happy for them, but there's a part of me that envies them. I wish I still had what they have and are about to have once they get married. I don't know if I can be Leah's maid of honor feeling this way. I told her I'd do it, but I don't know. Things are hard enough as it is. I know it's terrible. I hate feeling this way."

Alexander let his wife speak this time. "Andrea, do you think what you're feeling is uncommon?"

Confused, Andrea looked at Ellen.

Ellen went on. "Do you think that other people in your situation perhaps feel the same way?"

Andrea's response was slow in coming. "I don't know. I haven't really thought about it."

Ellen said, "Seeing people with something you once had and cherished but no longer have can trigger memories of what you lost. You're missing a huge chunk of what made you happy and whole. Jealousy or envy is a natural human tendency that someone in your situation may go through.

"Again, you don't want to feel this way, but you do, so talk to God about it. And you know, since you felt open enough to discuss your feelings with Alex and me, now we, too, can pray on your behalf regarding these matters. God wants us to pray for one another. Remember, there is strength in numbers."

Andrea felt as though several huge weights had been lifted off her shoulders. Alexander and Ellen prayed with her before they left. Before she went to bed, she got down on her knees and poured her heart out to God.

"Oh, Heavenly Father, it's been a long time since I've really talked to you. I'm so sorry for the way I've been acting—how I've treated everybody, especially my sister Leah. Please help me to deal with my negative feelings so I can get on with my life. In Jesus' dear name, I offer this prayer. Amen."

Though it was all she could say for now, it was a simple, yet earnest, plea to her Creator.

Chapter 28

Andrea went to her first support group meeting on Monday evening. She was surprised at the large number of people in attendance. She supposed more were suffering from the loss of a spouse than she had realized.

Different ones shared their experiences. One woman who looked extremely young, perhaps in her mid- to late twenties, had been a newlywed on her honeymoon when her husband was robbed and shot. Andrea's heart went out to the young widow. She and her husband had not even begun to share their married lives with each other when tragedy struck.

An older gentleman's wife of forty-three years had died recently of cancer. They'd shared a lifetime. But did that make his loss any less painful? Perhaps more so.

Andrea glanced around the room, attempting not to outwardly scrutinize the many faces she beheld. Each had a story to tell. Some similar. Others different.

At the next opportunity, Andrea suddenly heard herself saying, "It's been over a year since my husband was killed by a drunk driver. I'm still not over it. I don't think I ever will be. There'll always be a hole in my heart. I've had many low moments since he's been gone.

"My family and friends tried to support me all the way, but I was so full of anger that I rejected them. I used to think my faith would help me endure anything. It has been put to one of life's ultimate tests, and it almost failed. My heart and prayers go out to each one of you—that you not give up in your fight to live, even though your loved ones are gone."

After the meeting, Andrea found herself mingling for a few minutes, conversing with different people. She still had a long way to go, but it felt good to have people to talk to who could understand what she was going through. Again, her mother had been right. She couldn't help but wonder: if she hadn't fought against getting help for so long, how much progress would she have already made by now?

When Andrea went to Leah's to pick up the children, her sister asked, "So how was it?"

Andrea leaned back against the sofa, watching Kayla play with Clayton on the floor.

The experience could be summed up in one word. "Soothing."

Leah smiled. "That's good." She was thrilled that her sister had finally found the support she so desperately needed.

Wednesday morning, Andrea dropped the children off at day care. She decided to go walking in her neighborhood. It wasn't an easy decision, though. She would much rather have gone straight back to bed. However, she was ready to get on with her life. If she didn't start now, she feared she would waste away.

Leah and Devin's wedding was now just three days away, and she was looking forward to her parents' arrival tomorrow.

When she returned from her walk, there was a message on the machine from Leah. Andrea was still a little stressed about the wedding and couldn't talk to her sister right now. She took a shower. When she was done, she put on a pair of black jogging pants and a white T-shirt. She grabbed her journal and pen and sat down in her chair facing the window. For a moment, she just sat staring outside.

From where she sat, she could see two squirrels scampering up a pine tree. They appeared so free and happy—not a care in the world. She hadn't felt like that in a very long time. She began her entry in her diary.

Leah's wedding is three days away. She and Devin are about to have what I lost with Clay. I'm happy for them, but sad for me—because the more I see how much they love each other, the more my heart aches from not having Clay in my life. I'm not sure I can go to the wedding let alone be in it. I'm a horrible sister. Leah really stood by my side when I needed her, and this is how I repay her?

Andrea closed the book, got up, and ambled over to her night-stand. She opened the drawer and dropped in the journal and the pen.

A few minutes later, Glenn called. It was so good to hear his voice. They hadn't talked since she'd gone on leave two weeks ago.

Andrea smiled. "Glenn, hey. How are you?"

"I'm fine. How are you doing?"

"I'm holding on. It's so good to hear your voice. How's everyone at the office and your family?"

"Everybody's fine—at home and at the office. We miss you. Your patients are always asking about you. They miss you, too."

"I miss them. I miss you all."

Glenn felt the urge to ask Andrea if she had any idea when she might return to work, but he didn't. He had no desire to make her feel pressured into coming back before she was ready.

He asked, "So how are Kayla and little Clayton? I bet Clayton's growing up a storm."

Andrea smiled again. "They're fine. Yes, he is."

They talked a few minutes longer before saying good-bye.

Andrea began to think about all the special people she had in her life. So many people in the world were totally alone with no family or friends who loved them. For the first time in a long while, she felt truly blessed.

The next afternoon, Kayla sat looking out the window of the family room, anticipating the arrival of her grandparents. As soon as she saw Leah's car pull into the driveway, she yelled, "Mommy! Mommy! They're here! Mee Maw and Paw Paw are here!"

Andrea almost ran from the kitchen. "Okay. I'm coming."

The two ran outside to greet Anna and William. After everyone had their hugs and kisses, everybody went inside.

"Kayla," William said, "you look like you've gotten taller since the last time I saw you. You been eating your spinach?"

Kayla frowned, "Paw Paw, you know I don't like spinach."

William tickled Kayla. "Don't like spinach. Shame on you. Where's my grandson?" he asked of no one in particular.

"He's in his room," Kayla happily informed her grandfather.

Anna whispered, "Is he asleep?"

Andrea answered, "Probably not. When I laid him down a minute ago, he was wide awake. He was playing when I left."

Anna proudly offered, "I'll go check on him."

Everyone else went to the family room. A moment later, Anna walked in carrying her grandson snugly in her arms.

William smiled. "There's my little man looking like his Paw Paw."

Everyone laughed as William went over and removed Clayton from Anna's arms. "What are y'all laughing at?" He pressed his face up against Clayton's little chubby one. "Look. Now doesn't he look like me?"

Anna was the only one brave enough to say, "Yeah, on the bottom of his feet."

Everybody laughed.

William playfully moaned, "Oh, that hurt." To Clayton, he asked, "Did you hear that, sport? Mee Maw made a funny. It was so funny, I forgot to laugh."

A huge grin spread across the width of Clayton's face.

"Oh," William said to Clayton. "So you think it's funny, too. You're gonna take your grandma's side against me. Okay. I see how it's gonna be now. That's all right. I bet your sister wouldn't do me like that. Kayla, whose side are you on?"

Kayla sat on the sofa between her mother and aunt, grinning and shaking her head from side to side. "Sorry, Paw Paw. You're on your own. I'm stickin' with the ladies."

Laughter filled the room.

"Okay," William jokingly rebutted. "You're gonna need me. One day when you're old and gray, you're gonna say, 'Paw Paw. Paw Paw. I need you, Paw Paw.'"

Kayla laughed. "Paw Paw," she moaned.

"What?" William chuckled.

"Nothing, Paw Paw."

Soon the laughter had subsided somewhat. Andrea loved her father's sense of humor. She had forgotten how to laugh. He was helping her to rekindle her happy spirit. She wished her parents lived closer. Her children needed them. She needed them.

Chapter 29

Anna gave the beef stew she had prepared in the Crock-Pot for lunch a quick stir. With Kayla at school, Clayton asleep, and William having lunch with Leah and Devin, mother and daughter had an opportunity to talk.

Andrea sat at the kitchen table sipping on a cup of hot peppermint tea.

"It's going good," Andrea said. "I mostly go online. The group meets twice a week on Mondays and Wednesdays in Atlanta. I went Monday. It was an eye-opening experience. Hearing other people talk about what they've been through helps me to see I'm not as alone as I previously felt. I mean, I know I wasn't the only one on the face of the earth suffering in this way, but it sure felt like it."

Andrea gave her mother a tender gaze as she went on. "You were right, Mama. If I'd just listened to you, I wouldn't have wasted all that time feeling sorry for myself and being angry at everyone who tried to help me. There's no telling how far along toward recovery I'd be. I'm so sorry for everything I put you and Daddy through." She bowed her head in shame.

Anna set two bowls of stew topped with corn bread on the table. She sat down. "Andrea, look at me," she kindly demanded.

Andrea willingly obeyed.

Anna said, "Don't go through life worrying about the things you should have done. You'll drive yourself crazy if you do. You had to make the decision yourself as to when to seek help—because you had to do it for you, not for me. You're making progress one day at a time. You can't do everything all at once, but you'll get there, so don't worry about the past. You just take care of the here and now."

"Thank you, Mama."

Anna smiled. "You don't have to thank me. I'm your mama, but you're welcome. Excuse me a moment." Just as she closed her eyes and bowed her head to say her blessing, Anna felt Andrea's hand on hers.

Anna intertwined her fingers in her daughter's and said the blessing out loud, after which they both concurred, "Amen."

It filled Anna's heart with gladness to know that Andrea was praying again.

Andrea calmly announced, "Dr. Murphy said that setting goals helps fight depression. She said it'll help me to regain a sense of control over my life. I'm trying not to set them too high, though. I need to start small and work my way up."

Anna smiled as she closed her eyes briefly and uttered a quick expression of thanks to God for giving her daughter what she needed in order to get on with her life. "So what are some of your goals?"

Andrea sensed that her mother was keenly interested in what she purposed to do, and it made her want to share her plans with her, even though the only two things she'd written down might seem somewhat silly and childish to the average person. Grinning sheepishly, she replied, "Well, I'm making a list. Let me show you." Andrea sprang up from her chair, hastened toward the computer, and clutched a piece of paper in her hand. She hurried back to her seat, where she plopped down and passed the list across the table to her mother. "Read it."

When Anna glanced down, she noted mentally that Andrea had

written only two items. She read in an undertone, "One: get out of bed. Two: face another day."

Andrea wasn't kidding. She was starting small, but these were things that had probably seemed insurmountable to her months ago. Anna's face beamed as she looked adoringly at her daughter. "This is wonderful."

In the next instant, Andrea was laughing.

Not knowing quite how to respond, Anna finally joined in the merriment.

Andrea chuckled, "I told you I was starting small."

Anna smiled. "This is good, honey. I'm so proud of you. You've come a long way. Can you imagine the number of people in your shoes who don't make it this far? You keep it up." She wondered if her daughter had considered when she'd return to church. Of course, she'd be there tomorrow for the wedding, but that would be different than sitting through an actual service.

Leah was ecstatic that the wedding rehearsal was going smoothly. She hoped it was an indication of how the wedding itself would go.

It had been about three months since Andrea had set foot in church. She felt strangely out of place. She envisioned God looking down on her disapprovingly. Immediately, she recalled some of the things Alexander and Ellen had shared with her during their recent visit to her home. The anxiety began to subside. Surprisingly, she made it through the rehearsal. Afterward, everyone met at the restaurant. During dinner, Andrea felt a pain in her heart when she unwittingly observed Leah kiss Devin's cheek.

Andrea quickly scolded herself. *What's wrong with you? You've got to get over these feelings so you can be there for your sister tomorrow.*

Chapter 30

As Andrea sat at her bathroom vanity attempting to get ready for her sister's wedding, she told herself over and over that she couldn't go through with it. She had tried. She had prayed and asked God to help her do it, but she guessed He still wasn't listening to her prayers.

It was almost one o'clock. The wedding started at two, and they were to be at the church at one-thirty. They needed to be going out the door by at least one-fifteen.

Everyone else was ready. Anna had helped Kayla get dressed, while William had tended to their grandson. Anna went to check on Andrea. When she saw her simply sitting at the vanity in her robe and with rollers still in her hair, Anna couldn't believe her eyes.

She stood in the doorway, staring at her daughter as she attempted to choose her words carefully. "Andrea, honey, we're supposed to leave in fifteen minutes. Is there a problem? Do you need some help?"

Andrea simply stared back at her reflection in the mirror, not responding to her mother's questions.

Anna walked over and gently placed her hand on her daughter's shoulder. "Honey, what's wrong?"

Still, Andrea would not speak.

Anna pulled down the lid on the toilet and sat down. "Andrea, talk to me, please," she pleaded. "Tell me what's wrong so I can help you."

Andrea did not respond. Anna decided to go get her husband. When William entered the bathroom, he asked, "Andrea, is something wrong? Why aren't you dressed?"

Tears streamed down Andrea's face. "I can't do it, Daddy."

William was confused. "Can't do what?"

"I can't be Leah's maid of honor. I can't go to the wedding. I'm staying home."

William couldn't believe what he was hearing. Andrea couldn't miss her own sister's wedding. He panicked. He couldn't let this happen. "Your sister's counting on you to be there."

Andrea shook her head. "I can't."

"Andrea, please," her father begged as though his life depended on her being present. "Leah will be heartbroken if you don't show up at all. You don't want that to happen, do you?"

Andrea said nothing this time.

William went in search of Anna. "She says she's not going to the wedding."

Anna's eyes were huge. "What? Why not?"

"She won't say. She just said she can't go. Listen—why don't you and the kids go on? We were gonna go in her Jeep. I'll ask her for the keys. You and the kids can go, and I'll talk to her. Maybe I can get her to change her mind, and she and I can come in Clay's car."

Anna protested, "You'll both be late if you don't hurry up and leave."

"Well, there's no sense in all of us being late." William looked at his watch. "It's almost one-fifteen. If you and the kids leave now, you'll make it to the church by one-thirty. The wedding doesn't start 'til two, so even if Andrea and I don't leave 'til say one-thirty,

218

we'll still get there before two. There'll still be time for us to get in line. Okay?"

Anna wasn't liking these last-minute adjustments at all. She agreed reluctantly. "All right."

After William brought her the keys, she gathered up the children, and they were out the door.

William went back to talk to Andrea. She had moved from the bathroom to her chair in the bedroom. He pulled up a chair and sat beside her.

"Andrea, come on," he pleaded. "Please get dressed. We still have a few minutes, so we can still make it to the church before two. You don't have to be in the wedding. You can sit with Clayton and your mother and me."

"Daddy, you don't understand."

William took his daughter's hand. "What don't I understand? Tell me so I can try."

Andrea didn't answer. She was too ashamed.

William asked, "Is it because you're still grieving over Clay and a wedding right now will make you sadder? You know, that happens to lots of people. You've been through a lot. We all understand that. Your sister understands, but this is her special day, and she wants you there. Sometimes we have to face our fears in order to overcome them."

Andrea could listen no more to her father's assumptions. She had to tell him the truth no matter how disappointed in her he'd be.

Before she realized it, she was blurting out, "I can't go because I'm jealous of Leah and Devin."

William was shocked. He had not expected this. Growing up, Andrea and Leah never appeared to be jealous of each other.

Andrea mistook her father's silence for disappointment, as more tears streaked her face. "I told you you wouldn't understand. I know you're disappointed in me, and I'm sorry. I don't want to feel this way. I can't help it. I've tried to stop. I've prayed about it, but the feelings won't go away. I just . . ."

219

"Stop," William politely ordered his daughter. "I'm not disappointed in you. You have been through one of the most devastating things that a person can go through. You still love your sister. I can see how much this is hurting you—how it's tearing you apart. I'm sorry I was pressuring you. I didn't know you were having these feelings.

"Now that they're out, you can talk about them. Keeping them bottled up inside only made it harder for you to deal with them. You have a good heart, Andrea. Stop torturing yourself. No one in their right mind would condemn you for what you feel. At some point in our lives, all of us have probably been jealous of someone we love."

Andrea felt like a little girl again. "Oh, Daddy." She grabbed her father, clinging to him tightly. He held her and let her cry.

When she finally broke their embrace and spoke, William felt his heart drop. "Please tell Leah I'm sorry for missing her wedding." Andrea trusted her father not to tell her sister what she'd just confessed to him so she didn't see the need to make that request of him.

Disappointed, William stood and glanced at his watch. It was one-thirty. Sadly, he replied, "I'll tell her. Is it okay if I drive Clay's car?"

"Sure. The keys are on a green key ring on the peg in the kitchen."

"Thank you."

"You're welcome."

William leaned down and kissed his daughter's cheek before leaving. When he arrived at the church at about a quarter before two, Leah practically ran to him when she caught sight of him.

"Where's Andrea? Mama said she was having some problems getting ready." Looking around, Leah asked again, "Where is she?"

It broke William's heart to give his daughter the news. "She asked me to tell you she's sorry—she's not coming."

Leah went into a panic as she stared at her father and bombarded him with questions and expressions. "Not coming. What do you mean she's not coming? Are you serious? I don't understand. How could she do this to me?" She choked back tears, throwing herself into her father's arms.

William gently rubbed Leah's back. He urged, "Don't cry. You'll mess up your makeup. I know it's not easy, but it's hard on your sister, too. You know she'd be here if she could."

William was able to calm Leah down somewhat. While she went to touch up her makeup, he informed his wife that Andrea would be a no-show.

Anna couldn't believe this was happening. Just when it seemed that things were getting better, this had to happen.

Sadly, Leah began her walk down the aisle. This was supposed to be one of the happiest moments of her life. Instead, it was one of the saddest. As she walked arm in arm with her father down the aisle, she gazed lovingly at the man who was about to become her husband. Devin's grin was huge as he smiled at her. She managed to return his smile, despite how she was feeling. Now she felt she could finally relate to how Devin felt without his brother beside him as best man. The only difference was that Clayton had no choice. Andrea was capable of physically being there but had chosen not to. Leah felt a piercing pain in her heart.

As she and her father got closer to the attendants, Leah looked at the spot where Andrea would have been. At first, she thought her mind was playing tricks on her. She looked again, and there was Andrea standing in her position. When their eyes met, Leah detected a faint smile on her sister's face which grew larger as Leah smiled back at her.

With the bride and father of the bride now in place, the ceremony began. After the bride and groom had been pronounced husband and wife and allowed their first kiss as a married couple, Leah gave her sister a powerful hug. Andrea's embrace was just as strong. Then Leah took her husband's hand as they made their way up the aisle.

The reception was extravagant. The chocolate fondue fountains—another one of Leah's yearnings—made a hit with everyone. White, dark, and milk chocolate spilled up and over the fountains as guests covered fruit and other bits of sweet treats underneath the smooth creamy substances. Devin had to admit that he was extremely pleased with the whole affair, even though it had been expensive.

Later, an announcement was made that Mr. and Mrs. Devin Scott Hamilton were now going to have their first dance as husband and wife to Larry Graham's "One in a Million."

As Andrea watched the happy couple, her eyes welled up with tears of happiness at the love the two had for one another. After her father had gone, she had poured her heart out to God, begging Him to give her the strength to go to her sister's wedding. She had needed to be there as much as she needed the air she breathed. Being present meant that much to her. Fortunately, she had been able to catch a neighbor at home who brought her to the church.

When the newlyweds' dance was over, Leah slipped away from her husband for a brief moment to talk to her sister.

Leah sat down on a vacant seat beside Andrea. "Thank you. I'm so glad you decided to come. I'm so sorry. I should have known how difficult the wedding would be for you. I was so wrapped up in myself and what I wanted that I forgot about what was best for you."

Andrea spoke from her heart. "You have nothing to be sorry for. It was your wedding. Why shouldn't you have been happy? I'm sorry for stealing your joy."

Leah smiled. "It's all in the past, so let's just put it behind us."

Andrea smiled. "Okay."

When "My Girl" started to play, Devin grabbed Kayla by the

hand and led her out onto the dance floor. Andrea and Leah watched them dance.

Andrea commented, "That girl loves her some Uncle Devin. Look at 'em."

Leah's smile broadened. "Yeah. He loves him some Kayla, too. She's a special little girl, Andrea. She has a strong spirit. She got a double dose from the Washingtons and the Hamiltons."

Andrea agreed wholeheartedly. "I know. There were times I wanted to give up, but she wouldn't let me."

Leah grabbed her sister's hand as they watched the loves of their lives dance.

Chapter 31

The next day, Andrea drove her parents to the airport. The ride home was anything but quiet, with Kayla chattering away in the backseat. Andrea smiled. Leah was so right. Kayla had the Washington spirit. Mixed with the Hamilton blood, she was an incredible little girl.

"Mommy, when's Aunt Leah and Uncle Devin coming home?"

Andrea answered, "They'll be home Saturday."

"Why do they have to take such a long honeymoon? I miss them."

Andrea giggled. "Well, honey, they've only been gone since yesterday. Be patient."

"I wish it would snow."

That was kids for you. Talking about one thing, and the next minute, on a totally different subject. "It's a little early for snow. We usually don't get our first snow 'til January."

"But Mommy, it doesn't usually snow in April either, but you told me one time it did. Remember?"

Yes, Andrea remembered that day in 1987. It was uncommon, but it had happened. "Yes, I remember. So who knows? I guess it could snow, but don't get your hopes up."

On Wednesday, the Knights babysat the children while Andrea went to her support group. This was only her second meeting, but already, she was beginning to feel its healing power.

On Friday, Andrea went to school and read to Kayla's class and helped make games and books. At lunchtime, she ate with Kayla. Andrea enjoyed her visit to the school as much as her daughter. Andrea and Clayton had always been involved in activities at Kayla's school. However, after Clayton's passing, Andrea had lost the will to stay involved. Now her spirit of giving was being rekindled.

As Andrea put a forkful of spaghetti in her mouth, she thought of Jesus' words quoted by the Apostle Paul as recorded in Acts 20:35: *It is more blessed to give than to receive.* Andrea agreed wholeheartedly.

After lunch was over, Andrea and Kayla said good-bye. Kayla hugged her mother tightly around her waist.

"Thank you, Mommy. I'm so glad you came."

"You're welcome, baby. I had a good time. See ya this afternoon." Andrea brushed her lips against the top of Kayla's head.

"Okay."

They were still waving as Kayla turned the corner to return to her classroom.

Andrea felt good. On the ride home, she hummed all the way.

"So, how was Hawaii?" Andrea asked the newlyweds as they all sat around the dining room table.

"Fabulous." Leah grinned. "The islands are so beautiful. It's like being in paradise." She burst out laughing. "You should have seen Devin doing the hula dance."

Devin laughed. "What's so funny? You were dancing so hard, I thought you were gonna hurt yourself."

Everyone laughed.

Leah said, "Don't listen to him, y'all."

Devin said, "It's true. You should have seen her." He slid his chair back, stood up, and began to do the dance in imitation of his new bride.

More laughter filled the air.

Kayla bolted from her seat and began imitating her uncle.

Andrea and Leah were laughing and shaking their heads. Soon they, too, had joined in. From his carrier seat on the floor, Clayton kicked his feet and waved his arms in the air, shaking his rattle to his family's movements. A minute later, everyone plopped back down in their seats.

Leah said, "Sis. Lil Bit. Dinner was delicious. We couldn't have had a better welcome-home gift. Thank you."

"Yeah," Devin agreed. "Thanks. It was good."

Andrea and Kayla smiled as they responded in unison, "You're welcome."

In the family room, Leah and Devin passed out the souvenir gifts they'd brought for everyone. Kayla got her own little hula skirt. Andrea loved her hand-painted porcelain pin which displayed her name in black next to a bunch of brightly colored flowers. Clayton's gift was a little straw hat with his name on it.

When Leah and Devin prepared to leave, Andrea felt her heart drop into the pit of her stomach. She didn't want them to go. Their happy spirit was rubbing off on her.

At the front door, Leah said, "Lil Bit, we'll pick you up in the morning at nine-thirty. Okay?"

"Okay." Kayla grinned.

Andrea now began to feel a different pain in her heart. Kayla had stopped asking her when she was going back to church. Had her little girl given up on her?

Over the next couple of weeks, Andrea continued to make progress as she attended her support group once a week, joined in the online discussions, and took her medication. However, she still felt that something else was lacking in her life. God. She'd lost the closeness she once felt toward Him. It had been so easy to drift away. Coming back was the hard part.

Andrea had decided that this Christmas she and the kids would go to New York to visit her parents. She knew she had probably given them the shock of a lifetime with that news.

Now as she sat in their living room, staring out the window, her mind raced with thoughts of the past fifteen months. New York was a beautiful city. Her parents lived in a nice neighborhood. Andrea could see why they had come to love it. Still, she wished they'd move back to Georgia.

Her thoughts were brought to a conclusion when Kayla burst into the room shouting, "Mommy! Look at what Mee Maw and Paw Paw gave me."

Andrea's eyes fell upon the most beautiful black porcelain doll she'd ever seen. She carefully grasped it in her hands. "Oh, sweetie, she's beautiful. Now you need to be really careful with her so you don't break her."

Kayla nodded in agreement. "I know. Mee Maw and Paw Paw told me. I'm gonna start me a collection."

Andrea smiled. She was glad her daughter had found a new interest. "That's wonderful."

Kayla grinned as she carefully removed the doll from her mother's grasp, turned, and skipped away.

Over the next few days, Andrea enjoyed just being with her parents. Since the weather was so cold, she and the children didn't get in much sightseeing, but Andrea didn't mind. They got to see some of her parents' friends and church members, whom she hadn't seen in a while, when they stopped by for a visit. Most of them confessed that they'd heard she and the children were visiting. They also wanted to meet Clayton II, whom they'd never seen, except for pictures the proud grandparents had shown them. They also desired to see Andrea and Kayla, since quite some time had passed since their last visit. When they gave Andrea their condolences regarding Clayton's death, she choked back her tears. She appreciated their sentiments, although their acknowledgments still stirred up painful emotions.

When it came time to go home on Friday, Andrea hated to leave. At the airport, she found it extremely difficult to pull away from her parents' embraces. Kayla's constant chattering on the plane ride home kept her mind occupied.

As soon as Leah spied her trio, she ran to embrace them. "How was your trip?"

"It was good," Andrea said, smiling.

"Yeah, Aunt Leah," Kayla interjected. "I had fun. Just wait 'til you see what Mee Maw and Paw Paw got me. You'll love it."

Leah smiled as she hugged her niece. "Well, you've got me all excited. I can't wait to see it." She reached over and playfully pinched Clayton's cheek. "How ya doing, sport? Did you have a good time at Mee Maw and Paw Paw's, too?" The baby awarded his aunt a smile.

The next night, Andrea allowed LeaAnn to sleep over. She wished she had the energy the girls had. When she finally got them into bed around nine o'clock, Kayla moaned from her bed.

"Mommy, why can't we stay up and see the new year when it comes?"

Andrea responded, "Aren't you and LeaAnn going with Aunt Leah and Uncle Devin to church in the morning?"

"Yes."

"Well, you need to get your rest so you can get up early."

"But, Mommy . . ."

Andrea's voice was stern. "Don't 'but Mommy' me. Go to sleep. Good night," she said as she kissed Kayla's forehead.

"Good night," Kayla said, pouting.

After pulling the covers up over her daughter, Andrea went to the twin bed where Kayla's friend was lying and gently pulled up the covers for her. She leaned down, kissing the child on her forehead. "Good night, LeaAnn."

LeaAnn smiled. "Good night, Ms. Andrea."

Andrea turned out the light and partially closed the door on her way out. In the family room, she tried reading the Bible, but was soon fast asleep. When she woke up, she looked at the clock on the wall. It was 12:43 A.M. The new year had come. She felt as though she had aged about ten years just in the past year.

The next morning, Andrea arose early and helped Kayla and LeaAnn get ready for church. Later, as she sat rocking Clayton to sleep, she began thinking about returning to work. It was a new year. She was feeling much better. Now would be a good time to go back. *What about church? When are you gonna go back there?* She didn't know the answer.

Andrea decided she would give Glenn a ring later in the afternoon and talk to him about returning to work. For the moment, she put church out of her mind.

Chapter 32

It felt so good to be back at work—doing something she loved. Andrea had been back for almost two weeks. January was almost over. She grinned as she eyed her display of cards, scattered about the family room, which her patients had sent to the office while she was on leave.

Lionel Redding, her favorite little patient, was a gifted artist and had drawn her a lovely picture of a field of flowers surrounding a huge tree with birds flying overhead. Andrea had it framed and hung on the wall of the family room, along with a picture of a beautiful mountain scene that Kayla had done last year in school.

She hadn't yet had an opportunity to listen to the day's messages on the answering machine, so as soon as the kids were in bed, Andrea played the messages, sitting down with a pen and pad of paper. She smiled as she listened to the one her sister had left about how she'd burned her and Devin's dinner. She said her house smelled like a smokehouse. Devin told her he liked his potatoes a little on the charred side—it added flavor.

Her parents had called. She'd call them back after she retrieved all her messages. The next voice Andrea heard was that of a male who identified himself as Walter Oglesby with the Alabama

District Attorney's Office of Cleburne County. The man responsible for Clayton's death was going to trial in March for the offense of vehicular homicide. The district attorney's office wanted her to go before the judge, the jury, and the defendant and tell them how her husband's death had affected her family.

Andrea grew still as she sat with her hand over her mouth. She was not expecting anything like this. She didn't hear the remaining messages as they played. Her mind digressed back to that tragic night. Clayton had been to a seminar in Birmingham and was on his way home. He'd made it as far as Heflin, Alabama, on Interstate 20 when he'd been hit by the car.

She was just getting to a point where she was trying to put Clayton's death behind her and get on with her life. The wounds were slowly beginning to heal. Andrea wasn't sure her heart could take reopening them. What would she do?

Andrea returned her parents' call. She didn't hesitate to tell them of the DA's phone call.

Anna was afraid for her daughter. She didn't think it was a good idea for Andrea to take on such a huge task. Andrea had made great strides in her recovery, and Anna didn't want her to have a relapse.

"Are you going to do it?" Anna asked, praying the answer would be no.

"I don't know. It's such a shock. I wasn't expecting this."

For the next few days, Andrea could think of nothing but the DA's phone call. This was a decision that needed prayerful consideration, and she had been praying all week long. She'd finally been able to come to a decision.

When she went to lunch on Friday, Andrea dialed the DA's telephone number on her cell phone as she sat in her car before going into Wendy's. She'd probably picked a bad time to call. Maybe the man was at lunch as she was. Then she remembered that Alabama was on central time, an hour behind Georgia, making it a little after eleven there. But some people went to lunch at eleven o'clock.

The telephone was answered on the third ring by a pleasant-sounding woman. When Andrea asked if she could speak to Mr. Walter Oglesby, she was surprised when she was immediately transferred to another line, which was answered on the second ring. She had expected to be put on hold for a few minutes.

"Walter Oglesby. DA's Office."

Andrea suddenly grew speechless. "Ah . . . Mr. Oglesby, hi. My name is Andrea Hamilton. You left a message on my machine Monday regarding the vehicular homicide of my husband, Clayton Hamilton."

"Oh, yes, Ms. Hamilton. I'm glad you called. I was going to call you back today, since I hadn't heard from you. I'm so sorry about your husband. We really need your help, especially in the closing phase of this trial. Will you be there?"

"Well . . ." Andrea stuttered, "I don't think I can sit through the actual trial itself." She did not wish to hear all the awful details of what happened that night. "Can I just come for the closing?"

Walter understood. Some people felt the need to know every detail of what took place; others didn't. "Sure, Ms. Hamilton, that's fine. Whatever you want. We just need you to make everyone in the courtroom aware of how your husband's death has affected your family."

"Okay. I'll do it."

"Good. I'll keep you posted, and thank you for calling."

When the call ended, Andrea wondered if she had done the right thing.

When Anna hung up the phone, she shook her head sadly. "She's gonna do it," she said.

William took his wife's hand in his. "She'll be all right. She's been through a lot. Maybe this will be part of the healing process. I'm sure it wasn't an easy decision for her to make, but she probably feels it's something she has to do."

Anna looked at her husband, tears in her eyes. "She doesn't *have* to do it, William. Nobody's forcing her. She could have said no. Why is she putting herself through this? I worry about her so much. This just may be the thing to really push her over the edge. You saw how things got between her and Leah."

William thought about what Andrea had told him the day of Leah's wedding. About how she was jealous of Leah and Devin. He still had not mentioned it to Anna or Leah and had no intentions of doing so. He didn't see the need to. He often wondered how long after Clayton's death Andrea had been carrying those feelings around. Perhaps speaking at the trial would allow her to unload some more emotions she was burdened down with.

Saturday morning, Leah expressed disapproval at breakfast regarding Andrea's decision.

"She doesn't need to do this. She's just beginning to get on with her life. Now it's gonna be like reliving Clay's death all over again. I just don't understand her."

Devin looked adoringly at his wife. He admired her perseverance and love for her sister. Yet Leah had to understand that this was Andrea's decision, and she needed their support. "Baby, calm down," he urged. "Do you think this is going to be easy for her?"

Leah felt defeated. She dropped her fork onto her plate. "I don't know. I guess not," she admitted. "It's just that the last year and a half have been rough for her. Why does she want to go stirring all those feelings up again?"

Devin responded, "She probably doesn't *want* to stir them up. Sometimes we have to go through something painful in order to get better. Like an operation, for example. After it's over, you're in a lot of pain, but once the healing begins, you start to feel better."

Leah could go on and on about this. However, she chose not to. Hard as it was, she remained quiet. Nothing else was said until she got up to go to work.

She asked, "What time are you going to Andrea's?"

Devin answered, "Ellen's picking Andrea up at five, so I guess I'll try to be there about a quarter 'til, so I'll leave here about four-thirty. You still coming over when you get off work?"

"Yeah. My last appointment is at five-thirty. I should be finished by seven o'clock. What if I get a pizza on the way and bring it? I'll call the order in. It'll probably be after seven-thirty before I get there, though. Think you and Kayla can hold out that long?"

Devin grinned. "Yeah, I think so."

Leah smiled. "Okay. I'll see you later tonight then."

Devin rose to his feet and grabbed Leah's hand. The two newly-weds walked to the door, then stopped to share a hug and a kiss before saying good-bye.

Later that evening, Leah joined Devin and the children at Andrea's. Leah was glad that someone had finally been able to get her sister out of the house for something other than her support group.

As they sat at the kitchen table stuffing their mouths full of pizza, Kayla exclaimed, "Mmm . . . this pizza sure is good."

Leah and Devin smiled and nodded. Leah reached down to where Clayton sat in his carrier on the floor and gave him a spoon-ful of mixed vegetables from the baby food jar. He gobbled it down and smacked his lips together. Next, she spooned up a bit of sauce from a slice of her pizza and gave it to him. The baby smacked his lips again.

Kayla declared, "Clayton likes it, too."

Leah agreed, "He sure does."

Devin asked, "Babe, should you be giving him that?"

Leah replied, "It's okay. It won't hurt him." She turned back to Clayton, saying, "Baby needs something with some taste, doesn't he? Yeah. That's right."

Clayton grinned.

After supper, Devin and Kayla cleaned up the kitchen while Leah gave Clayton his bath. Then they gathered in the family room where they sprawled out on the floor with Clayton and played Old Maid, Kayla's favorite card game. Kayla laughed hysterically when Devin got stuck with the old maid.

At nine-fifteen, Leah instructed Kayla to get ready for her bath. It was already forty-five minutes past her bedtime. Devin removed the sleeping baby from the floor and put him in his bed. After Kayla finished her bath, she said her prayers. Then she got into bed, and Leah read her a bedtime story.

Finally around nine forty-five, Leah and Devin were able to sit down and relax. The evening had been fun and exhausting.

Leah said, "Man, I'm tired. Those two little buggers really tire you out, don't they?"

Devin agreed, "Yeah, but they're fun."

Leah's heart went out to her sister and all the single parents around the world. "I don't see how Andrea does it every day. She goes to work, then comes home and takes care of the kids and the house. She really has a lot on her plate. And now, there's this thing with the trial."

Devin wished Leah wouldn't start harping on the court proceedings again. They'd already had this conversation once today. She and Andrea had finally been able to weather the storms that had crossed their paths, and he wanted no more disturbances. He hoped his wife would keep her opinions regarding the matter to herself.

He said, "Don't get yourself all worked up. You're stressing yourself out. I know what you need." He stood, pulling Leah up with him. "You need one of my soothing back massages. Lie down on your stomach." He helped her onto the floor, knelt beside her, and began massaging her back.

Leah felt her tense muscles begin to relax. "Your fingers are magic. That feels so good."

Devin grinned. "I'm glad you like it."

Once the massage was complete, the couple returned to their

seat on the sofa. The next thing Devin knew, Leah had fallen asleep with her head on his lap. When Andrea walked through the door at ten-thirty, Leah was still sound asleep.

Andrea commented, "She conked out on you, huh?"

Devin smiled as he looked down into the face of his sleeping beauty. "Yeah. She's tired."

While Andrea went to look in on the children, Devin woke Leah. When Andrea returned, they had on their coats.

Andrea gave each a hug. "Thanks, guys. I really appreciate you babysitting."

"You're welcome," Leah and Devin replied in unison.

"Anytime," Leah added.

After the couple had gone, Andrea got ready for bed. She opened up the drawer of the nightstand to retrieve her journal, but it wasn't there. Then she remembered she'd put it in the top drawer of the chest after her last entry.

Andrea went over to the chest and pulled open the drawer, gently lifting up some items of clothes as she searched for her journal. *There it is.* As she grabbed hold of it, something in shades of orange and yellow caught her eye. It was the brochure that Alexander and Ellen had given her after Clayton had died. The pamphlet on bereavement support groups the ER doctor had given her the day she found out she was pregnant was there, too. Underneath it, she saw something else that she had forgotten about. She pulled it out. Clayton's wallet. She had placed it there after her mother had moved some of her things to the chest.

Andrea took all the items she had taken out of the drawer over to her bed. She plopped down and picked up the wallet, then opened it. She meticulously eyed the contents: Clayton's driver's license, photos of her, Kayla, and the rest of the family. She peeked inside the money section at the five twenty-dollar bills.

Andrea closed the wallet and held it to her heart for a fleeting moment. Then she put it down and picked up the brochure. She opened it up, revealing the table of contents. She scanned the list and stopped at *How Can I Live With My Grief?*

She flipped through several pages, quickly scanning them before turning to the next one. When she saw the subheading *Help From God*, she felt a huge lump well up inside her throat. It mentioned the scripture at 2 Corinthians 1:3 where God was called *the God of all comfort.* It went on to say that divine help didn't eliminate the pain but could make it easier to bear. *That does not mean that you will no longer cry or will forget your loved one. But you can recover.*

All of these items had been within her grasp, but she had forgotten them. Would they have made a difference in her recovery? Maybe. At the time, though, she wasn't ready to get over Clayton or get on with her life—until now. Perhaps she had suffered so she could be of help to someone else when their time to grieve came.

With tears streaming down her face, Andrea closed the brochure. This time, she cried, not simply because she was sad, but because she felt a huge sense of relief in knowing that God would help her through her pain.

Chapter 33

The next morning, Leah and Devin were getting ready for church when the telephone rang.

"I'll get it," Devin offered.

When Leah came out of the bathroom, Devin was hanging up the phone. "Who was it?"

"Andrea."

"What did she want? Is everything okay?"

"She said not to pick Kayla up for church."

"Why not? Is she sick?"

"She didn't say."

Leah was getting upset. She wanted to know what was going on. Her voice reeked of irritation when she asked, "Well, Devin, did you ask her?"

Devin stared disapprovingly at his wife. He didn't appreciate her tone. "No, I just asked if everything was all right, and she said yes. I figured if she wanted me to know anything more, she'd tell me."

"You should have asked. Something's obviously wrong. I don't understand how something can be right under a man's nose and he not see it. Why does it always have to be the woman who takes care of everything?"

"Leah, don't get mad at me. I told you I asked if everything was all right. What more could I do?"

"Never mind. I'll call her."

This was a side of Leah he didn't care for. "Do what you want," Devin said and walked off.

When Leah called Andrea's house, she got the answering machine. She left a message, but Andrea still had not returned her call by the time she and Devin departed for church.

Tension filled the vehicle as the newlyweds rode in silence.

Finally, Leah asked, "Can we go by Andrea's after church?"

Devin gave her a flat, "Sure," refusing to say anything else.

This was their first spat since their marriage, and though they both felt horrible, neither one was going to cave in to the other. Leah had no right to get upset at him because he refused to give Andrea the third degree as she always did.

Because of Devin's lack of discernment, Leah would have to sit through the entire service wondering what was up with her sister this time. All he'd had to do was ask a few simple questions to see what was going on.

Devin pulled the car into the church parking lot. Once inside the building, he and Leah stopped to talk with other parishioners before finding a seat. After locating two vacant chairs near the front, Leah got up to go to the restroom. On her way, she thought she saw someone who looked just like Andrea. She had to be mistaken. Her eyes did a double take. The woman had a baby in her arms. When Leah spotted Kayla beside them, she knew without a doubt that it was her sister.

Leah forgot all about the restroom and rushed over to greet Andrea. She changed her mind, though, when she saw the crowd of people gathered around her and the children. Some of them hadn't seen Andrea in months, and everyone seemed excited to see her and the baby. Leah went to the restroom.

When she returned to her seat, Leah whispered to Devin, "Andrea's here. That must be why she didn't want us to pick up

Kayla. I'm sorry." She felt horrible for jumping to conclusions and taking her frustration out on her husband.

Devin still felt annoyed, but knew how protective Leah was of her sister. "It's okay."

After the service, Leah got her opportunity to speak to Andrea. "It's good to see you. Welcome back."

Andrea smiled. "Thanks. It's good to be back."

On the way home, Leah felt the need to have a heart-to-heart talk with Devin. She turned slightly in her seat so she could see his expression as she spoke.

"Honey, I'm sorry about this morning. I was worried about Andrea. I know that's not an excuse for my behavior. I realize that if I want our marriage to work that I'm going to have to start working on myself. I know sometimes I jump to conclusions and speak without thinking. I love you. I don't ever want you to have any regrets that you married me. I want to be with you forever."

Devin looked at Leah for a brief moment. "You know, when we had our pre-marriage counseling session, Alex said a successful marriage is based on love, trust, honesty, and respect. But he said, most of all, we have to have God in our marriage. I feel we have all those things and more. Now that we're married, we're going to be discovering things about each other, and we won't like everything we find out. But as long as we keep the lines of communication open and talk like we're doing now, I think we'll be all right."

Leah smiled as Devin reached over and took her hand in his. "I think we will, too."

They felt much better now. They could see that marriage was hard work, but they were determined to make theirs last forever.

As Andrea prepared her and Kayla's plate for lunch, she felt a spiritual healing. It was as though God had lifted her up and wrapped her in His arms like a shepherd would for one of his little lost sheep. With that image in her mind, she immediately thought of

Isaiah 40:11 where God was referred to as a shepherd who gathers His lambs within His arms and carries them in His bosom.

Making her mind up to attend worship service this morning had been easier than she had anticipated. She had said a simple heartfelt prayer begging God to help her to get up, get ready, and make it out of her door and through the church doors. She appreciated how—instead of everyone asking her where she'd been, which would have torn down her spirit more—most hugged her and expressed how much they had missed her. She had missed them, but had not realized until that moment how much.

Andrea and Kayla had finished eating and were clearing away the table when the telephone rang.

Andrea asked, "Sweetie, will you get that?"

Kayla ran over to Andrea's desk nearby, grabbing the phone off the receiver. "Hello? Mee Maw!" the child squealed. "Guess what? Mommy went to church today."

Andrea smiled at her daughter as she made her grand announcement. Maybe it wouldn't be on the six o'clock news, but Kayla would probably shout it to the world if she could. Kayla talked a few minutes to both her grandparents before handing the telephone over to her mother.

Andrea placed the receiver to her ear. "Hello."

Anna said, "Kayla's excited, isn't she?"

Andrea smiled. "Yes, she is."

Anna asked, "How do *you* feel?"

Andrea drifted her eyes heavenward as she pulled out her chair and sat at the desk. "I feel at peace with myself and God. I'll never get over losing Clay, but I suppose the pain of losing him will become more bearable. I still hurt, but when I look back over how much I hurt in the beginning, the pain's not as great, although it's still there."

Anna proudly stated, "You've come a long way, baby. And that's what's so encouraging. You had a whole lot of bumps along the way, but you're coming out on top. You're a fighter, Andrea. You always have been. You and Leah both. None of us ever gave up on you, but your sister—she fought with you all the way. You know, people say twins have a special bond, a strong connection that allows them to feel each other's pain. I don't know if that's true, but I do know this. You girls love each other, and I admire your devotion to one another."

Andrea smiled. "What you just said means a lot to me, Mama."

"Well," Anna said, "I'm not going to hog up all your time. Your father wants to talk to you, too. He's always complaining that I take up all your time and only leave him a minute or two to talk to you."

Andrea snickered. "Okay. Bye, Mama. I love you."

"Bye, baby. I love you, too. You take care."

William took the phone from his wife. "Andrea."

Andrea's face was beaming. "Daddy . . ."

Three and a half weeks later, Andrea and Ellen sat in the mall's food court eating lunch.

Andrea looked sadly at her friend. "Ellen, the woman you told me about who lost her husband and children in the accident, who is she? Do you know where she lives? I'd like to talk to her."

Ellen's response was delayed.

Andrea felt terrible. She never should have put her friend on the spot like this, but Andrea had been hoping for some time now that Ellen would tell her on her own.

Andrea reached over and sympathetically touched Ellen's hand. "The woman is you, isn't it?"

Ellen couldn't speak or look at Andrea. She simply nodded her head.

"Oh, Ellen, I'm so sorry. Why didn't you tell me?"

This time, Ellen looked Andrea squarely in the face. "I don't know. It was a long time ago. I've put it behind me. I guess I was afraid that because I made it through, I would put too much pressure on you to try to get over your loss before you were ready. As much as it hurts us, we have to let people grieve in their own way. Your pain is your pain. Mine is mine. God created us as individuals. We don't all think and act alike."

Andrea spoke freely from her heart. "Thank you so much for not giving up on me. I pushed away so many people—the people I love the most. Some stopped calling and coming around—not that I blame them, considering the way I was acting. But you and Alex and my family and Glenn never once left my side. I just want you to know how much I love you and appreciate having you as one of my dearest friends."

Ellen spoke through tears. "I love you, too."

For the moment, nothing more needed to be said.

Chapter 34

Andrea clapped her hands. "Go, baby, go!" she yelled as Kayla ran in the open field near their home with her kite high in the sky coasting in the March breeze.

Andrea looked down at Clayton who was grinning and clapping his hands from his stroller. When he smiled, he revealed his one baby tooth that had already come in before he had turned eight months old two days ago.

The wind felt pleasantly cool as it swept across Andrea's face. In two and a half weeks, it would be spring again. With the trial relating to Clayton's death about to get under way, Andrea needed this day with her children. She was having second thoughts about speaking during the closing. However, she hadn't expressed her apprehension to anyone. She felt confident that when the time came, God would help her to make up her mind and go from there.

Kayla headed back toward her family with her kite. She passed the string over to her mother, who gradually rolled it around the thick chunk of wood until it was down low enough for Andrea to grasp it in her hand.

Kayla exclaimed through a wide grin, "That was fun!"

"Yeah, it was," her mother concurred.

Kayla leaned down and kissed her brother's cheek. "Did you like that, Clayton?" she asked.

Grinning, Clayton reached up with both hands and touched his sister's cheeks.

Andrea smiled at her offspring. They were so adorable and truly loved each other. "Okay, guys, let's go."

Andrea watched as Kayla pushed Clayton's stroller back to the car, which was parked in a clearing off the road. After the children were securely buckled in their seats, she unlocked the trunk and lifted it open. Carefully removing the kite from the car's roof, she laid it flat in the trunk.

After they had lunch, Andrea took the children outside to the backyard to play. Leah and Devin had recently bought Clayton a toddler playground set. While Kayla swung on her swing set, Andrea played with the baby on his.

It was a beautiful, sunny day. The dogwoods bursting into bloom in shades of pink and white and the different shades of tulips blossoming in the flowerbeds had given Andrea spring fever. She couldn't wait to start digging in the soil with the kids and putting some flowers in the ground.

After a few more minutes of playing, Andrea took the children with her to the mall. The jewelry store was working on something for her and had promised it would be ready today.

At the store, Andrea greeted the clerk with a smile as she handed him her ticket. "Is it ready?" she asked with anticipation.

The clerk returned her smile. "Yes, it is, Ms. Hamilton. I'll go to the back and get it for you."

Andrea was on pins and needles. She couldn't wait to see it.

The young man reappeared and placed the item on the counter. "Here it is."

Andrea reached down and carefully picked up the small, brown, cedar jewelry box which was trimmed in gold along the edges. It had belonged to her husband. She had asked the jeweler to insert a small diamond-shaped gold piece in the center. In an undertone, she read the inscription that was now engraved inside the diamond.

Andrea smiled and her eyes filled with tears. *CLAYTON DAVID HAMILTON II, 07/02/05*. "It's beautiful."

The clerk smiled. "We're glad you're pleased."

Kayla said, "Let me see, Mommy."

Andrea held the box down lower so her daughter could view it. "Oh, Mommy, it *is* beautiful. . . ."

Andrea's heart was filled with a newfound joy. The money that remained from Clayton's wallet after paying for the jewelry box would be put in the baby's savings. She paid the clerk. This was one of the best days she'd had in quite a long while.

On Friday, Andrea was quiet as she ate supper with the kids at Leah and Devin's. After supper, Devin took Kayla and Clayton into the den, while Andrea and Leah cleaned up the kitchen.

Wiping off the table, Leah eyed her sister suspiciously as Andrea placed leftovers in plastic containers. "What's wrong?"

Andrea looked at Leah. "Hmm."

"I said what's wrong? I can tell something's bothering you. What is it?" Leah asked sympathetically.

Andrea decided to share her apprehension with her sister. "The DA's office called me today. The trial will soon be coming to a close."

Leah smiled. "Well, that's good. Soon you'll get to have your day in court and tell everyone what you've been through."

Andrea didn't say anything.

Confused, Leah asked, "That's what you want, isn't it?"

Andrea confessed, "I'm not sure anymore. I've finally started to get on with my life, and I don't know if my heart can take reopening those wounds."

Leah was surprised that her sister was having these kinds of feelings. Andrea had seemed so sure about her decision. Leah admitted that she initially was against it, but she was beginning to think Andrea should go through with it. Here was the opportunity for her sister to have a little more closure to this terrible experience and try to close this chapter of her life and move on.

Leah encouraged her sister, "You just have to put your trust in God and leave everything in His hands." She added, "Whatever you decide."

Andrea thought back to a time when Leah would have given her her opinion whether she wanted it or not. At this point, she wished someone would tell her what to do, but Andrea supposed she had to learn to trust wholeheartedly in God again.

On Saturday, Andrea worked in her flower beds with Kayla while Clayton watched from his stroller. Every now and then, a squirrel would scurry up a tree, and Clayton would point and giggle.

It was a nice day for working in the yard. Andrea felt the sunshine and exercise would do her good. Besides, she really needed to get the beds ready for her spring and summer plants.

When a car pulled into the driveway, Kayla jumped up, yelling, "Poppy! Nanna!" She left her mother and brother slowly trailing behind her as she dashed to greet her grandparents.

Andrea hugged her in-laws. "Hey. Why didn't you let me know you were coming? This is a pleasant surprise."

Lizzie said, "We just decided on the spur of the moment to venture out. We just left Devin and Leah's."

Andrea smiled. "Really? That's nice. Well, come on inside. The kids and I were just digging around in the flower beds."

Edward said, "We don't want to keep you from what you were doing."

Andrea responded, "That's okay. We're almost done. We can finish up later."

They went inside.

Andrea asked, "Are you hungry? I haven't been to the store yet, but we can scrounge up something."

Lizzie suggested, "Why don't I go shopping with you." She

looked at her husband. "Dear, you don't mind staying here with the children, do you?"

Edward ruffled Kayla's hair. "'Course not."

Kayla smiled as she clung to her grandfather.

"Okay," Andrea agreed, "but I've got to shower first."

Lizzie smiled. "Sure. Take your time."

Andrea showered while Lizzie and Edward played with the kids. When she was dressed, she grabbed her grocery list off the kitchen counter, and she and Lizzie were out the door.

As Andrea maneuvered the vehicle over the highway, Lizzie couldn't help but notice how much happier her daughter-in-law seemed. Losing Clayton had taken its toll on her, but now she appeared to be back to her old self. It made Lizzie regret what she was about to say. Apparently, Andrea hadn't yet heard the news. She remembered, too, that Andrea had told her she didn't watch the news much anymore, since she always saw something that depressed her.

Lizzie decided to go ahead and get it over with. "Did you see the news last night?"

Andrea gazed at her mother-in-law. "No. Why?"

Lizzie hesitated momentarily as she attempted to choose her words carefully. "They had a piece on the news about the man on trial for Clay's death. They said it was his fifth DUI."

Lizzie was still talking, but Andrea had stopped listening. She had heard all she needed to hear.

Andrea was about to be called to present her testimony to the court. Leah, who was sitting beside her, slipped an envelope into her hand. Andrea looked at it, confusion evident on her face.

Leah answered her sister's questioning gaze. "Kayla asked me to help her write something. She wants you to read it when you give your statement."

As Andrea looked around the courtroom, it seemed as though all eyes were on her, including those of her family: her parents, Lizzie and Edward, Leah and Devin, and even Alexander and Ellen.

Andrea rose and walked to the front of the courtroom when she was called to present her statement. She stood behind the podium and looked out over the audience. *Oh, Lord, please help me do this.*

She had made an outline of what she wanted to say, to help her recall her thoughts. Andrea began, "October 12, 2004, was the worst day of my life. That's the day I received the phone call that my husband, Clayton David Hamilton, had been hit by a drunk driver." She felt a huge lump in her throat and tried to swallow.

Andrea fixed her eyes on the sad face of a woman in the audience. "By the time I got to the hospital, Clay was already gone. Our last good-bye, our last hug, our last kiss had been two days prior to that. Only we didn't know it at the time."

She looked briefly at her notes before allowing her eyes to roam the courtroom again. "The day after my husband's funeral, my mother took me to the emergency room. That's when I found out I was four weeks pregnant." At this bit of information, Andrea observed sad and shocked expressions on many of the faces looking back at her. She continued, "Our son was born last year on July second. Our daughter was five at the time of her father's death. Her name is Kayla."

Andrea blinked back tears. "She is a strong-spirited little girl who has a lot of faith. I almost gave up on living, but Kayla, along with my family and friends, wouldn't let me. Even when I became angry at the world, including my loved ones and God...." Admitting to everyone present that she had been angry at God caused her to pause briefly, for hearing herself say it hurt her terribly.

"They all stood by me. Everyone handles tragedy differently. I never thought anything would happen in my life to cause me to seek professional help. To me, it would have been a sign of weakness, so I fought against it tooth and nail. Even when my dear mother kindly suggested it, I became angry at her and pushed her away." Andrea could hold back the tears no longer. She grabbed a couple of tissues from the box on the podium and wiped her face.

William patted his wife's hand as tears streamed down her face.

Fearful that if she looked at the defendant, she would go to pieces, Andrea focused her eyes on different ones on the back row of the courtroom. She had to do this. She had to finish what she'd started.

"Finally, I sought help, but only after almost tearing my family apart. It takes every fiber of my being to get out of bed every morning and face another day with my children without my husband. Little Clayton will never know his father in the sense that Kayla and I do. My husband won't get to see his children grow up and share their lives with him. Kayla at least has some fond memories of him.

"My sister gave me a letter a few minutes ago that Kayla wrote. I didn't know about it until she handed it to me." Andrea removed the paper from inside the envelope and unfolded it. "So at this time, I'd like to read it to you."

She looked down at Kayla's neatly printed letters she'd written on tablet paper.

"Hello. My name is Kayla Marie Hamilton. I am six years old. I miss my Daddy so much. He was funny. He always made me laugh. He had funny nicknames for me. Like Butter Bean, Tater Tot, and Snapdragon."

As Andrea read Kayla's letter, there appeared to be very few dry eyes in the courtroom. She dabbed at her eyes and wiped her nose with the tissues she still held in her hand.

"I have a baby brother, Clayton. Mommy and I made a scrapbook for him with pictures of her and me and Daddy. We want him to see what Daddy was . . ."

Andrea flipped the paper over and continued reading. "Like. My Daddy's gone, but I know I'll see him again one day when God brings him back to life." She blinked several times and looked up at the ceiling before concluding. "Then we can all be together again. Sincerely, Kayla Marie Hamilton."

Andrea refolded the letter, stuffed it back inside the envelope, and walked slowly back to her seat. When she sat down, Leah grabbed her hand and squeezed it.

As the verdict was being read, Leah still clung to her sister's hand. *Guilty.* The sentence would be imposed the following day.

As court concluded, Andrea's family and friends hugged her. She had done it. By God's grace, she'd made it through.

Epilogue

"Mama. Daddy. This house is beautiful," Andrea bragged as she looked around admiringly.

She was so glad her parents had moved back to Georgia. They had been successful at locating a small, two-bedroom house not far from her and Leah. They would be moving into their new home at the beginning of April. They had already sold their home in New York and had moved all their belongings to a storage building.

Anna and William had kept their plan to return to Georgia a secret from their daughters until after the trial. Andrea was thrilled that her folks would be staying with her until they moved into their house.

Anna asked, "You really like it? It's not that big."

"Oh, Mama," Andrea said. "It's big enough for you and Daddy. Isn't it about the size of the house you had in New York?"

"Yes," William said. "Your mother's just worried about there being enough room when all the family come over."

Andrea said, "Don't worry, Mama. Remember how we used to do when Leah and I were kids? Our house wasn't this big, but when we had get-togethers, there was plenty of room."

Anna laughed. "Yeah, we'd be packed in the house like sardines in a can. We were so close, we could hear each other think."

Andrea and William laughed.

Later that night after everyone was in bed and the house was quiet, Andrea took a bubble bath. As she soaked in the tub under the soft glow of her peach-scented candles, she thought about the sentence that had been handed down on the man who had taken Clayton's life.

Walter Oglesby had called that afternoon and given her the news. Because of his extensive record, the man was sentenced to thirty years in prison and thirty years probation. He would not be eligible for parole until the year 2020. Andrea was pleased with the sentence. She felt it was a small price to pay for the lives that had been shattered.

As she was getting out of the tub, she looked down at the white-gold bridal set she still wore on her ring finger. After drying herself off, she slipped into her pink nightgown and strolled over to her jewelry box on her dresser. She opened the right side and removed a silver Milano rope chain, which had belonged to Clayton, from one of the hooks. She laid the piece of jewelry on the dresser.

Slowly, Andrea began to slip the ring set from her finger. She placed the rings on the dresser and unfastened the chain. Then she put the rings on the necklace and fastened it around her neck so the rings would lie close to her heart.

Andrea walked over to the window and stared out into the night sky. So much had happened. Her life would never be the same without Clayton. But she had a lot of wonderful memories of him, and they would live on in their children.

Grasping the rings in her hand, Andrea held on to them tightly as she softly whispered, "Thank you, Heavenly Father, for helping me through this test of my faith."

A TEST OF FAITH

Maxine Billings

ABOUT THIS GUIDE

The questions and discussion topics that follow are intended to enhance your group's reading of A TEST OF FAITH by Maxine Billings. We hope the novel provided an enjoyable read for all your members.

DISCUSSION QUESTIONS

1. Think back to the day after Clayton's funeral when Andrea learned she was pregnant. Picture the scene in your mind's eye as she lies in the bed of the hospital examination room crying uncontrollably. Describe some of the things that may have been going on inside her head. How do you think you would have felt and reacted?

2. The day comes when Andrea's parents have gone back home, and Andrea and Kayla are the only ones in the house. After putting Kayla to bed, Andrea then walks throughout the house to each and every room. Why do you suppose she does this? What do you think would be the first thing you would do once you had that moment alone after things had quieted down?

3. In the beginning, Andrea consulted and meditated on God's Word for comfort and guidance, yet she did not keep up this spiritual routine—and later even eventually stopped attending worship services. Why did she start to question the truths she'd been taught from the Bible?

4. Despite what her sister was going through, Leah felt that Andrea was being selfish because she did not seem to share her joy concerning the wedding. Should Leah have been more empathetic and ceased trying to discuss her wedding details with her sister?

5. Andrea's family hurt so much for her and wanted her to get over her grief and on with her life. Do you feel that sometimes we put too much pressure on people to try to get over the death of a loved one?

6. Do you think that if Andrea had kept up her spiritual routine, joined the support group, and/or sought medical help for her depression that she would have spared herself a lot of pain and heartache? Or do you feel that simply a good spiritual routine would have been enough to sustain her?

7. Andrea made the decision to speak during the closing phase of the trial of the man who was responsible for Clayton's death. Later, she began having second thoughts, but felt confident that God would help her come to a final decision. Then Lizzie told her about the man's extensive DUI record. Do you think this new piece of information was God's way of helping Andrea to make a conscientious decision so she could finally get on with her life?

8. Did Andrea's speaking at the trial help bring more closure for her in dealing with her pain and grief? Why or why not?

Dear Readers:

By the time of this book's release, it will be a year since the release of my first book. As always, I look forward to hearing from you. I would love to hear your thoughts about Andrea's family crisis and how it affected her and her loved ones.

Please enclose a self-addressed, stamped envelope with your letter and mail to: Maxine Billings, P. O. Box 307, Temple, GA 30179. Feel free to e-mail your comments to *maxinebillings@yahoo.com*. Please visit my website also at *www.maxinebillings.com*.

In closing, I'd like to say that I thank you from the bottom of my heart for the support and encouragement you've extended to me. It's been an incredible journey. Thank you for sailing with me.

From my heart to yours,
Maxine